AMBASSADOR 9: RED CRYSTAL DESERT

PATTY JANSEN

CAPRICORNICA PUBLICATIONS

GET FREE EBOOKS

Visit pattyjansen.com
or scan the QR code below with your phone to get four series
starter ebooks for free!

DID YOU KNOW?

Ambassador 9 is also available in audio. Click the image or visit https://pattyjansen.com to find out more.

1

THE HOUSE LAY on top of a rocky outcrop in the fork of the valley.

It had sprawling rooms and a veranda that wrapped around the entire ground floor. The scent of fresh paint still lingered in the rooms but, from what I understood, its design and its location were almost older than humanity.

The windows looked out over both arms of the valley, broad canyons with sheer cliffs of rock, a boulder-strewn floor, and a faint haze of purple from the dust of the surrounding desert. The right arm of the canyon contained several glistening pools of water, the left a modest creek.

The latter amazed me most. This was Asto.

The river into Athyl, dry for so long it had lost its name, was flowing again. After fifty thousand years of desert, enough water fell in the mountains to produce a small permanent stream.

"What do you think?" a voice said behind me.

Asha Domiri, second in charge of Asto's society, commander of the armed forces and my father-in-law, came to stand next to me.

He had brought me here on a short flight from his residence

in the huge army base on the plateau that was just visible through the haze.

I took in the room with its smooth polished mosaic floor with patterns of light grey leaves in white marble-like stone. I looked at the sheer curtains ruffled by the breeze, and the exquisitely carved windowsills displaying the likeness of creatures that had been dead for thousands of years.

There was no more wood on Asto, but the artificial material looked so much like it that the difference was indistinguishable.

"It's very a nice house," I said. "I like the view."

"I thought this would be a good place as a base for you and your association while you're staying here."

"Here?"

For the past few days, since arriving on Asto, we had been staying at his household. He did not live in the Inner Circle as his status allowed him, although he had an apartment there. He had to live with the military that he led.

"Yes, it's big enough for your entire party. The little one can run and scream as much as he likes, your security team doesn't have to share resources, and I have organised for people to come today who can assist my daughter with the care of the child when it arrives; and, until it does, she can sit on the veranda and enjoy this beautiful view."

The view was indeed beautiful, but I was puzzled by this move.

He continued, "I know there is not enough furniture in here, but we'll bring some in."

Yes, only one room in the house—an upstairs bedroom— contained furniture: a bed without bedding, two chairs and a table. There were also a few pots and pans in the kitchen, but not enough for all of us.

And also, this was clearly not my own decision.

In Coldi society, one kept one's rivals and enemies close. Did that mean he trusted me, or did that mean he didn't want me to be anywhere near his association at all?

"Not to dispute your generosity, but I have a lot of business in the city. Wouldn't it be better if I stayed there? I can find some accommodation that won't upset your household."

He turned to me, giving me that intense look of his. "My household are not upset."

Was he miffed that I suggested I should look for my own place?

"Then is there a problem because your home is on a military base?" Because those stiff-faced people definitely didn't like visitors.

"My military officers are not upset. They will do as they are told."

Then why? "I'm not sure I understand. Does this house belong to you?"

"It doesn't, but I've secured permission to use it."

Well, that was as clear as mud. And one lesson I'd learned in Coldi society was that you *always* worried about who owned the place where you were staying, because this person also owned the listening bugs.

He must have sensed my apprehension, because he continued, "There are a lot of complications. Your coming to Asto may be controversial for some members of your party. I don't want to cause any major trouble for them and for you, especially since your stay here will be temporary, and I don't want to upset established hierarchies."

There we had it. He wanted us out of his household and army base because he feared that my presence would challenge the established power structure, which, in Coldi, was determined through hormones and the *sheya* instinct that could—and often did—react badly to a sudden influence from a person outside the power structure. In other words, a person like me.

But was it really about "members of my association" more than about me? I was yet without status in Coldi society, and part of the reason for my visit was to establish the place I would occupy in the many loyalty networks.

Although I could think of some of those people whose very presence would stir up conflict in the future, it was worth finding out his thoughts about these situations.

"I'm guessing that the Azimi clan will be interested in the little boy," I said. Ayshada was only two, but his very existence was the cause of more controversy than a two-year-old should have to deal with.

Asha nodded. "That whole range of your association is full of trouble. Because Nicha grew up with his mother, she thinks she can enforce her politics on him. She is, of course, in bed with the Azimi clan, and probably planted this little bundle of joy on you."

"Ayshada is still too young to cause trouble."

"He's a liability for you, a weakness in your association." His face was hard.

If I hadn't seen him, in an unguarded moment in the kitchen, sneak Ayshada a treat behind his father's back, I would have thought he hated children. "So, the Azimi clan will demand to see him or take care of him for a specific time?"

Asha lifted his chin, the Coldi way of saying no. "They will not come to you. They will come to my son, and they will try to pressure him into agreeing to have the boy spend some time with them when he's older."

"How bad would that be?"

"It's customary that children who are living with one parent spend at least some time with the other parent. That's not bad per se. We want to make sure that happens after he has gained an understanding of what the Azimi clan may be trying to do to him and his father."

"But Ayshada is still too young."

Asha agreed. "He is."

"And what is the Azimi clan's game at the moment? Anything in particular I need to worry about?"

"The usual stuff. Scheming to take power through gaining influence in the colonies, revenge politics based on slights that were supposedly done to people many years ago. I can give you a list. They have a variety of writs awaiting response, but even if no one responds, the Azimi clan doesn't have the people to enforce their threats."

The usual stuff, in that case. The Azimi clan found issue with a lot of things and issued a lot of writs. They were notorious on not following through with the threats outlined in those writs. I could handle it.

But as usual when talking to Asha, the most concerning issues hid behind layers and layers of rhetoric. Coldi were direct with their opinions, but guarded their serious problems like a rabid dog.

Yeah, I didn't like surprises, but the Azimi issue seemed under control. For now.

Next problem area. "Is the problem then about the position of Reida?" I asked.

Asha snorted. "There is that. He's Ezmi. Outer Circle. Many people are surprised that you have him on your team. But ultimately, it's your choice."

I never had much choice about Reida in particular. Nicha had picked him. But I liked Reida. He was a good kid—a bit unconventional, but useful, and I would defend him. "He's very good." At breaking into things, both physical buildings and databases. "I noticed that some of the staff at the base gave him hostile looks."

"Give me the names of those people, and they will be reprimanded."

"That's not really necessary."

"Believe me, it's necessary."

No, I didn't want that. I didn't want to be a tattletale getting people up in arms against me because I'd felt they could have been more welcoming to one of my junior workers. I hadn't come here to make enemies. Neither had I come here to thrust Reida in an unwelcome spotlight. He hated being singled out.

So I changed the subject away from Reida. "The Ezmi clan are not going to create any trouble while we're here?"

"Most of his family, if he has any left, would have no ties that link back to any of ours, no matter how far back you stretch it. Since he's contained within the structure of your association, that wouldn't create too much trouble, so just tell the little rascal to keep his head down, and he should be safe."

"He's been very well-behaved lately. He completed the Academy and got his full guard license. He is doing a lot of training in spyware and electronics." To be honest, I was quite proud of the young man, who had spent the first few months in my house trying to sneak into the bedroom windows of the girls in town.

"It's actually the other one in that *zhayma* pair I'm worried about."

"Deyu?" To me, Deyu was akin to a living goddess. She was always ready to do her duty, she did it better than anyone without complaining, she was the strongest in our team, the best fighter, the most impressive looking young woman I had ever seen. She was gentle, polite, listened well, loved animals and took all opportunities that came her way with both hands. Just to think that she used to drive trains in the city brought tears to my eyes. What an utter waste of talent.

"That's the one. Omi."

That was Deyu's clan. A clan mostly of workers and labourers. There were a lot of them. They were, in fact, the largest clan on Asto.

Asha continued, "Because you have taken her under your protection, her status has increased immeasurably. When she left Asto, she and her family had merely scraped into Eighth Circle. I understand her father still holds a furniture business."

"I understand he is fairly well known there."

"Yes. And politically active."

"What do you mean?" A cold feeling crept over me.

"He belongs to an ambitious section of the Omi clan. I know

the Omi clan don't get mentioned very often in discussions about politics, and that is because they are usually fairly quiet. But the Omi clan is massive, and because they are so big, their internal structure doesn't resemble that of our clans. They are divided into branches. Their leader normally comes from one of two different branches of the clan."

I could see where this was going. "I'm guessing Deyu's family branch is not one of them."

He gave a brief nod. "Sometimes I wonder why I bother explaining Coldi society to you. You seem to have a better understanding of it than many people on Asto."

"That's because failing to understand it will get me killed."

He chuckled, but we both knew how true it was. "Anyway, now that you're bringing her here, it has strengthened rumbles in the Omi clan. Some people suggest that someone should mount a challenge to her, because her position was never properly assigned."

"That's because Nicha rescued her from being a train driver."

"Things are different now."

"You mean her position has become influential and the clan want a say in who fills it?"

"Eventually, yes. I don't know that anyone ever warned you about collecting that many people from different clans in your association. The clans will all want a say. You're not yet on the radar of the other clans, but the Omi clan has keen eyes to increase their influence."

"Are you really suggesting that someone is going to mount a challenge to Deyu's position in my association, because Deyu is not from the approved branch of the clan?"

He met my eyes squarely. His irises were dark, with few golden spots. "That's one option. Because we are dealing with a clan that is not normally very much in the spotlight, there is no rulebook for what they will do. What is worse, they don't even have the script themselves."

I'd learned recently that there *was* an actual rulebook, mostly electronic and constantly amended, that described clan rules. Each clan had their own rules, especially when related to how they dealt with other clans. In combination with the *sheya* instinct, it was complicated enough to make my brain hurt.

"What are likely possibilities for what challengers will do?"

"If they belonged to any of our clans, they would simply show up here and demand a fight between Deyu and a challenger." *Our clans* meaning Palayi, Domiri, Vonayi, Lingui and even Azimi. "But because we know so little about them, we can't expect that's what they will do. One thing I do know: in the upper clans, fights to establish position are always fought with the opponents' bare hands. You don't use weapons."

"And I am guessing the Omi clan do?"

"They fight dirty." Not a direct answer. Was that meant to signify anything? Was he afraid? Was he ready to start a conflict? "We can expect anything. Attacks under the cover of darkness, attacks that involve more than one assailant, attacks that use a member of another clan as cover."

Something didn't make sense to me. "For what aim would they do this? Just because they're envious of Deyu's success? If we had committed a perceived slight, wouldn't they send a writ first to outline what our transgression is?"

He spread his hands. "I can't claim to understand the workings of the Omi clan. I do know that they're not as placid as they seem. I know that sections will be very unhappy."

"By us visiting here?"

"That, and other issues at play within the clan."

"Are those issues ones that Deyu is involved with?"

"That is hard to know."

Whatever he wanted to say, I doubted this was about Deyu.

I should by now be used to his way of informing me, and yet, after all these years, I *still* got angry when he spoke in vagaries like this. And yet I followed him, just as, all those years ago, I'd gone to Africa because he'd indicated that something there was important for me to find, not bothering to tell me he'd known that an Indrahui warlord had ensconced himself there.

I'd travelled deep into space because he got himself into trouble, even if he would never directly ask for help.

So here we were again. The same game. Except this time Thayu was heavily pregnant. I wasn't sure I wanted to play games right now.

"So, if Deyu is under threat from her own clan, what measures do you suggest we take?"

"I suggest you limit her exposure to the general population. I suggest you take the Vonayi and Palayi guards when you leave the safety of the house. This is also why I suggest you stay here. When you're here, you can see anyone coming from a long distance."

That was certainly true. And I had a whole new guard association trailing us so it wasn't as if we lacked the people to set up a safe perimeter. Sheydu Palayi had brought her whole association of six of her highly trained security guards. They were there purely to protect us so the members of my association could go back to their assigned roles.

Although—how would we be unsafe in his house inside the army base? How would challenging members of the Omi clan get into the base? They wouldn't, because they weren't members of the armed forces.

Something very strange going on here.

Asha continued, "Don't worry about feeling lonely. Most of us will be in and out of here all the time, because there are a lot of things we need to do and sort out."

That was also true. And had he really tried to make a joke?

Make no mistake: he wanted us here for some reason. At the same time, the practicalities were attractive. The whole house to ourselves, and one in as magnificent a position as this, did sound liberating.

There were plenty of spacious rooms for everyone, large open living areas, stone floors Ayshada couldn't damage or stain, no matter which wheeled vehicle he rode or which part of his dinner he upset. There was a security room near the door for Sheydu and her people, a large quiet private room for myself and Thayu with doors that opened onto the veranda, and that room even had its own washroom with hand-painted tiles. It held a comfortable couch, a basin with cool water that was refilled from an underground tank, and plenty of space for the items that would be necessary when Thayu gave birth.

This gorgeous house was much nicer than the functional but cramped and dark military bunker that served as Asha's household, where the desert dust blew in through the windows that looked out over dusty courtyards.

A military household, with military people and military efficiency. They weren't used to two-year-old toddlers, or a baby who had just learned to run but hadn't quite mastered the art of walking or listening. That was Ileyu, Veyada's daughter.

And we hadn't even spoken about the issue of Mereeni, Veyada's partner and the girl's mother, and the fact that she was a *Hedron* Coldi and they were even less welcome than all of the other people we had spoken about. And Veyada, whose father was Vonayi, and Vonayi and Domiri clan—which included most military people—did not have much time for each other.

My head hurt. I'd just wanted to come here for the ceremony. Thayu wanted to be home for the birth of our child. I had stacks of work waiting for me at home in Barresh, especially with the group we now called the Tamer Collective, who had been unofficially cleared to start a second Exchange network. Because they would do it anyway even if we didn't approve, and it was better to maintain a semblance of control and communication than to have conflict, but there were oh so many battles to be fought on that front.

It was not as if I were looking for additional things to worry about.

"I think we will accept and move to the house." I was pretty sure I spoke for most of my association.

He gave a brief nod.

"You'll be provided with plenty of help to move in and make other preparations. That also pertains to the ceremony. Now that I've explained that several people will be trying to goad you into a confrontation, it will start at your confirmation ceremony. People will try to get into your favours, get you to make promises or simply spy on you. I can't shield you from all of it; I don't think you are inexperienced enough that you will fall for many of these games, because they will be so obvious. But be on your guard. Everybody who is new and introduces themselves to you or your association is likely to want something."

"I understand. I will do my best."

And then he clapped my shoulder.

It was testimony to my transformation that I didn't buckle at the knees.

2

S O IT WAS DECIDED.

While we made our way through the living quarters back to the main entrance, I could already imagine the members of my association spreading out and relaxing here. It was a pleasant place.

The position was easy to defend. The house stood quite isolated on the hilltop. It was connected to the surrounding platform through a narrow tongue of land with steep drop-offs on both sides. The path from the door wound through a rocky garden to a paved area that was just big enough for two or three aircraft.

Asha's craft stood there with the two guards from his association, who travelled everywhere with him outside the military base. When we came back out of the house, they opened the door and let us in.

The craft was Asha's military vehicle, with the small inconspicuous military emblem next to the door. None of the men wore uniforms, as was customary. I had been assured that if there was conflict, they would.

Asha was a pilot, but he had chosen to let one of his staff fly the craft for the very short trip across the valley. We took our places in an alcove with a semicircular couch and table that I imagined might be used for discussing war plans. More realistically, the craft would most often be used to ferry Asha and his association to the massive military station that orbited Asto and to all the other military deep space vessels that I didn't know about.

Over his shoulder I could see the controls, and as we took off, the screen displayed the rocky surroundings, followed by the soft grey-purple of the valley floor.

It was indeed astonishing to see this landscape return to life.

We spoke about the growth of plants on the valley floor, and he said there was quite a bit of it. I should go and have a look. He was chatty, as if there wasn't some sort of plan behind moving us here.

The craft turned. Through the windows, I could see the skyline of the city in the distance. We were quite close to the outskirts of Athyl, known as the Outer Circle.

In the time that the rivers had contained water, this valley—if it had existed in its present form—would have been in a key position, since this would have been prime agricultural land.

"Why was this house built here?" I asked Asha. "It seems to occupy a highly strategic position."

"There was always a house at this position," he said. "We have uncovered evidence that the position was inhabited by figures of authority in the time of the Aghyrians."

Which of course didn't answer the question at all, because this house was new. "How are you going to use it?" I used possessive pronouns, assuming the house was his.

"It will be yours for the time being," he said. "As you have seen, you will have everything you need."

The tone of the conversation signalled the end of this line of discussion.

I wanted to know who owned the house, but property ownership was a very complex matter on Asto. One could own a house, own the land it stood on, or own the lease on either or both. Most property was owned by the entity that could broadly be called "the state" even if it was nothing like state ownership on Earth.

I wondered if in his haste to get me and my mixed-up association out of his vicinity, he had made some deals that Thayu would call "interesting".

It never ceased to amaze me how distant Coldi parents could be to their children. Thayu hadn't been to her father's house for many years. Being in the very last days of her second pregnancy, after the sadness of having lost all contact with her son, she needed some help right now, and the first thing he did was send her away?

But no, that was an Earth sentiment.

Despite his legendary bluntness, I knew that he was neither cold nor a dumb brute, and he must sense that his suggestions baffled and disappointed me.

He had *invited* me to join his clan and had planned the upcoming initiation ceremony for the sole reason that I could be there. Because of the position of the stars or something equally obscure.

The man continued to be an enigma.

The craft turned again, giving me another view of the magnificent rocky landscape and sheer cliffs that hemmed in the gorge on both sides. Then a collection of low blocky buildings on the clifftop came into sight. These were the outskirts of the vast military camp.

Not much later, the craft landed in the dusty compound of Asha's house in the military settlement.

The house was two storeys tall, a square blocky thing, nothing like the elegant designs of the buildings that housed the high society in the Inner Circle or the sheer historic grandeur of the house on the knoll. It was functional, and could serve as a bunker in case some imaginary war broke out.

As soon as the craft landed, one of Asha's guards opened the door. We descended the ramp into the hot and dusty courtyard, where a number of people approached us. These were all military officers who wanted replies from Asha about issues that had developed in our absence.

I went into the house, through the square open door and the dark low-ceilinged hallway. The house had no climate control, and the air inside was stale, hot and stuffy.

We had been given an entire wing of the house. There were now quite a number in our group. My association consisted of Thayu, Nicha—with his son Ayshada, who was a delight and a charming rascal at the same time—Deyu, Reida, the lawyers Veyada and Mereeni and their baby daughter Ileyu, who was nine months old.

Our group also included Sheydu and her own association of six security people, who, besides Isharu and Naru, were still a bit unfamiliar to me. At home in Barresh, they lived in the adjacent apartment. They had come with us on this trip for the first time.

We occupied the rooms at the end of the corridor, while Sheydu and her six-strong guard association had taken the rooms closest to the entrance. They had set up a security station—goodness knew why, because we were inside one of the most secure places on Asto—where, each time I passed, data scrolled over multiple screens piled haphazardly on top of one another, watched by Anyu.

She was sitting there now, a severe-faced woman with more wrinkles and grey hair than Sheydu. I had to admit to feeling a little intimidated by her, with her sharp observation skills, which she used to pick out one single anomaly in data that scrolled across the screen almost at the speed of light. She would slam her hand into the screen—making me fear that she'd break it—and then give a triumphant look, as if we should all know what she had just discovered.

Her earrings with the lime green gemstones—Vonayi—would dangle in the hollow under her earlobes, an oddly feminine display from someone I could hardly imagine less feminine.

"All is well?" I asked her, although I still didn't know what should be well, and what not being well would entail, and not really wanting to know about either option.

Deyu was also present, but I only noticed her when I stepped into the room. She leaned against the wall, her formidable arms crossed over her chest. She wore a dark form-fitting rubbery suit and a gun in each of her arm brackets and another—bigger—gun in a bracket on her thigh. She was possibly a third of Anyu's age but one and a half times the size.

"A message came for you," Deyu said.

"Oh? An important message?"

But it had to be, because back in Barresh, I'd fought a massive losing battle in favour of handling my own correspondence.

Anyu would not allow it, because it was how I'd previously ended up in trouble, according to her. She had studied my correspondence from the past years and determined patterns by which people who wanted ill could identify my words, could determine when I was being truthful or not, and could pinpoint where I was, because the encryption level of my various devices was "appalling".

Yet, Anyu sat here and failed to react to Deyu's mentioning of the message. It had to be a *sanctioned* message.

"Show me," I told Deyu.

"I took the reader to your room," Deyu said.

So someone had hand-delivered a message. Most likely, it would have come through a military courier.

Yes, this was important. I dreaded what it could be. Some disaster from Barresh?

I went into the corridor.

A squeal came out of a room further down the passage. Next, Ayshada ran out carrying a piece of construction foam with tubing attached to it so that the ensemble looked like a gun. When he saw me, he dropped it on the ground, sank to his knees, picked the mock weapon back up and pointed it at me, making shooting noises.

"Ayshada, what are you doing?" Nicha came to the doorway. Then he laughed when he saw me.

"Oh, it's you. I was wondering if it was that humourless housekeeper again. She already made two remarks today about Ayshada's supposed ambushes in the corridor. She says he bothers her with his screaming."

"Ah. Some people have no sense of humour."

"Well, normally I'd agree with you, but . . ."

"But what?"

"You wouldn't want to hear what he got into today."

"Let me guess: the maintenance shed."

Ayshada had been fascinated by this part of the building where weapons were taken apart and maintained. It was a classified military area, and Nicha had told him—several times—that he was not allowed down the narrow corridor that led from his grandfather's living areas to that part of the complex. Not even we could go in there.

"You guessed it," Nicha said. "Not only that, but the technicians thought he was cute and let him play with some empty gun housings, so now he has to have a gun to shoot everyone."

I laughed. "Apparently, the fascination of little boys with guns is universal."

"It's easy for you to laugh. The military officer who came to return him to me wasn't so happy."

I laughed even more. But yes, I could see how Asha preferred to get us out of the house. There were too many of us, from too many rival or unknown clans, and we took up too much space, made too much noise and upset this very orderly household.

Let me know who they are and I'll reprimand them, indeed.

The door to our room opposite Nicha's was open. "What's going on?" Thayu asked from inside.

"Ayshada keeps getting into all kinds of mischief," I said, walking into the room.

"Wait until Ileyu gets to that age." Thayu sat with her feet up in an easy chair by the window, overlooking a very dusty courtyard.

"She can't possibly be any worse, can she?" I couldn't imagine. Ileyu was such a cute girl even if at the moment she was a bit of an unguided missile.

Thayu started laughing. Her stomach, round to bursting, shook when she did this, and she placed her hand on it, as if laughing hurt.

We were getting so close to the birth that every sign of her discomfort sent a little chill through me. I'd even stopped asking her if she was all right, because she had told me to quit being nervous, and that she would definitely let me know if something was up.

"So, what was this trip all about?" she asked.

Before Asha had taken me out to the house in the valley, he had been quite mysterious, mentioning that he had something important to show me.

I sat down opposite her. "We went to see this rebuilt old house on the hill in the valley. Your father wants us to move in there."

"Yes. He has told me he was looking for somewhere else."

"Doesn't that disturb you?"

She frowned. "Should it disturb me?" She attempted to push herself up from her half-lying position, but she was so big that she couldn't sit properly anymore and proceeded to hang sideways in the chair. It looked intensely uncomfortable.

"You're just kidding me, aren't you?"

"No, I'm not. We're his guests. He can tell us to go wherever he wants us." Thayu had already gone through the legendary cranky period that Coldi women suffered before birth, and had been much better for the past few days.

"He can, but to me, it seems strange that he wants us out of the house. On one hand, this is a military settlement and we don't belong here."

"That would be an understatement. Ayshada is getting on people's nerves."

"But certain people do have children here. I've seen them."

"They are all children of military people."

"Yeah, and? They're still children. They're noisy and you can't always keep them quiet. And they don't always do as you say."

She shrugged, spreading her hands. I always found it hard to talk about aspects of her father's behaviour that puzzled me or grated on me. I didn't want to talk him down in front of her. He was obviously a capable man in his society, but I failed to understand him, and her answer to my questions about him would often be so indifferent that I'd been convinced she had a poor relationship with her father, only to find out later that I was completely wrong about that.

I breathed in deeply, trying to formulate what I found disturbing. "Part of me thinks that he wants us to be comfortable—"

"Rest assured, comfort has nothing to do with it. If he were concerned about our comfort, he would have left all this until after the little one was born. The initiation ceremony can be held a few times a year, and there is no reason that we needed to come to this one. You've deferred this a couple of times already."

That was another issue that had given me pause. He'd been very insistent that we should come to *this* particular ceremony.

"So why does he want us in this remote house?"

"I don't know. We can only go and find out." That was a typically Coldi attitude. Dive headlong into a troublesome situation, to find out what shape the trouble would take.

"But I don't really want to risk you in your situation."

"I'm perfectly fine." In a don't-go-there tone.

Yes, we'd had endless discussions about the cruelty of some Coldi birth rituals. At least I thought it was cruel for a young mother to stumble into the desert, give birth alone and cover the child with sand while it was still wet from the womb.

Thayu said it was a very old custom that had become popular

again with women in the army. She said it was powerful and symbolised the strength of women. I suspected we'd never agree.

"I just don't like all the continued travel and disruption," I said.

"It doesn't take long to get out there."

But it was very isolated. The hand of panic clamped around my heart. I didn't want Thayu to be some sort of martyr giving birth in between reloading her weapon in a fight, or alone in some cave where she was hiding because of something stupid I'd done.

Because, from all I had heard about it, Taysha Palayi, the father's brother, had locked her in a room in his house after an argument, probably about how and when his brother's contracted baby would appear, and Thayu, being Thayu, had been stubborn because she hated the brothers who had never stopped humiliating her. And crashing the birth party by refusing to perform had been her only power. So after the guests were gone and there was still no baby, they locked her in a room without food or light. Coldi women could delay the birth, but not indefinitely, and the longer they waited, the more uncomfortable they grew.

She had told me that, sitting there in the dark, she had contemplated killing the child but, although this often happened, she realised that it would put herself and her father in a lot of trouble. And that was an admirable level of clear-headedness for a young and frightened woman in pain. So she had held out as long as she could, and when biology dictated that the child could no longer wait, had given birth and had painted insults with her bloodied hands on the walls. Then she had climbed out through a window, leaving the child on the floor in the room.

I couldn't even get my mind around the cruelty.

I wanted to avoid all reasons for her to compare this birth with that terrible situation. I wanted to be there with her, although the thought that no one else—like doctors—would be there terrified me.

"It all happens by itself," Sheydu had said to me when I voiced this concern. "Nothing you men can do anyway."

And she, being Sheydu, had probably given birth to Veyada in between reloading her gun.

I didn't think any of my association realised how deeply traumatised Thayu was by her previous experience. I didn't even think I'd realised quite how bad it was until it was too late, when she woke up with nightmares, clamping her hands around her stomach, pleading with someone not to take her child.

She had only been seventeen that first time.

Why had she given herself to that family, I wanted to know.

Because she wanted to be independent from her father, who was a hard taskmaster, something I could understand. Because a lot of powerful men leered at her, she needed money and a place to live, and had crudely sold her virginity to the highest bidder.

Because she wanted to be a spy, and the household of Athyl's lewdest and most corrupt official was a rich ground for information that had eventually launched her career, even though, to make reparations—apparently the insults written in blood on the walls had been too much—she would be required to give the family a second child.

I had paid out that contract. She cried the day I showed her the official declaration that he ceded all claim to her. But whenever mention of her son came up, her eyes misted over.

I would do better, much better.

Change of subject. "Deyu told me that she brought a message to you."

"Oh yeah, she did. Wait."

With a groan, she heaved herself from the couch and reached for a reader on the cabinet against the wall.

I jumped up. "I could have gotten that."

"I'm not incapacitated, just slow."

I touched her stomach, the skin hard and stretched under the loose shirt that she wore.

She handed the reader to me.

The moment I saw it, the sleek style, the message on the screen to hold my finger against the screen, I knew where this came from, and why there was so much security related to this message: when we were in Barresh, Chief Coordinator of Asto Ezhya Palayi could walk into my office and enjoy a meal with us. In fact, he very much enjoyed the freedom of doing so. When he was on Asto, he had to justify each move, because each of his interactions with other people had potential consequences.

The huge webs of loyalty that held society in check only worked in one direction: upwards. For the person, or people, at the top—Ezhya, Asha, Natanu and most of the Inner Circle— interacting with those in the outer parts of their loyalty webs was fraught with danger. Because if they spoke to a worker on the street, that worker's status might increase as a result of the interaction, causing an instability in the worker's environment that had the potential to work its way up the chain.

When I was in Barresh, Ezhya could easily speak to me. On Asto, every one of his moves was scrutinised. So he contacted me in secret. I'd been expecting this for some days.

I sat on the chair by the window that looked out over a dusty yard with a couple of vehicles. I put my finger on the screen. The message made room for a few lines of text.

Ezhya's message was short—very short.

It said,

Welcome to Athyl. I hope you find your accommodation to your liking and the ceremony pleasing.

I stared at it.

What?

No reply to any of the questions I had formulated so carefully before leaving for Asto?

"Anything wrong?" Thayu asked.

"Everything is wrong. Why did he even bother sending this?

He's not even telling me whether he will be at the ceremony. No reply to my questions about seeing him." I spread my hands.

And I'd wanted to see him. He'd entrusted me with an important function at Tamer. There was so much I needed to tell him about the alternate exchange movement of the Tamer Collective and the people who advocated it. In particular that sneaky, extremely smart Minke Kluysters. I needed to tell him about the last days of the great Aghyrian captain Kando Luczon and the direction of the remaining Aghyrians. All those things that weren't easily discussed via messages.

And instead he sent me this?

"Is he so scared that someone will read what he says and, heaven forbid, might think I'm trying to take their positions?"

"You don't understand."

"Obviously not."

"He sent you this message because he knows you expect a message, because that's what you've been taught to expect."

"Just to please me?" This was getting really strange.

"He is being *polite*." She used the Isla word, because there was no Coldi word that captured the same sentiment.

"He doesn't need to be polite to me."

"Yes, he does, and your reaction proves it."

"I want a *real* reply from him, that he will meet with me, or come to the ceremony and talk with me afterwards. You saw the things that are going on at Tamer. You've met Minke Kluysters. You know about all the data Jasper Carlson has been collecting. You've seen the Aghyrian ship. You heard their stories about a civilisation left behind in another galaxy. You know that these people have the capability to come back one day. He needs to know this, and not the filtered, sanitised version he'd get through *gamra*."

"Yes."

And then she left one of those infuriating silences where I wondered what she knew and was or wasn't able to tell me.

Eventually, she added, "There will be a time to talk about these things."

"And that time isn't now, when I've made an effort to come here?"

"I don't know what goes through Ezhya's mind. I honestly don't know."

And Coldi trusted their leader to make the right decisions at the appropriate time, always. This was one thing—possibly the only thing—that I'd have grave trouble accepting. I might have developed some of the *sheya* instinct that placed me in their society and caused people to have dominance or subservience reactions to me, but the transformation only went so far. It could not erase years of experience with people at Nations of Earth and *gamra*. There would always be the little voice inside me that said, "But, hang on. . . ."

The door to the room opened, and Veyada strode in. He stopped and looked from me to Thayu and back "Am I disturbing anything?"

"No, we were just talking," I said.

But Thayu said, "Yes. He is still worried that Ezhya has not made a commitment to talk to him."

"Oh." Veyada turned to me. His eyes were very dark, with a few gold flecks. He looked healthy and relaxed. "Ezhya will be here."

"That's what I said," Thayu said.

"No, you said that he'd make up his own mind."

"And why would you think that he won't come to see you?" Thayu asked.

Yes, why indeed? Because I hadn't heard anything from him for a long time. Because I was supposed to work for him and had things to tell him. Because some communication would be nice.

But he clearly didn't see the need.

He never spoke of his plans anyway, that was not his style.

And I should banish those last shards of *Earth* manners to

the place where they belonged: in the past. Ezhya valued me, because if he didn't, I would have noticed.

Ezhya would be here. At some time, of his own choosing. And I'd deal with it.

"Anything going on?" I asked Veyada.

"Time for training."

I protested. "But we already had a walk this morning."

And walk was quite an understatement for the mad scramble up a loose rocky incline with a bag of rocks on my back that he had made me do not once but twice.

"You need to gain more strength. You're still weak."

With a sigh, I heaved myself off the couch. It was true that in the last couple of years of my life I had become fairly disgusted with myself at how lazy I had become. With the laziness had come a certain softness of the body, and most of that had left me under Veyada's training that he'd started after we came back from Tamer. He seemed to be keen to give me the full military treatment. To what aim I didn't know, but Veyada rarely did anything just for fun.

Thayu assured me that she would be fine, so I went to the bedroom, changed into my outdoor training suit—a body-fitting one-piece, with tough patches on the knees and elbows—and followed Veyada out of the house.

"What are we going to do?"

"We'll have another wrestling session."

For the past few weeks, he had seemed quite keen on those. First he had me wrestle inert opponents like bags filled with sand. I was required to punch them, to pick them up and carry them across the room, flip them over my shoulder and lift them above my head.

Then he had switched me to wrestling him.

Veyada was quite tall, but he wasn't one of those Coldi power machines, mountains of muscle and flesh, like Deyu had become.

He was Coldi however, which meant he was naturally stronger than me.

Or I should say, he was stronger than I had been in my normal human form.

The first time we engaged in a wrestling match, his body had hit mine with the full force of his strength, and I hadn't fallen over. I had been so surprised by that I'd let him pick me up and slam me onto the mat.

After a number of days of daily sessions, that didn't happen anymore. These days, our strength was much more evenly matched.

He dragged the mat out of the storage room that normally seemed to hold items for simple maintenance on the vehicles in the courtyard: brushes and dusters to remove desert sand from nooks and crannies, a few rubbery panels, cutting tools and pots of adhesive to repair the caterpillar traction bands.

The wrestling mat was made of a smooth dark material that got very hot in Asto's unrelenting sunlight and, if anything, my efforts in wrestling Veyada sprang from determination not to end up on the mat with any exposed skin.

We grappled. He tried to push me over and trip me up, but I managed to block him until he left me an opportunity to swing him over my hip onto the mat.

"I win."

He grinned, getting to his feet. "You're becoming too good. I have to get you a different teacher."

"But I am not training to be in the military." I slapped dust off my suit leg.

Veyada picked up one corner of the mat and I picked up the opposite corner.

A couple of Asha's people had been watching us. They now went back to whatever they had been doing before.

We took the mat back to the storage room, never quite managing to get it off the ground. The black material was so hot that I had to keep swapping hands.

We dumped the mat in the corner of the room.

"Do you think this is what the military does? Wrestling?" Veyada asked.

"It has to be in the basics of the training, isn't it?"

On closer consideration, what was the need for wrestling when you had thousands of electronic weapons at your disposal?

Veyada said, "I've never been in the military but those who have tell me the first thing a prospective soldier learns is to blindly trust the military structures and associations. Fairly soon after signing up, all recruits get to do something that would kill them if it wasn't for their new military association. They learn to put their lives in the hands of others. Without that, you never have a military. They don't start off their training with fighting. Many of them never pick up a weapon."

"Then why is it that you're so keen to train me?" Because it couldn't just be for my health. This went beyond that.

"Do you remember when we were on our mission to Tamer, how we came into the craft that would take us to the planet and you had a tussle with the pilot?" His dark eyes met mine.

I nodded. I remembered that well enough. I remembered the overwhelming urge to attack him, and how I had managed to push the man into the wall, thus winning the confrontation, to my own surprise.

"That is why," he said.

"Is this to settle dominance disputes? Are there going to be that many?"

"Probably not, but your instinct is firing like that of an adolescent boy. I don't want you to lose any fights that you don't need to lose."

And with Veyada, that could mean anything.

While strolling back into the house, I asked Veyada if he had heard of the house in the valley, and told him that Asha wanted us to move there. And I added, "I've agreed, because it's very nice."

"You do know it's not just a house, right?"

"It's a historic recreation, as far as I can tell."

"Yes," he said, in that infuriating way that indicated there was more to it that he wasn't telling me. "I'm sure we'll find out a lot more about it."

"You agree with us going?"

"It's not up to me to agree or disagree. You've already committed."

"But do you think it's a stupid move?"

"No. What will happen will happen. But it will be interesting."

"Can you all just stop being so infuriating? If there is anything I need to know about this move, or about the house, or anything else, can you please be up-front with it and tell me?"

"There isn't anything. I could speculate on why the house was built, or why Asha wants us there, but it would be nothing but speculation. There are many possible issues. None that stick out to me as important right now."

Trust your superiors. That was all.

Shut up. Do as you're told.

3

———————

A**FTER WRESTLING** in full sunlight, the house seemed cool. Strange how one's perspective could change.

It was almost time for the late afternoon break, traditionally the time of day where people officially stopped work and came inside to deal with family matters. And Asha's household was highly regimented and traditional. You were not supposed to turn up at the table unwashed, especially if you had been working outside, so I ducked into the bathroom after Veyada had used it.

The bathroom, too, was very traditional. In line with the scarcity of water in Athyl, the "bath" part was just a stone bowl that barely held a bucket's worth of water, which was refilled from a spigot in the wall. There would be a water tank behind that wall, also a part of the mechanism to keep the house cool.

The bowl sat on a bench where stacks of folded washers lay as well as bottles of soaps. You were meant to wet yourself, spread the soap with one towel, then rinse yourself with another towel from the pile. Afterwards, you poured the water in a sink, from which it was filtered and recycled.

Thayu had walked me through the procedure. Was this common in houses in Athyl, I had asked.

No.

But the army was rigid and traditional and, while they spent lots of effort on technology in space, living quarters on land didn't factor into the equation.

"They expect to be fully space-based within twenty years," Thayu had said. "They have to conserve resources up there, so they consider the austere conditions in the bases practice for living in space."

One was also supposed to turn up in traditional clothing, a wide, loose-fitting garment and calf-length trousers, both in the traditional colour known as *shessyu*.

Coldi eyes didn't see the colour red. After my transformation I had gradually lost that ability, too and it had finally solved the enigma that Coldi used the *shessyu* colour in all ceremonial fabrics, but couldn't see its rich maroon pigment. Now that I couldn't see it either, the fabric was navy blue.

The traditional garments lay in the bathroom, neatly folded for everyone to use.

Nicha had managed to get even Ayshada into one of these outfits. Not that he liked it, mainly because Nicha had also told him that he couldn't bring his toy gun, at which point Ayshada started screaming. Nicha picked him up while we walked through the hallway to the main part of the house. I wanted to tell Nicha about the house, but Ayshada's protest screams killed all chance of a conversation.

I was tired from Veyada's training and would honestly have preferred a quiet afternoon.

On previous days, the afternoon gathering had been held in the kitchen, but today it was moved to the formal dining room.

The plain table was set with a feast of salted mushrooms, pickled vegetables, protein cubes—made from a kind of plant-based cheese that was set in a flat dish and cut into cubes—and other things that I recognised, and things I didn't.

Asha waited in the room, seated on the bench near the window. When we came in, Nicha still carrying the screaming Ayshada, he got up. "Come here," he said in a non-negotiable voice.

Ayshada stopped screaming and turned around.

Asha reached into his pocket and pulled out a tiny model of an aircraft. It was a sleek model of a small craft with large wings, designed to carry a lot of weight. I hadn't seen this type of craft before.

Ayshada's eyes widened.

"Come," Asha repeated. He dropped to his knees.

Nicha put Ayshada on his feet.

He carefully made his way over, eying alternately his severe-faced grandfather who scared him and the beautiful toy in his hand. Ayshada's eyes still lacked the gold flecking that adult Coldi developed, and it was almost impossible to distinguish his irises from his pupils. Right now, he was all big black eyes.

Asha held out the model, and Ayshada reached for it, taking it in his hands and clamping it against his chest, as if afraid that someone would take it off him.

Asha smiled and got to his feet.

"We'll have trouble getting that off him later," Nicha said.

"He can have it," Asha said.

Ayshada took in an audible breath, his mouth wide open.

Sometimes I wondered about his ability to understand what we said, but he definitely understood that.

"Will you say thank you?" Nicha said to his son.

Ayshada had to tear his gaze from his new treasure, but he bent his head and bowed. Asha stroked his head.

Then Ayshada ran off to the corner and started playing airplanes, the thought of food forgotten.

We all gathered around the table. The scene I had just witnessed filled me with an odd kind of warmth. It was always good to have it confirmed that, underneath the quaint habits and harsh judgements, Coldi adults felt the same way about young children as people on Earth did.

"This is quite a selection of good food," I said as we gathered around the table.

"Yes. I am not a bad host. I don't want you moving to the house because I dislike sharing my house with people—no, don't tell me that you haven't been contemplating that, because I know you have. Also don't tell me you don't think that my staff feels upset by your presence. I also know that to be true. And they are unused to having young children around and likely find them testing."

"Then what is the reason that we should move, other than that the house is comfortable and big?"

"No one can visit you here. There are many people you need to talk to, and you're off-limits to them when you're staying here."

This was also true. I still didn't fully believe that this was an important reason, but I let it ride. Thayu was right: we would find out the true reason. It had always been like that with him.

Asha told us that he would arrange for some people to come and help us move tomorrow. He had everything planned out in great detail. He handed Sheydu, as head of my security team, an extensive set of plans of the house, its internal structures and possible places for bugs, and a map of the surroundings.

Then I spotted him speaking to Reida, who looked uncomfortable, and Deyu, who was a bit more self-assured.

He even went to Mereeni, who held Ileyu. Ileyu looked around with a dopey look on her face, her gaze following Ayshada who ran around the room with his new toy.

Mereeni stood close enough to me that I overheard some of the conversation: he apologised for any hostile remarks by people at the base.

It was very strange.

Then I wondered if maybe he felt *lonely* in this stiff military household. I'd seen no evidence of companions, male or female, and had no idea what he did with his spare time.

I asked Thayu about it when we got back to our room. It felt as weird as asking a person about their parents' private life could feel.

"No, there is no special woman as far as I know," Thayu said.

"I had the impression he was trying to be friendly to everyone, especially Mereeni."

"I saw that, too," she said. "No, I don't know why he made such an effort to talk to them."

"Sometimes I think your father is as much a mystery to you as he is to me."

"He's not a mystery. There is always a reason. He never does anything without a reason."

"It would just be nice if he told us about it."

"Why? He tells you all you need to know when you need to know it."

I considered: had he ever deliberately withheld information?

Often, but not information that I needed. Thayu was absolutely right in this. It was just that I lacked the blind trust in people that let the others accept not knowing things.

But as Veyada had already said about military training: Coldi people needed to trust their superiors with their lives. I had no other option than to trust Asha to make the right decision.

The next morning, a couple of men arrived with a large craft to take us the short distance from the plateau into the valley.

When we got into the craft, Sheydu slipped into the seat next to me to let me know that she had the security issues under control—were there issues? I wasn't sure what she was talking about—and oh, she thought it was high time that we had our own transport. Apparently Leisha, one of the two men in her new association of guards had spent some time as combat pilot instructor. He could both be our pilot in the short term and train me and a few others to become accredited pilots.

Since our numbers had increased so much, I saw little sense

in disagreeing with her, even if it seemed so much bother to own a craft and buying tickets was so much easier.

But each time we travelled, the bill for our tickets became ever more horrendous, and for this latest trip we'd only needed to arrange permission to travel from the Exchange to the army base, because Asha paid for our transfer—and for crying out loud, why did transport companies charge so much? If we had to pay for commercial off-world tickets on top of that, things would get very expensive.

But owning an aircraft was expensive, too, and cumbersome.

Sheydu gave me a stern look. "No. I know what you're thinking when you have that look on your face. You need to do it. Don't delay and delay this like buying a weapon. Most of the aircraft are sold in Eighth Circle. I will plan a trip there after the ceremony."

We spoke about types of aircraft as we glided across the valley, circled the rocky knoll where the house stood, and landed on the small piece of flat land on the narrow spit that connected the knoll to the cliff.

Ayshada was beyond excited. He yelled and pointed out the window and jumped in his seat so much that Nicha had to restrain him several times, because the craft turned a few tight corners.

Mereeni sat behind Nicha, holding Ileyu, who had done the only sensible thing a nine-month old could do—she'd fallen asleep. Mereeni's dark eyes roved over the landscape and I wondered what went on in her mind.

Two hundred years ago, her ancestors had fled the regime that oppressed them, the outcasts from the Ezmi clan, and they had started a new colony on the metal-rich world of Hedron that had turned into a formidable mining empire.

While Asto and Hedron had ceased to behave like toddlers to each other, the relationship was cool and, growing up, she would never have thought—or wished—to visit Asto. But, seeing her clan still on the outside of Asto's society, I was sure she felt *something*.

I would have to ask her, when I had a moment.

Then the craft landed and we all got out, Ayshada running up the path to the door and Nicha running after him. Did that kid ever stop?

It appeared that overnight someone had been in to place furniture inside the house. The big rooms that had been empty yesterday were now furnished with soft couches and inviting beds. A set of low couches and ottomans stood in the living room. I recognised the heavy, blocky style from the Coldi households I had visited in Barresh. There was even the traditional little table in the hall directly opposite the entrance. It was as yet empty, but I would have to put someone in charge of placing an artistic arrangement of vases, bowls, dried flowers and rocks there, according to the unwritten rules that assigned meaning to the arrangements.

I wondered who in my association could do that.

Ayshada ran around the house screaming because he liked the way his voice echoed in the stairwell. Nicha told him a few times to shut up, to little effect.

Nicha and Veyada insisted that Thayu and I take the large room downstairs. Thayu first went into the bathroom of our suite, and found that a full birthing setup was already installed.

Mereeni approved very much of the situation. "This is really nice," she said while walking around carrying Ileyu, who was still asleep, drooling over her mother's arm.

I let my team divide up all the other rooms on the ground floor and upstairs.

Sheydu and the security association took up the front of the house where the path from the small landing area came into the door. They set up the room to the left of the entrance as their security station, with a bewildering array of electronics that had taken up more than half of our travel luggage when we came here, and had been added to since.

Naru Palayi and Isharu Vonayi, the *zhayma* pair directly under Sheydu, were giving directions to set up their equipment using the maps provided by Asha. They had dumped their small sacks of personal belongings in the two adjacent rooms on the right hand side of the front door. I assumed they would sleep there.

The *zhayma* pair under Isharu, Anyu and Leisha, were doing something with wires. Zyana and Sevayu, the other *zhayma* pair, under Naru, had dragged the table into the middle of the room and looked to be calibrating scanners, or something like that.

I asked if I could help them, but was told that everything was under control.

I observed them for a while from the door, happy that my security was in good hands, happy that Sheydu finally seemed content to do everything her way.

The house might be in a visible position, but with Sheydu in charge, people were unlikely to spring surprises on us.

For now, they were all very busy.

I returned to our ground floor bedroom, where Thayu was asleep on the bed. She lay on her side, her face away from the door. From this angle, the only way to notice that she was pregnant was that she no longer had a waist.

I sneaked to my bag to retrieve my reader. Time to do some work.

I took the device out to the veranda, where the air was warm and dry, but no longer hot to my skin. Although it was what passed for winter here, before my transformation I would have had to wear a temperature-retaining suit, take a double dose of adaptation medication and use a tank with cooled air to be comfortable. I was beginning to see the huge advantages of Coldi people. A few biological modifications had made life much better.

A bench ran along the wall in front of our room and the living room. I sat down with my reader on my lap and opened one of the documents I was working on, a long declaration of *gamra*-member entity rights and responsibilities that I was translating for approval by Nations of Earth. In the past months I had sent them reams of such documents, and translating them meant a lot more than just translating the words. The meaning of the words often did not become clear without context, and the first document I sent was two-thirds footnotes and one-third actual document. It was a very long and tedious process, because Nations of Earth would come back to us with questions and demands for further explanation.

This was just the formal process.

And it was with brief discomfort that I was reminded of the tasks I had left behind in Barresh. If ever I'd thought that having Earth formally accepted as a prospective member of *gamra* would solve problems, I'd been disabused of that notion soon enough.

A hacking scandal of the feeder data via Exchange coverage for the *gamra* island had rocked *gamra* to its foundations. Not so much the hacking itself—everyone knew that happened. Espionage at *gamra* was a gentleman's agreement. You allowed bugs in your house to protect yourself as much as other people wanted to know what went on. The Exchange wasn't secure and everyone knew that.

For years, the heavily top-down societal system of Asto and the lumbering democratic system of *gamra* had worked alongside each other. Asto officials made fun of *gamra*'s lack of quick decisions and *gamra* officials staged mock outrage at Asto's brash rudeness. But the fact was, they knew the beat. They knew each other's scheming and politicking.

What neither Asto nor *gamra* had ever seen was the sheer amount of commercialism that Earth brought to the equation. The looks on the faces of the *gamra* officials at the news that people listened in to conversations and used information gathered this way to *sell* it so that manufacturers and political activist groups could target customers was enough to let me know that we had a problem, a large, looming, cultural problem. The art of selling and especially marketing was not one of the *gamra* people's strengths.

Oh, they bought and sold, but it wasn't for nothing that the Trader Guild was the most respected organisation outside the official channels. If there was a local dispute and no law enforcement was present, a Trader would do. Like *gamra* delegates, they were allowed to carry a weapon, and on top of that, they had the mandate to arrest people and take them to the nearest law enforcement office.

Traders were highly respected people, and if ever they weren't —because let's not pretend that didn't happen—oh, boy, the Guild dealt with them swiftly.

So the *gamra* worlds knew commerce. The Trader Guild was the oldest trade association, preceding the pyramids on Earth by thousands of years. It was highly commercial.

What they didn't know was blatant, tacky, subversive, disruptive, deceptive commercialism of the type that was rife on Earth.

To those people who said that most *gamra* societies were not susceptible to it, I'd answer that one only needed to look at the subculture of well-off Asto businessmen and their collections of plastic figurines from 20th century Earth movies and cartoons. It was disturbing to come into a Coldi household somewhere in Athyl and be faced with a collection of faded plastic toys depicting characters that were popular in my grandparents' youths.

These collectors were ripe for the picking: gather their names and then find a way to send them lists of plastic junk for sale. And then send them increasingly politically motivated stuff. And jack up your prices under the guise of scarcity.

Right now, the structures didn't quite allow this to happen, but I didn't imagine it would take very long for those barriers to come down, seeing as Earth was an official prospective *gamra* member.

Would I have to stand up in the *gamra* assembly and declare: Look, I know I campaigned hard for this world to join, but now that they're here, watch your back and your pockets, because these people are really dangerous and will screw you over if you give them half a chance?

Yeah, that would go down really well.

And there was still the risk that things would go spectacularly wrong. Especially since the Tamer Collective, the group of entities that contained representatives from the Pretoria Cartel, had gained some legitimacy and were proposing to build a second Exchange that would be properly encrypted. A fairly large section of Earth business put their money on that system—because they didn't like the open Exchange—and it might be that, in the end, Earth never fully joined *gamra* at all, because the cultures were incapable of complying with the system of trust that had been developed over hundreds of years at *gamra*.

It was that fear that kept me awake at night. The fear that, having come so close to full cooperation, things would fall apart at the last moment. That we would end up with a situation worse than we started with.

It looked like this alternate Exchange was going to get off the ground some time sooner rather than later. The *gamra* delegates considered it a second-rate system, a cheaper version of the Exchange, that would deal with and allow entities that did not meet its stringent requirements to trade and travel to other worlds.

That part of the argument they understood. I wasn't sure how much they understood of the danger of encryption and other technological features that the builders of the proposed system were planning to add. What both worlds desperately needed was a connection between them to link each to the other, and an agreement that described what each could do and the other could not.

But so far all my calls for such an agreement had been met with blank looks from the stodgy *gamra* delegates, and I figured that something bad needed to happen first before they understood the danger.

Oh, they understood the potential for misuse. But they argued that they would just deal with perpetrators. I didn't think they understood how bad it would get, and what was more, that we had no laws that would allow us to prosecute these people.

After my plea to deal with this sooner rather than later, a delegate had asked, "But supposing that someone was really so mad as to spy on everyone to see what they do and buy, what would they do with all those useless figures?"

And I'd felt a ripple of agreement going through the audience.

My frustration had hit peak point right then, because it was not a matter of *if.* This was already happening. Jasper Carlson in Barresh was collecting this data. No one stopped him. No one said anything about what he could use it for. In fact, this data had already been used to show the Tamer group and Minke Kluysters in a good light, so that now we had to view them seriously.

These were not nice people. These people were *criminals.*

But collecting and using personal data—the only thing they could be accused of in *gamra* worlds—was not a crime and no one would realise how it could be used until it was too late.

And while I was here, the time bomb still ticking, and I was cut off from a number of my regular channels.

This trip would not be terribly long, but all of a sudden, while sitting here staring over this dusty valley, the threat of all the things that could happen overwhelmed me.

I recognised the feeling. Thayu would poke fun at me, saying that I couldn't possibly solve all the problems of the universe by myself, and that trying to do so would only end badly for me, and nobody else would care.

I knew I worried too much.

After the brief feeling of elation when the vote for Earth to join *gamra* was passed, a lot of worry had returned with a vengeance, and I'd not even had the heart to speak about this to the fresh-faced Earth delegates who had arrived in Barresh to join Melissa Heyworth in representing their home world.

It was all too depressing.

I shut down my reader and went for a walk around the house.

A glance through the window revealed that Thayu was still asleep. A strand of hair had come loose from her ponytail and fallen over her face. Her cheeks were rosy and the thin fabric of her dress showed the tight curve of her stomach. I was keen for this wait to be over and meet my daughter. No doubt Thayu was keen as well.

I didn't want to wake her, so I walked over to the veranda where a couple of steps led into the front yard of the house.

While there had been an attempt at landscaping, with the paved path from the front door to the landing area winding between large rocks, the lack of vegetation made the selection of materials monotonous. The choice was small rocks, medium rocks, large rocks, and very large rocks. To aid matters, they came in a variety of shades of grey.

I wondered if there was any other way of getting to the house than this narrow tongue of land that connected the rocky knoll with the top of the plateau. A narrow path led away from the landing area to the mountain ridge behind it, but it was nowhere near wide or substantial enough to carry land vehicles.

Asha had said that there was a path that went into the valley, which I had seen from the front veranda.

While I stood there, a craft circled over the house and came down.

Our pilot Leisha had not landed our craft economically, and there was barely enough space for the other craft, a clunky, dusty and well-used vehicle with the emblem of the Couriers' Guild on the side.

The crew proceeded to unload a number of dark boxes onto the ground and then left again.

Sheydu's people tromped out of the house, carried the boxes into the room that was meant to be their bedroom and proceeded to unpack them. More cameras, tripwire, sensor plates, motion detectors, smell detectors and drones. Great.

I wasn't sure why it was necessary, but meanwhile, everyone seemed to be waiting for something to happen. My induction ceremony, the birth of our daughter, and events that would happen as a result of us moving to this house. Whatever they were.

4

———

I WANDERED THROUGH the house, taking in its glorious design and exquisite craftsmanship.

Since wood had pretty much ceased to exist on Asto after the meteorite strike, builders used a synthetic material that could be made to look like wood. Usually, it had a cheap and tacky feel, but the windowsills and panelling of the living room looked so much like real wood that I spent quite some time studying them, running my finger over the grain, and I still wasn't sure if this was real wood or not. Whatever was the case, a lot of money had been spent on this house, and that was an unusual occurrence for Coldi society, without any clear aim.

A bit later, glancing into the hallway, I spotted Nicha walking through the house wearing full armour and a fearsome gun at his side.

Nicha did not normally wear weapons; in fact, he was the least likely in my association to do so.

I went into the hallway, where I found Veyada also in battle gear. "What are you all wearing that for?" I asked.

"Training," he said, his standard answer to everything.

"Do they really think that's necessary?" I asked Sheydu as she walked past, carrying a pack bristling with electronics.

She said, "Out of all the places we have been, this is probably the least safe, even if it's easier to defend."

That was Sheydu in her element—defending places that were not safe, making those places safe again, while complaining about how everyone was oblivious to security risks.

Of course she hadn't been able to do this at Asha's house. He'd be insulted if someone called his military base unsafe, although I was sure that Sheydu could have found thousands of ways to establish just that.

It was how she rolled.

"Are you going somewhere?" I asked her.

"We need to set up a wider perimeter."

She ducked into the security room and picked up a box full of gear.

"In the valley?" I followed her out the front door.

By a perimeter they meant an invisible line around a clearly demarcated area from which, once detected, a visitor, friendly or otherwise, would reach our position in a certain time. That period was usually the length of time it would take the team to grab their gear and be ready to defend their position. So they set the perimeter, with warnings at something like five minutes, which meant that from the time the system registered the visitor, my team had five minutes before the visitor would be with us.

I was following Sheydu down the path through the front yard. She stopped so suddenly that I almost ran into her.

She asked, "Do you want to come? You look kind of lost for something to do."

"If you'll have me."

I had also learned to take those types of invitations from Sheydu very seriously, so I asked her what to wear, and she said just walking clothes.

I was wearing comfortable house clothes, too thin to go into the burning sunlight, too light-coloured not to get covered in red dust, so I went into our room to get changed. Thayu had woken up. She was looking at something on her reader and turned to the door as I came in.

I told her about Sheydu's invitation.

"You should go. She probably wants to show you something."

"I wonder what she could want to show me out here?"

"You'd be surprised."

Walking clothes in Sheydu's terms usually meant to bring light weapons, so I strapped on my arm bracket and inserted the gun. Sheydu nodded appreciatively when I came into the hall.

Her entire association was waiting there as well. All of them were trained at the elite spy academy and looked the part, with the customary dark clothing and packs bristling with weapons and equipment. Reida stood with them, carrying a pack that looked too big for him.

But none of them looked as impressive as Deyu, who was also with them, a fighting machine of muscle, carrying an array of weapons, body and leg armour, explosives, trackers, wire, a rope and a veritable hardware store's worth of picks, knives and hammers. She had recently received a higher accreditation in her guard level, and I understood that she had passed the entire course with flying colours, even if no one spoke much of these things.

Anyu was in control of communications and wore an infrared visor, even if it was in the middle of the day, and carried all the things I could think of being useful in communications and quite a few things that I could not.

We went outside, walked down the path from the front door to the landing area, and turned sharply to the left. After squeezing ourselves between a couple of rocks, we found a narrow path that zigzagged its way down the steep rocky descent into the valley.

We walked in single file, and I had to admit to leaving the checking of our surroundings to others, because the footing was treacherous. Not only was the path steep, but the ground was hard and covered in fine gravel, and the drop-off into the valley very steep. On top of that, once we swung around below the house, the rock wall caught the full force of the afternoon sunlight, and it was hellishly hot. Wiping sweat out of my eyes while trying not to slip on the loose gravel was quite a feat.

But gradually, the ground evened out and the valley floor came closer.

People in Barresh joked about Asto as a dead planet. It was true that some areas on Asto were dead, but this was not one of them. Every crevice between stones was full of little plants and mushrooms. Most of them looked like some variety of lichen or moss, but there were some larger ones.

"We should come out here at night," Veyada said. "All these little plants come out and they sit on the rocks soaking up the warmth from the day."

I had learned that these moving plants had always been part of Asto's flora, but they had become much more prevalent and indeed the only wildlife to survive in many areas after the meteorite strike.

As the riverbed down the valley came closer, more types of plants appeared. Some tufts of vegetation looked like grass.

I stopped to take photos. In my youth I used to collect photos of wildlife around my grandparents' beach house in New Zealand and recently started doing it again. It was a relaxing occupation, especially in Barresh, where wildlife was abundant and poorly documented.

Reida had been much bemused by this activity of mine, and had started to collect rocks, specifically ones with fossils.

The closer we came to the bottom of the valley, the more humid the air became. That was also surprising to me.

The boulder fields now stretched out before us, and from down here they were not quite as desolate as they looked from up on the hill. There was a surprising amount of vegetation, something that would have been unheard of even last time I visited, even if most of it looked grey, dry and inedible.

"This is quite something," I said, crouching down to take photos.

"It started around the time of your previous visit,' Veyada said. "There were some big rains that year, and some of this vegetation appeared after rain was becoming more prevalent."

"Where does the seed come from?" I thought I already knew. I remembered the parties of scientific people from Asto visiting the Barresh Delta to collect plant material, because Barresh was one of the places where the Aghyrian refugees had gone, and it was clear that the vegetation in and around the city bore a very strong resemblance to that of their own world before the meteor struck. No megon trees were left on Asto, but if you compared the agricultural crops of Barresh with the rainforest plants the Pengali harvested, it was clear that they were different. Megon trees had not ventured further up and down the coast because they were not native to Barresh. They had been brought there by the Aghyrian refugees.

Not only that, but the megon trees of Barresh bore a very strong similarity to the paperbark trees on Earth.

But Veyada gave an answer I didn't expect. "Most of this vegetation is from seed deposits found in the aquifers. It's still native vegetation."

Some people on Asto objected to plants from elsewhere being transported to their world. They would only allow it if the plants could be shown to be the same as species that had existed before the meteorite strike. Of course, that was nigh impossible, depending on who you asked.

We walked through the rock-strewn meadow that was situated on what appeared to have become a floodplain. In places, there were dips where water had lingered for longer than in the surrounding dry land. Some of these places still contained a lot of poisonous salt that had been washed out of the soil, leaving patches of pink, white and yellow at the bottom of these depressions.

The river itself was clear. It wasn't particularly impressive, and not very deep, but presence of open water on the surface of Asto was surprising enough.

I asked Veyada if I could touch it.

He laughed. "You're now just as Coldi as all of us. There is no place on this world that is unsafe for you."

"Not even the Crystal Wasteland?"

"Well, maybe the Crystal Wasteland, but even that is fast becoming habitable."

So I crouched and dipped my fingers in the creek. The water was warm. I licked my fingers and recognised the slight metallic tang. Asto was high in fluorides and most water bodies were on the acidic side of the scale.

The creek made soft burbling noises while it made its way across the rocks. I wondered how long it would be before trees would grow here again.

A voice echoed over the floodplain. The security team had stayed behind at the base of the hill. They had set up an installation on a tripod on one side and someone was holding up a device. I could see lights blinking.

"What are they doing?" I asked Veyada.

"They need to calibrate the instruments for this area. Their security location file does not include the full landscape map, so they need to make one."

Sheydu took her job very seriously. It never ceased to amaze me how much preparation went into some of these tasks of protecting me and my team, which I thought would be fairly simple but apparently weren't.

We sat on a rock on the bank of the river watching them. The light from the two suns descended further towards the ridge of the valley, casting more and more of the opposite side in shade.

"I wonder what poisonous mushrooms we'll have for dinner." I was beginning to feel a little bit hungry.

I could see the top of the house from where we sat, but it would be a long and hot walk back up there.

Of course our regular cook Eirani had not been able to come with us, because she was keihu and couldn't visit Asto.

Instead, Asha had lent us a cook, someone I also suspected of being a partial spy. But that was how things went in Coldi households.

It seemed like the security party had completed their work, and were packing up their gear. We got back to our feet and had a leisurely stroll across the field to the bottom of the hill.

"You got what you wanted?" I asked Sheydu when we reached them. I still hadn't found out what, if anything, she wanted to show me down here. Maybe it *was* nothing more than a stroll into the valley.

"The maps for this area are rubbish," she said, in typical Sheydu fashion. She did not make small talk.

She shouldered her pack, a big rectangular box that had contained some of the equipment. She was carrying this on top of all the weaponry. It had to be heavy and Sheydu was not young, but she showed no signs of age.

The column slowly made its way back up the small path. This close to the hillside, I couldn't see the house any more. The going was tough. The afternoon sunlight beat down on the slope, the path was steep and loose rocks meant I was always one step away from an embarrassing and dusty slide back down. I followed Deyu. Reida walked in front of her, both their packs smaller than they had been coming in, now that some of their equipment had been installed in the valley.

Reida carried a bag full of rocks, most of them with fossils, and he kept adding to it while we climbed.

They were in good spirits and were joking and goofing around, and Reida was telling Deyu that he was interested in the creatures that had been immortalised between layers of rock. Deyu told him that she preferred live creatures over those that had been dead for many hundreds or thousands of years.

All I could do was put one foot in front of the other and take care not to slip. Clearly they were in better condition than I was. Veyada probably had a point with his training.

We were about halfway up the hill, when a section of the compacted earth came loose, and Reida who walked in front of Deyu shouted.

He fell flat on his face, and slid down the steep slope. Deyu managed to jump aside but he slid right into me.

I fell, too, like a bowling pin, landing on top of him. Together we slid through the treacherous loose dirt until we came to a halt against a boulder.

Oof.

I sat up and Reida did the same, a sheepish expression on his face. We'd both been wearing body suits and I had only lost a bit of skin off my left wrist. Reida sported a scrape on his cheek. He laughed.

"Here I was thinking that I was the clumsiest in our group," I said.

He reached for his shoulder. Then he looked around. "Where is my bag with rocks?"

The bag had gotten caught a bit further up the slope. The straps hung around a rocky outcrop and some of the contents had fallen out. Rocks lay strewn about, recognisable because their colour and texture were different from the gravelly hillside.

Deyu and I helped Reida pick up as many of his treasures as we could find.

Reida had affixed a small tag to each rock, the same type that security used to determine precise locations. I assumed that the tag had recorded where the rock had been found.

I piled rocks into my hand, but then my foot slid on the gravel. I managed to stay upright, but two rocks fell. One rolled down the hill, the other split neatly in half.

It fell into two equal sides, clean-cut. Something glittered inside.

What the. . . ?

I picked up both halves of the rock. The inside of one half

had been hollowed out so that there was some room for a tiny electronic chip. Well, what the. . . ?

"Have a look at this." I held out the rock so that Deyu and Reida could see it.

They scrambled up and down the hillside respectively. The typical chemical scent of the body suits, mingled with that of Coldi sweat, enveloped me.

"It's a bug," Reida said, confirming what I already suspected. He mentioned a make and model. "Same type the military uses."

"Where did you find that?" Deyu asked.

"It was inside one of the rocks Reida collected."

Reida took the rock from me and passed it over the scanner in his belt. "I found it a bit higher up the slope on the way down."

"Would it be a military bug?" Deyu asked.

The military base lay across the valley. They could see what happened at the house if they wanted to. The sky was turning golden. A few aircraft flew at high altitude, on their way to the airport in Third Circle, or other places.

There was no sign of life in the rest of the valley or sides of the canyon.

"I don't know," I said, and I didn't. I couldn't imagine Asha placing bugs to spy on us. If there were any, they would be in the house, and Sheydu and her team would have removed them. At this distance, halfway up the slope where Reida had found the rock, it was hard to imagine that the tiny microphone would pick up anything useful.

The others had stopped a bit further up the slope when they noticed we weren't following. Most of them were still waiting, basking in golden sunlight, but Sheydu was on her way back down.

Reida showed her the rock when she reached us, and told her briefly, and in jargon, what we had found.

Sheydu shook her head. "It can't be military. They've shared their network with us. We would have picked up the location.

We went down here because there *wasn't* any coverage. Those bugs are used by just about everyone around here."

"But who would have placed it?"

She shrugged. "Could be a lot of people." She jerked her head at Reida. "Take it up to the house and have a look at it."

She handed the two halves of rock back to Reida, who put them in his bag.

We continued up the hillside. When we came to the house, Reida went straight into the security room, where I spotted him talking to Anyu though the open door.

Wonderful smells spread through the hallway and Asha's cook—a friendly-faced young man—reminded us that dinner was almost ready.

I met Thayu in our room, and told her of the strange find.

"It wouldn't be a bug that belongs to my father or the army," she said.

"No, Sheydu already told us that. But I wonder who it does belong to."

"It could be orphaned, no longer operational, no longer needed."

"It looked quite recent."

"Things don't age in the desert the same way they do in Barresh."

That was true. "But who would put this in the middle of the desert? What would they listen to?"

"So many possibilities."

"What? Do you think it could belong to *zeyshi*?"

Thayu had lived and worked with those desert rogues, many of whom still lived in desert caves. "It's a possibility."

"But I thought there weren't any *zeyshi* in this area." Asha had told me so.

Thayu raised her eyebrows. "That's what people in power like to say."

"So I'm guessing it's not true?"

"It *could* be true, but likely it's false. One thing about *zeyshi* is that the smaller groups move around all the time. Many in the Inner Circle make the mistake of thinking that these are insignificant poor people on the outside of their own insignificant clan, but that's not true. Because they're smart and nimble, these groups have wide-ranging contacts everywhere, including with the less savoury elements of the Inner Circle. We've seen that during our last visit, yet the Inner Circle still peddles this view that they're insignificant, petty criminals."

She tended to get a bit fired up about this subject—I should have known better than to mention it. "Could you find out who they are through your contacts?"

"I don't know that it would be any help. The Ezmi clan is not united, and you'd be surprised to hear how many of my former contacts have died since I was involved with them. I'm not sure that my interference would be of help. More of a hindrance, probably, because I had little status when I was there, and now I have a much better position. They won't trust me and won't tell me the truth."

Even acknowledging that Thayu *might* have *zeyshi* contacts was a confirmation of her previous position, which was something I hadn't been terribly sure about. I knew she had worked as a spy in the Outer Circle and that her posting was based on material she had collected when living with Taysha Palayi and his family. She had uncovered significant misconduct.

Taysha Palayi—who had been Ezhya's second—was dead. I had shot him in defence of Ezhya's position.

This event and its deadly result was a highly sensitive subject, and one I expected to hear more about during this visit.

"So what can we do about these bugs?"

"Let Reida handle it. Then go through the proper channels."

Whatever those were.

We went to dinner, which was an agreeable enough event, with many mushrooms and other dishes that I had never seen or tasted. Someone must have passed on to the cook that I was partial to fried worms, because there were plenty of those.

Neither Reida nor Anyu came to dinner. I told the cook to make sure they got something to eat.

After dinner, Sheydu's people got up from the table as one and went down the hall. Not wearing a feeder and being privy to their communication, I assumed they'd been commanded there or something was about to happen, so I followed them. Thayu insisted on coming with me.

We found Reida and Anyu in the security room, fiddling with the large screens and the display on his reader.

I noted with satisfaction that two empty bowls stood on the corner of the desk, with the accompanying scent of cold food.

Reida jumped up from the only chair in the room, which he'd occupied because he'd been using the equipment, and offered it to Thayu. She didn't even refuse, and sat like a queen in a ridiculous—compared to her usual no-nonsense style of clothing—pale green dress, but for once looking alert and interested.

Naru sat on her knees under the desk while Leisha and Zyana were hooking up some equipment. I wondered what all of this was, but it was clear they'd made an interesting discovery.

5

—————

THE REST OF THE TEAM also came in.

The security room was small and the equipment took up a big part of it. Aside from the chair, now occupied by Thayu, it held no furniture.

Nicha and Deyu stood at the far end against the wall. Sheydu sat on the floor. Anyu was still fiddling with screens, and Sevayu and Isharu had retrieved a tray with cups of *manazhu* from the kitchen, which they distributed around.

Veyada and Mereeni came in last, because they had put Ileyu to bed. They had to remain near the door, because the room was full.

Ayshada was still running around the hall with his newly acquired model aircraft, making zooming noises.

Sheydu turned down the light in the room.

Darkness had fallen during dinner, with only a faint glow of daylight remaining over the opposite side of the valley.

As I had suspected, Sheydu's team had been setting up a projector.

Sheydu began, "We made a surprising discovery and need to show you a few things. The bug we accidentally discovered in a rock Reida collected is not a regular listening bug. It's a repeater bug. For those who don't know the difference—"

She looked at me, because I was likely the only one who didn't know the difference.

"—a listening bug sits in the ceiling or inside the wall plaster of a building. It's activated through voice and will either record or transmit what's being said. A repeater bug is always on. It listens for transmitted codes, and when it finds one of those codes, it will pick up and resend the signal. It stores a limited amount of data before sending it to another place every day, using the repeater bug. This happens at sunset, triggered by a diminishing of light and running down of the battery. It actually sent this information today while we were investigating, soon after we brought it here. More about that later."

She touched a screen and a projection sprang up in the air.

The setup was quite large, taking up most of the empty space in the middle of the room, including the top of Thayu's head and the corner of one of the equipment boxes.

At first, it was hard to figure out what I was looking at. The light was off, and the projection was also quite dark, with just some patches of light, as if this was recorded somewhere in a cellar where dark . . . things . . . were stored in rows. Sparse lights on the ceiling gilded just a few of the items, but the image quality was too poor for me to guess what they were. It would have been handy had there been a reference point, like a person, to see how big those things were. We could be looking at rows of chips on a circuit board for all I knew.

"What is this?" I asked. "Where is it?"

"This is the image that we took off the device," Anyu said. "It's paired with a surveillance bug, so it takes an image at regular intervals, and if there is no change, it starts looping them and overwriting them. We found over a thousand images in the device's storage. They're all identical. The quality is better than you would expect from the visuals, since it records heat as well, and we ran them through some manipulation programs. We came up with a remarkably better image."

She touched the screen in front of her a few times and a new image sprang into the air.

With the new image, the cavern's size became apparent. With flat surfaces and clean angles of walls and the ceiling, the structure was clearly artificial. The low ceiling was supported with many pillars.

On the floor stood rows and rows of . . . machines, like a parking lot.

Most were low, ground-hugging things with wheels or caterpillar mechanisms. One nearby machine had an identifiable cabin for a driver with a bank of solar panels on the roof. Any markings or features where these things had come from had been covered with a layer of dust.

On another machine, when Anyu enlarged the image, a badge had clearly been removed, because there were holes for screws in the metal. There was something vaguely familiar about the design of this thing, with long arms on either side, now folded against the body of the machine like wings on a bat.

They reminded me of the lumbering machines that put down road surfacing. I remembered a crew with these machines coming into the little town where my father lived, in New Zealand. On Earth.

But if I was right, or even if I was wrong, what the hell was this all doing here?

The members of my team stared at the projection.

"What the hell are all those things?" Nicha said, his voice low.

Isharu pointed at the screen. "That looks like a Damarcian design."

Sheydu had told me that she had chosen Isharu for her team because her family had a long history, back to the time when *gamra* headquarters were in Damarq over a hundred years ago, and still had very strong ties there.

"More importantly, where is this?" I asked. "I presume it's extremely unlikely that someone recorded this elsewhere and just happened, accidentally and randomly, to drop this bug here where Reida happened to find it." Those surveillance bugs had to be close to their paired repeater, because their reach was small.

Sheydu snorted. "I've seen stranger things happen, but no, there is a likely explanation."

She wiped the image and replaced it with yet another scan. This one I recognised as a three-dimensional projection of the valley. The knoll in the fork where the house stood was clearly recognisable, although this image had been made before the house was built.

But I noticed that the scan also showed the existence of structures in the ground, under the cliffs. They were faint lines that petered out a short distance into the rock.

"What's this?" I pointed.

"There are many of these caves in this area," Thayu said. The projection of the valley floor—without the creek that ran there today—touched her hair. "They're the remnants of the old city of Aghyr, buried after the meteorite strike and cemented together with the molten rock that flew out from the impact site."

"I didn't know those ruins went as far out of the city as this."

"Oh, they go all the way to the Crystal Wastelands, where the heat was too great and evaporated all the structures it hit there. None of the cliffs you see here are natural."

I hadn't known that. Now I wondered about the dark clefts and holes in the rock wall on the cliff that faced us. People could be watching us from those caves and we would never know.

"So . . . what does this image show?"

Sheydu said, "A lot of caves are in the area, some likely underneath this house; the scan Asha gave us doesn't have the detail to show us where the caverns are, and likely the bug Reida found was reporting on something close by."

"You mean that someone has hidden all these . . . vehicles in a cavern somewhere and no one knows about it?" That seemed absurd. "Why would anyone do that, in the middle of the desert?"

"It's not as strange as you think," Thayu said. "For many centuries, sections of the Ezmi clan, ones that have been known under the names *unclean*, *pirates*, or *zeyshi*, made their living from selling stuff they found. People in the Inner Circle bought a lot of it. It is, for one, the main reason why Coldi society has advanced so much. They studied and rebuilt the technology."

Reida was nodding. His family had strong connections with these people.

"Over the years, the good finds became rarer and the practice of collecting more competitive. The *zeyshi* warlords were pitted against each other in savage battles over ground and the right to explore cavern systems, until the market collapsed. Then the *zeyshi* went into producing their own technology with their own expertise, especially in health care, since their clan has some unique genetic issues that make them unlikely to have the *sheya* instinct and that come with a range of other problems."

Specifically, some of the Ezmi clan were Aghyrian throwbacks, and they had been treated appallingly throughout history.

Thayu pushed herself straight on her chair. "But the trade in historical items never died completely, and these holding rooms still exist. This particular one is a bit too far out of the city for my network to be familiar with, but I've seen similar setups. The established opinion is that *zeyshi* are brutes eking out an existence in the desert where they kill each other over access to muddy wells and abduct and rape girls to keep their numbers up, but the reality is very different these days. These are sophisticated operations and there are many of them. The *zeyshi* communities survive through trade and, since their main source of items to trade—old Aghyrian artefacts that they dug up—is almost depleted, they've moved to different types of trade, mostly of technology, because that technology also improves their own lives." She looked at me. "On our previous visit, it was *zeyshi* technology that saved your life."

I'd been aware of that.

"That's all very well, but one thing doesn't add up," Sheydu said. "It seems to me that many of these machines have been collected from other worlds."

"We also know that Asto has been opened up to visits from other worlds," Veyada said. "It's why we're here. While our visit has been sanctioned by authorities, let's not pretend that there won't be any unsanctioned visits, especially because the *zeyshi*, who are still on the outside of society, are people who would benefit from those off-world contacts, and the Tamer Collective group now offers a means of doing so without being tracked."

Off-world Aghyrian visits to the *zeyshi* warrens, we'd known about those, too. There was no reason other people couldn't have visited illegally. Business interests, other Aghyrians, Jasper Carlson, Minke Kluysters. The thought made me shudder.

Thayu nodded. "Yes. Let's not forget that these are the people a group of whom, two hundred years ago, escaped from here and founded Hedron, which is now the most technologically advanced world of *gamra*."

She let that statement hang in the air.

Mereeni—who came from that highly technologically developed world of Hedron—lifted her chin as if daring anyone to speak.

Most people from Asto's inner circles considered Hedron an affront to their authority. And yet the fact that Mereeni had been allowed to come with us was definitely a sign of relaxing rules.

I wondered how much effort Sheydu had to put into getting her highly traditional team to accept that this feisty lawyer from Hedron was part of the association they were supposed to protect. Knowing Sheydu, she would have made this expectation very clear. Veyada had chosen Mereeni as partner and he was Sheydu's son, and I didn't doubt for a second that Sheydu would die for him. She had decided to accept Mereeni and would protect Mereeni and Ileyu, too.

I asked the group, "Do you think Asha knew about this storage cavity when he sent us here?"

Isharu said, "I don't see how he could have. He could have noticed some activity, and might have known that something was happening here, but we discovered this by accident. I don't even know how important it is."

Again, Thayu shook her head. "He knows. Possibly he hopes that we will find out what it's about."

"Is that why the house was built?" I asked. "Presuming he built it."

Now Deyu spoke up. "The house was built by a historical organisation led by a woman named Rashanu. She is part of the group of people who believe that Coldi should be proud of their culture and honour their history over importing foreign technologies and habits. In their quest to find shining examples of culture that did not come from other worlds, they came across the plans of this house. It's amazing because the plans were completely untouched by the disaster, and the house had been planned for this locality. So they decided to build the house that was never built back then, as a symbol for our culture and resilience."

After fifty thousand years. Talk about a holdup in acquiring a building permit. "Does the house belong to her?"

"People don't own land out here, so it's built on communal land. Through a stroke of luck—and probably because authorities weren't paying as much attention as they should—Rashanu managed to obtain the right to use the land, and paid for the construction, but she is old and has plenty of funds. She gives a lot to people who teach people to have pride in their own culture. I would assume that she lends the house to people who want to use it to help her cause."

"Just to be clear, Deyu, this woman is one of the philanthropists in the Inner Circle?" But in that case, how did she even know about this?

"Not at all. She lives a few houses down from my father's factory." She held up her chin. "Her full name is Rashanu Omi."

Several people gasped at once.

"The leader of the Omi clan?" Anyu asked, sounding incredulous.

"Yes," Deyu said, sounding defiant. "We are not just dumb workers, you know. We have plans, too."

I held up my hand to silence them.

Deyu and Anyu had already clashed once before over this matter. Anyu—as oldest in our group—could be a little dismissive of anyone who didn't fit her own highly trained Inner Circle experience. She'd referred to Deyu as "just a train driver" at which Deyu had reminded her that even if she would have never stopped being a train driver, she still would have been responsible for the safety and comfort of far more people than those who guarded a single wealthy person in Inner Circle.

Yeah, that discussion ended well. Pardon my sarcasm.

It seemed this trip was really going to test my ridiculous idea of gathering people from all those clans in one household.

In one stroke, I'd learned more about the house and valley than Asha had ever revealed. I wondered how he had secured permission to use the house for us, and wouldn't be surprised if this involved intentional planning.

Maybe we were here to discover things.

"So what are we to do about this strange discovery?" I asked.

"Without further information, probably very little," Sheydu said. "So the Ezmi *zeyshi* have a storage facility somewhere. The bug sent a message to a place in Eighth Circle to report its daily activities. We've disabled it and now it will stop sending. I don't know if the *zeyshi* will get upset about it. We'll find out their next step."

"There is only one issue," Reida said. He didn't often speak up, and people listened when he did. "They're not Ezmi or *zeyshi*."

"How do you know that?"

"Because I asked."

Anyu said, "The Ezmi clan doesn't have a leader or a clan representative."

"That doesn't mean I can't ask respected people about this find."

True. Again I held up my hand to ask Anyu to be silent.

Reida continued, "I have consulted with them. They tell me it has nothing to do with them. In fact, they tell me they're curious about who owns the contents of the cavern, because they shouldn't be there, according to a long-standing agreement, which my clan adheres to."

"What sort of agreement?" Mereeni asked, but I'd heard Asha mention it.

Reida said, "An agreement was made long ago between *zeyshi* groups and the Vonayi clan that the *zeyshi* would stay out of this valley, because it's important for the water supply of the aquifers. In return, the *zeyshi* tribes were granted the use of Taivi and Origin Hill."

I was unfamiliar with those names and frowned at Veyada.

"Let him explain," Veyada said.

Reida's cheeks coloured. His eyes met mine. "The *zeyshi* are proud to trace their ancestry down to the ancient settlement of Pakkatish."

That name rang a bell for me. "Weren't they considered to be rivals of the so-called 'rational' Aghyrian government?"

"Yes. The women of Pakkatish," and then he used a word, *negari,* which I had never heard before.

"What does that mean?"

"*Negari* is a *zeyshi* word for a wise woman who advises young men what to do and how to behave, how to be a good person."

"Like a *priestess?*" I used the Isla word, because Coldi didn't have any language for spiritual positions. Coldi people could be extremely superstitious, but they had no organised religion.

At the same time as Reida said, "I don't know what that means," Thayu said, "Yes."

Reida continued, "There are stories that when the meteorite approached, the *negari* of Pakkatish took babies into survival life support chambers deep underground. Many died but some survived. Many were found by the early Coldi people who had survived in these chambers themselves. But these people were different. They were descendants of the original people of Pakkatish that you would call Aghyrians today. They are the roots of the *zeyshi* people and the Ezmi clan. So the hill in the centre of Pakkatish was important. The Inner Circle denied us access to it for a long time. They feared that allowing us back on the hill would make us likely to create trouble. So they proposed an impossible deal: the hill or access to secure water."

I noticed how his language shifted from describing a neutral historical event to *we* and *us*.

Then another thought. "You knew this, coming into this valley?"

He straightened. "Every Ezmi child knows this."

In the corner of the room, Mereeni nodded. "I remember. I didn't realise it was this particular valley, but we were taught about this cruel bargain. And we were taught that the Ezmi clan is proud and resourceful, and that this was why our ancestors chose the hill and not easy access to springs."

Reida continued "And that surprised them, because they expected us to choose the easy option."

Mereeni again, "And they wanted us to do the farming—"

Reida interrupted, "For no pay of course, other than the right not to be chased around."

Mereeni again. "For the right to remain hungry and desperate."

"Our ancestors were proud people."

They met each other's eyes across the room during this

extraordinary exchange. Veyada had his hand on Mereeni's shoulder. No one else spoke. The treatment of the *zeyshi* and the people in that group who had so much Aghyrian blood that they didn't look Coldi and didn't have the *sheya* instinct was a black stain on Asto. It had all happened at least two hundred years ago, the *zeyshi* had recovered to some extent, as I had already seen, but they *still* lived on the edges of society.

They had struck out once and had settled at Hedron. If anyone thought that Hedron had forgotten about them, here was the evidence that they hadn't. Children were taught this shared history in both communities.

Well, that was . . . chilling, powerful, interesting.

Speaking into the uncomfortable silence, Reida continued, "So all we're saying" —he again used inclusive-we to indicate himself, Mereeni, and the Ezmi clan— "is that this storage isn't a *zeyshi* construction, because we stick to agreements. And besides, for people in the Inner Circle, it may seem that Eighth Circle and the Outer Circle are all the same, dusty settlements full of poor people, where they can't travel without an army of guards. But as someone who has lived there, I can tell you, there is no bigger boundary than that between Eighth Circle and the Outer Circle. When you're in Eighth Circle, you're a citizen, you're legal, you can take part in the concourse, you can improve your position, your community gets trains and hospitals. In the Outer Circle, we get nothing."

Now Deyu was nodding.

"So, we traced the location back to Eighth Circle. It's unlikely this went to a place controlled by the Ezmi clan. That's all I have to say about it."

6

———

THE MEETING BROKE UP soon after that and everyone went to their rooms.

Reida and Deyu went upstairs together and didn't speak to anyone. I'd have to find some time to speak to them individually. I wanted to ask Deyu about this woman Rashanu and Reida about the movements of the Ezmi clan and whether he could lead us to some of his contacts, or any suggestions where we could find this cavern. I wasn't sure whether to believe him that the Ezmi clan had nothing to do with the storage cavern, but even if he was right and they didn't have anything to do with it, they might know who did own it, or at least give us some pointers.

If I was going to find out—and even Thayu's suggestion that Asha knew about its presence made sense—I would need to use Reida's and Thayu's contacts. The fact that Asha knew about it meant that I *had* to find out what this was about, because that was likely the reason he'd put us here.

And I had to make sure nobody got killed in the process.

When we moved into the house, Sheydu and her association would have done a good sweep of the house to check for listening devices, but I asked them to do it again just in case.

They spent most of the evening crawling in the spaces under the house, scanning walls, investigating window frames, sticking their heads into ceiling vents and rummaging on the roof. They didn't find anything.

Personally, I found Asha's warning about the Omi clan and the fact that one of that clan owned this house—even if one couldn't really own anything out here—far too convenient a coincidence.

I agreed with Thayu: Asha knew that something was brewing and had somehow managed to get the owner to agree to our use of the house.

Something to do with the Omi clan, which he was trying to keep in the good books of, or foster some sort of relationship with. And that in itself was unusual enough.

While Thayu rested, I went upstairs to talk to Deyu. After I knocked, she came to the door, her expression flustered, as if she'd been having an argument or making love, and I wasn't game to ask which.

She told me that she didn't know why the house was built. She knew the Omi clan leader Rashanu, who was a prominent businesswoman in Eighth Circle who headed some sort of historical society.

"But my information is likely a couple of years out of date," she added.

"Could you set up a meeting with her?" I asked.

Deyu replied that she would try.

Other than that, we could do nothing except wait and see. From my experience, waiting and seeing was very much what security did. They made reactive decisions and were rarely proactive other than when a clear threat had already developed.

I wasn't even sure I wanted to investigate this actively.

So we waited.

Later in the evening, Thayu asked me to rearrange some of the things in the bathroom.

The traditional birthing outfit consisted of a hammock chair, a contraption that could be folded out to look like a barrel and could be filled with water, and various boxes with towels and sheets. Newborn children slept in another type of hammock that came with a frame and a satchel. This thing stood in the corner of our room, sowing anticipation and a small measure of fear in me whenever I passed it.

What if I was really terrible at being a father?

Thayu wanted the chair in the bathroom to be moved to the other corner so that she could move the rubbery mat that was also part of the package into the light that came from the window.

She looked on while I did this—and the thing was solid and quite heavy.

She gave an air of confidence, but small things, like her tendency to be quiet in our security meetings, made me think that inside she was very fragile.

I closed her in my arms, smelling the hot scent of her skin.

She said in a low voice, "You will now definitely have your initiation ceremony before the child comes."

Four days. I'd read that Coldi women could delay the birth by five days. I understood this was what she had done previously.

I couldn't console her by saying not to worry about the ceremony, because it was important and the only reason we had come here. But it seemed she worried about it more than I did, and I had the niggling suspicion I was missing some vital information that might have been dropped to me, but I'd put aside because I had been too worried about Thayu.

Becoming a parent was exhausting and I had the easy part.

To be honest, now that we were on the very pointy end of this part of the process, I couldn't wait for the next phase.

Everything was ready. We had the name picked out and had notified the register that we would be using the name. We'd prepared a room in my apartment, even if the little one would be sleeping in our room for the first few months. Thayu had brought a bag full of tiny shirts, a few of which had been sent by my father, and all we could do was wait.

Wait, in this spacious, luxurious, out-of-the-way house in a place that puzzled me to no end, while there didn't appear to be anything to do except wait for the ceremony or for our daughter to make her appearance.

Or for someone to object to our presence and send us a writ.

Or for a territorial war to break out around us.

That evening, while Sheydu and her team were still scoping out the house, I attempted to do some work, but the climb down the hot hillside had made me very tired, and I joined Thayu for an early night.

It was still dark when I woke up.

Someone was running through the hallway and the footsteps made the floor shake. A door banged against a doorframe. Somewhere outside a voice shouted.

What was going on?

I sat up in bed, but it was so dark I couldn't see anything.

Thayu was still asleep, and I didn't want to disturb her. I climbed out of bed and went to the window.

But the window looked out over the valley. A light was on out there, but it was across the canyon, a long way from where we were. The sound I'd heard came from behind the house.

I jumped into some clothes, went into the hallway, remembered that I had been drilled to always bring a weapon, and went back to get my gun. I strapped it on while I went into the corridor.

As I was about to shut the door, there was a bang, and then the very distinctive sound of the discharging of a gun.

"What was that?" Thayu said in the room. She sat up in the bed.

"You stay here." I wasn't having her involved in anything dangerous.

"Fine." She got up and put on clothes.

I very much wanted her to stay here, safe, but I also knew

that it was foolish to try and stop her. She was out in the corridor with me in seconds. She had even brought a weapon.

Once security, always security, no matter how pregnant.

On reflection, she was probably as concerned about me as I was about her, and I resolved that we should probably stay inside the house, for the safety of both of us. We had a full contingent of proper security people to deal with whatever disturbance had developed.

The action appeared to be at the entrance of the house.

The light was off in the security room, but the equipment was in operation. The full bank of lights was blinking, indicating that the team were all awake up there and using their receivers.

The boxes and crates inside the room stood open, the content gone. Sheydu's large guns and explosives. The rocket launcher.

I peered out the window.

Out in the darkness of the night, I could see very little. Thayu had a gun out and used the infrared sensor on it to scan the surroundings. I did the same with my gun. The screen was tiny, and only allowed the user to see the small part of the scenery. Making anything out in the grainy picture was an acquired skill.

"Is that a person kneeling behind a rock?" I asked.

"That's Sheydu," Thayu said.

No doubt her gun was attached to the bank of security equipment in the room behind us in a way mine wasn't. I opened the channel on my feeder, and heard some garbled speech. Sheydu, I thought.

". . . over there. Put a marker on that rock as well."

Someone else responded. Reida, I thought, or maybe it was one of Sheydu's people.

"What are they doing?" I asked Thayu, keeping my voice low.

"Someone was stupid enough to try to sneak into the house. They tripped the perimeter and woke everyone up with the alarm." *Everyone* probably included the security team, but not me.

"Why would they break into the house? I thought they would send a writ first."

"Depends on who they are. It could be a warning. It could be they don't have enough manners to send writs; it could be that they *were* coming to deliver the writ but were clumsy enough to run into the perimeter."

"In the middle of the night?"

"Unlikely, but it could be anything. We will only find out when we catch them. I trust Sheydu will do that." Her voice told me she was sad not to be doing any of the catching.

Sounds of a rapid exchange of gunfire crackled through the night.

"Hmm, two weapons firing," Thayu said. She was scanning the hillside on the other side of the aircraft parking area.

Heart thudding, I aimed my gun in the direction of the hill, and was hit with a blast of white light from the screen. A moment later, the rumble of an explosion shook the ground. "Holy crap, what was that?"

"That would have been one of Sheydu's explosives," Thayu said.

In the visor of my weapon, when I set the magnification to the highest setting, I thought I could make out a couple of figures lying on the ground, judging from the shapes. Or maybe they were just rocks that retained the heat better than the surrounding sand and they showed up better in my infrared visor.

I peered at the tiny screen, willing a clear picture to emerge. Damn this poor night vision.

From my previous visit I knew that nighttime was unlikely to be very dark. It was common that a layer of mixed fog and dust blanketed the city and surrounding areas, and that the city lights reflected back to the ground.

I knew where the city was in relation to our position, but

couldn't, for the life of me, see the glow of light in the distance. Having experienced better night vision before my transformation, I knew what I had lost. I felt like I was blind.

It was frustrating. I panned the scanner over the area where I thought the action was taking place. At one point I wasn't even sure if I was still looking at the hillside behind the house.

But then I spotted someone coming out from behind a rock, carrying a long object resting on the person's shoulder. A second person also carried a long thing, but in a shoulder sling.

Armed people. Sheydu and her association?

Another figure came into my vision from the direction of the house. This person was tall and broad shouldered, and clearly armed.

"Is that Deyu?"

But I knew it was. Coldi women only grew this formidable if they started training young. Not even Mereeni at the Hedron guards had developed that impressive physique.

Deyu picked her way along the hillside, stopping at each of the figures I had seen lying on the ground, went through their clothing, turned them over, presumably photographed their faces and collected their weapons.

Thayu said, "Watch out."

Another figure approached from the other side.

Careful, Deyu.

Deyu straightened and looked around. Thayu's warning had reached her.

The attacker wasn't so lucky.

Deyu raised the gun, and ruthlessly fired at him. The gun had to have been set on the most lethal setting, because the white beam of light—to my vision—went straight through the attacker's body, exploding in a spray of light gobs. The person fell backwards.

Deyu fired two more shots in a direction out of the narrow view of my visor. Then she jumped onto a rock and continued firing.

I searched the hillside for her target and found a person standing as frozen, glowing in the vision of the visor, just as Deyu hit the figure another time.

Why was she doing that? Because when you hit someone repeatedly with a charge gun, the body cooked from the inside and exploded from the pressure—don't ask me how I knew that.

No, she didn't go that far, but the next figure she hit only lit up partially, and then something giving off a bright glow went rolling down the mountainside.

His head.

She'd set the gun to an even more precise beam.

Two more attackers ran down the hillside. Deyu made short work of them.

She had emptied the gun. She stuck it in her belt and grabbed another one and continued firing. I couldn't even see the targets.

At this point, two other people joined her, returning fire from further up the hill. One of them carried a cannon which he placed on a stand.

I kept my visor trained on Deyu. She used the cannon to blow up a rock, and when the people hiding behind it went running, she picked them off, not missing once. Soon, the hillside was covered with glowing bodies, already fading after the heat from the charge was seeping into the night.

A chill went down my spine. This gentle young woman was a killing machine.

Eventually, she had flushed out the last person and calm returned.

I let go of the veranda railing that I didn't realise I'd been clutching so tightly. "What the hell was all that about?"

There was no reply.

I looked around, realising that Thayu no longer stood next to me. Where was she?

I went into the house, but didn't know whether I could turn on any lights. In the pitch dark, I could see and hear nothing.

Were all the members of my team outside? I could hardly believe that. For one, Thayu was in no position to go out there. Or I would get very angry if she had.

Then I spotted a little pool of light on the other side of the paved area where the aircraft stood. I could see the outline of a couple of people backlit by a light. They were surrounded by bodies on the ground.

I thought one of the people walking around was Sheydu. Thayu was there, too, in the typical pregnant woman pose with her hands by her sides.

Fear clamped around my heart. No one from my team was injured, were they?

I wanted to run over there and find out.

But Veyada's lessons at all those security drills came back to me. Never do anything unexpected. Never go out alone without telling anyone. I should always scan the area for where everyone was. I should always make sure that none of the enemies were still in the area.

It had gone quiet and Sheydu, still walking around between the bodies, didn't seem to be particularly concerned about danger.

I made sure I collected all the necessary equipment from the security room: receiver, helmet, locator. I checked my gun and went down to the veranda.

The night was very dark and quite cool. The path from the main entrance to the aircraft parking area was paved, but I remembered there were some steps and I didn't know where they were. I walked very slowly, because I didn't want to turn on a light. I scanned around me with the gun visor every few steps.

I reached the aircraft not much later and uneventfully. I hid myself behind its bulk and put on the helmet and turned on the visor. The projection inside the visor showed me a number of light dots with their identification. These were members of my team. I wasn't aware of all the numbers but one of them I recognised as Deyu. With her number came a long list of weaponry she carried.

I turned to the house, and the helmet showed me a point there, too.

Anyu, now at the security station.

"You appear to be using at least some of the training we did," a voice said nearby.

I gasped.

While I was looking at the surroundings, Nicha had come up behind me.

I asked, "Do you have to sneak up on me like that?"

"If you'd been paying attention to all your channels, you would have realised I wasn't sneaking."

That was right, of course. I had not been watching the partner channel. "I didn't have a partner in this," I said.

"We started this venture as *zhayma*s. Partners are for life."

Also true. I asked. "What's going on?"

"Someone tripped the perimeter alarm, and when Sheydu's people went out to check, they were fired on. When they defended the path to the house, the assailants went into a full-blown attack."

"Who are these people?"

"We need to find out. But many of them won't be answering any more questions."

"Yeah. I saw that." The brutality with which people defended their positions in Coldi society still disturbed me, even after all those years. How could someone as gentle as Deyu go on a killing rampage?

"Let's go and look then."

7

WHEN WE GOT to the other side of the aircraft parking area, the smell hit me. I'd smelled the sickly scent of cooked flesh before, but the higher temperature of Asto's night made it all the more noticeable.

I pushed away unbidden thoughts of that one time I'd seen this happen in front of my eyes, when my *gamra* employed security guard Evi—who was not Coldi, couldn't come to Asto and was manning the skeleton staff at my apartment in Barresh—had repeatedly shot Romi Tanakan, the Indrahui war lord who had killed his family. That was a good number of years ago. I still couldn't think of it—or eat soup with too much meat—without feeling ill.

I stopped, not wanting to give in and appear weak but not wanting to go any further. Sweat rolled down my back.

A dark figure was coming towards me.

I recognised the familiar broad shoulders and tall build: Veyada.

"You're too late. All the action is over."

"Nobody woke me up until you were all running through the hall. I thought you were handling it well."

"That's what we're for. I'm joking. I think I would have been upset if you had come out with us. It's quite the situation."

"Is it safe now?"

"As far as I know, yes."

Meaning that the team members were still scanning the surroundings. "Who were these people?" I asked.

"We're trying to work that out," he said. "That said, it's highly likely that they're *reychi*."

Those were nameless fighters, people whose lives were forfeit because of some transgression, and they were paying back their duty to the person or clan they wronged for the chance at dying honourably. It was an odd habit. The concept of the Tamerians was the same and I'd seen those type of fighters before: those who had attacked us when we were at my father's house in New Zealand. People with next to no identity, whose only aim it was to carry out orders, usually of violence, and often to die themselves in the process.

"How many are there?"

Veyada replied, "A lot. More than we initially thought. We were heavily outnumbered."

Which might have explained some of the viciousness of Deyu's actions. If someone sent *reychi*, either you killed them or they killed you. There was no compromise. They would not negotiate.

Which made me swear to never challenge Deyu in a fight.

Behind Veyada, I spotted someone dragging a body down the hillside. It was Isharu, one of Sheydu's people. She dropped the body in the dust, undid the belt and searched all the pockets. She gathered a couple of devices, which she dumped in a pile of electronics and went back up the hill for the next body.

I could see this clearly now because the sky was turning blue and sunrise wouldn't be far off.

"Are any of them still alive?" I asked Veyada.

"If they are, they're not around here."

But, being *reychi,* they would rather die than flee, because there was nothing for these people to flee to. "Can I do anything to help?"

Veyada said, "I don't know that you want to see all this. Deyu made a bit of a mess."

The nauseous feeling returned. "I can handle it." I had long since decided that I would not shy away from any mess that my team created on our behalf. So I braced myself and followed him across the paved area around the side of the aircraft.

While we walked, I noticed that he held his hand on his weapon, just in case.

Deyu and Reida stood at the area where the pavement met the rocky slope on the other side of the aircraft.

A bumpy path led up the hill that we hadn't investigated yet. I assumed that the path led up to the platform and from there to some of the far Outer Circle communities, but a map I had seen had shown the nearest community quite a distance away.

The attackers must have come from there, since there didn't appear to be a vehicle involved, all of which made the *reychi* theory more likely. Someone had a grudge against us, but these attackers wouldn't give us any clues as to who it was.

My team had dragged a number of bodies down the hillside. I helped search their clothes for devices, and the container with electronics became two containers.

Some of the bodies where mutilated, and there were drag marks in the dust from blood. That brought me another uncomfortable question: what did people on Asto do with a mess like this? In Barresh, the island security would take care of it, contacting the families and disposing of the bodies in orderly fashion. If families couldn't be located—which was often the case for Tamerian mercenaries—the bodies went to a funeral house in town where they were incinerated under pressure— since one couldn't make fires in Barresh—and the remains kept in a little jar with a tag, in case relatives ever turned up.

I didn't know why this suddenly seemed important to me. I guessed it was my too-sensitive human sensibilities taking over. Because I wanted to do the right thing, because, damn it, this type of carnage *upset* me, as it should upset decent people, no matter that the *reychi* had "attacked first" and without warning. We were perfectly in our right to defend ourselves and were very capable of doing so. Dare I say, we had probably been allowed to use this house for that reason.

Sheydu and Thayu were walking back to the house in a serious discussion. I'd have to ask Thayu about it later.

If Deyu felt anything about the carnage she had inflicted, her face didn't show it—a reminder to never, ever, project human feelings onto Coldi. They just didn't work that way.

"Most of them aren't wearing any clan designation," Reida said.

"Reychi?"

"Or Ezmi clan."

Coming from him, that sounded particularly grim. Theirs was the one clan that did not normally wear clan designation, the earrings with coloured stones. It was Reida's own Ezmi clan, even if he wore the amber earrings these days. Many of those people did not have the *sheya* instinct quite as strongly as a lot of other Coldi, and many rejected the rigid structure of Coldi society.

"Why do you think that?" Deyu asked as she walked past. "You said yourself that the Ezmi clan has no involvement in this valley."

That was right. He had said that.

Deyu continued, "What offense have we committed that the Ezmi clan would get upset about? Because otherwise, why would they send people trying to kill us?"

"We discovered their bugs," Reida said.

"Which you investigated and just yesterday said *weren't* Ezmi."

"Then whose bugs can they be if not the Ezmi clan's?"

"Are you saying that you don't believe what you told us last night?"

"There could be many possibilities."

Deyu and Reida faced each other. Deyu had been dragging a corpse, and it lay between them.

I held up my hands. "Wait, are you two really going to have an argument over who gets to be the bad guy?"

Reida glared at me. "It always *is* the Ezmi clan anyway, out here at least."

"Well, the Ezmi clan doesn't have the monopoly on doing bad things," Deyu said again.

"Is there something about this you know?" I asked her.

"No." But her reply sounded like a challenge—for me to find out.

Something was going on, but this likely was not the place and time to discuss it.

So I left them and went to the others.

There were twenty-three bodies in all, and some had clearly been stripped of their identification. Not just earrings, but also identifying code in their readers.

Some of the bodies were badly mangled, others merely looked asleep.

I found it hard to believe that a single person could have killed most of them. Deyu had not a scratch on her.

"They weren't very well trained," I said, looking at the macabre collection.

"Of course not," Sheydu said. "If they were going to train them well, they wouldn't have sent them on such a stupid mission."

"Any indication what they wanted?"

"I'll have some vids to show you, and you can make up your own mind."

Yes, definitely something there.

While all this had been happening, the faintest glow of sunlight appeared on the horizon. The smell of cooking breakfast wafted from the house, and because I had nothing else to do, and Sheydu assured me I wasn't needed except to carry some equipment back to the office, I walked up to the house for breakfast.

The members of my team were so confident that they had caught all of the people that they let me walk alone. But for some reason, as I crossed the area where the aircraft stood, walked along the path that zigzagged up to the house, and gazed over the wide expanse of the valley with the little creek down below, I had a feeling we were being watched. I checked over my shoulder, but couldn't see any sign of people on the rocky cliff face, although there were plenty of hiding places.

This was a lonely place. It was a place where you stood out, where you couldn't find this presence that you knew was out there, and where everybody could see you from a distance.

The house was comfortable and the view was pretty, but I wasn't sure I was terribly happy with it. Our enemies could be watching from the ridgetops across the valley. They could be watching from the ridge behind us. They could be watching from a satellite for all I knew, but someone was watching.

I found most of the others of the team around the table in the kitchen. The cook provided by Asha had produced an amazing meal, and the smell was heavenly.

The talk in the kitchen, however, was all about danger and murder. Nicha had made a large sheet of all the potential threats to our group. I knew about many; some threats were more likely than others. For example, much as the Azimi clan didn't like us, I thought they were too sophisticated to send such a crude operation. If ever they found it necessary to kill us off, they would send some people who actually had a decent chance of completing the job.

I didn't know enough about the Omi clan to judge whether they were likely to have sent this group, and the only member of that clan we had was still outside. Then again, I had no idea why the Omi clan would have any beef with us, except for being nervous with Deyu's presence, which I very much doubted to be serious enough for an action like this. After all, one of their members had lent us the house.

But the Omi clan had *branches*, Asha had told me.

Still, Nicha dismissed it. "They wouldn't use *reychi*. That's not their style." He judged that the Ezmi clan, who might own the storage inside the mountain, were too disorganised and poorly resourced.

"I don't know that I agree with that," I said. "Everything I'm seeing from the Ezmi clan is more sophisticated than I've been led to believe. And they were organised enough to put together a claim for Asto and communicate with the Aghyrian ship."

"That's just a part of the clan, and that is the problem. They're not united, and those people we met on our previous visit probably don't care one bit about this valley. The ones who do care are unlikely to have the resources to have a bunch of *reychi* in their pay. Besides, they gave up their claim to this valley, and there is no sign that they ever breached that agreement."

"They wouldn't be so stupid as to suddenly show such a sign," Anyu said.

True. "But they also wouldn't be dumb enough for such a clumsy invasion."

"It's a warning only," Isharu said. "Some clans do this a lot."

Nicha said, "Clans in the Inner Circle, yes. Ones who have plenty of money."

"Then what do you think is going on?" I asked him.

"Oh, they're *reychi* all right, but you're looking too far afield. They've been sent by people who object to *your* presence here in particular." He met my eyes.

I snorted. "*My* presence? What sort of people would they be?"

"You don't think everyone in the Domiri clan is happy to have you as their member? There are quite a lot of purists in the military. They would never go against you while you were in Asha's household, but now you're fair game."

"Then why didn't Asha keep us in his house?"

"To protect himself from a challenge from them?"

"I don't think that's true at all," Thayu said.

"So you don't think certain sections of the Palayi clan are pressuring Asha to back away from our association? Because that is happening."

"Asha made the decision. He is the leader."

Nicha and Thayu glared at each other across the table. It was hard to imagine they were talking about their father.

My head hurt. Too many people could have sent this warning party.

We were spared further arguments when Sheydu, Reida, Deyu and Veyada trooped in.

Both Reida and Deyu were very dirty, their faces caked with dust that had stuck to their sweaty skin. Deyu sported several dark stains on her suit. They sat down without saying much and started eating.

Veyada also looked tired.

I glanced at Sheydu, signalling for her to start talking about what she had seen or what she knew, but she said nothing and simply started eating.

As leader of the association, I felt I had to say something about the attack. I thanked them all for their work, and spelled out a couple of arguments about who might have been behind the attack. I asked Sheydu if she had anything to add, but she shook her head. Well, either I was wrong or this was one of those frustrating occasions where people wouldn't say anything because they weren't sure.

Oblivious to the tension, several members of Sheydu's team debated possible origins of this group and the reasons for the attack: that it might be because people objected to us, to our presence here or to the presence of the house.

"It doesn't make sense that it's a group of people who

object to the presence of the house," Anyu said. "When Rashanu Omi was building it, they would have had plenty of opportunity to destroy the project. They did nothing and let the builders finish their work. This is not about the house or the land it stands on. It's about us or about the people associated with us."

Several people agreed in an annoyed, tired way. It had been a long, hard night, and confusion and tension was mounting.

I had to break that mood, because it started people sniping at each other. "Well then," I said. "When I don't know who is related to what, I usually draw doodles."

"Doo—what?" Sheydu asked.

It wasn't often that I used Isla words anymore, but an equivalent Coldi term escaped me. Coldi didn't doodle.

"Watch." I pulled over my reader, wiped the screen, set up the projector stand that enlarged the image on the screen—or, at this point in time, the lack thereof on the white rectangle of light—onto the surface of the table.

A quick check of my pockets revealed that I had left behind or lost my stylus, so I drew on the table with a spoon.

"This is our association." I drew a circle in the middle of the table. Then I drew a number of smaller circles inside the bigger circle.

"These are all the interests that are represented in our association: Palayi, Domiri. . . ."

"Vonayi," Sheydu said.

"Azimi," Veyada said, looking at Ayshada, who was wolfing down the leftovers from Thayu's plate, oblivious to the tension.

"Ezmi," said Reida. "The *zeyshi* group and Hedron." He glanced at Mereeni, who was usually quiet in situations like this, where she felt her presence might upset people.

For each clan representation, I wrote the name in one of the little circles. It was hard to write with the spoon, and the writing got messy.

Then I drew a number of bigger circles outside the central

circle, each with a corresponding name and a line to the smaller circle inside the central circle with the same name.

"These are all the clans that we have connections to, and people who could possibly have a disagreement with us. Azimi is likely to want reparations for perceived slights. Omi clan might want to settle a score with Deyu."

"Not that urgently," Reida said. "Rashanu is a popular leader and she'll keep the position for a few years yet."

That was not entirely how I had heard it from Asha, but then again, Asha might not have the full story. Most importantly, Deyu herself said nothing. And she had just single-handedly killed twenty-three people without as much as a peep.

I continued, "Vonayi clan might be upset about the house as well, but they may have already made a deal with the owner of the house. I'm not sure that's relevant to our situation. I cannot, for the life of me, think of what problem the other clans might have with us."

Nicha spoke up. "As I said, I think there are some elements in the Domiri clan who don't like our association and object to your becoming part of the clan."

"But Domiri clan is an Inner Circle clan. They would use a writ to express their displeasure before doing anything else."

Several people nodded.

Domiri clan people were all over the military base on the other side of the canyon. If they wanted to come here and talk to me, they could just do it. Palayi clan people were all in the Inner Circle. Ezhya was the clan leader and he was so busy with whatever he was doing that all he'd done was send me a lame message. They didn't look interested.

We all stared at my messy drawing.

"I think you're all looking at it in the wrong way," Deyu said.

She held out her hand and I gave her the spoon. She rubbed out the Domiri and Palayi circles and the connecting lines between my association and those main clans in power. Then she drew a bigger circle and put those clans in it.

"This is the Inner Circle," she said, and then she pointed at the empty space around it. "We are out here with all these clans that people like you and Asha have little connection with." She glanced at Sheydu and Isharu. They were Palayi and Vonayi respectively. "We, our association, are the only connection between what is happening out here in the desert and the Inner Circle. Maybe someone doesn't want us to develop these connections."

Well, crap. It took Deyu to make a disturbing observation like that.

And also, it made a lot of sense, but if it was true, it meant that the attack was a lot more about me and my unusual team than I liked.

That moment of intense, deep realisation was shattered by the sound of an aircraft engine. Sheydu got up and left the dining room. I realised that Anyu and Isharu had already left while we were talking.

Zyana remained at the door to the dining room, and Naru stood at the windows. Guarding us.

Something had obviously tripped their alarm. I didn't say anything for fear of disturbing their task.

Next I could hear people talking at the door. I thought for a moment that these were Asha and his guards coming in from outside, but I didn't recognise any of the voices, and I didn't think that any of Asha's people would spread such a sickly sweet smell of fragrance around them.

I glanced at Thayu, and she looked just as alarmed as I was.

We had visitors.

A moment later a woman came into the door of the dining room.

I vaguely remembered having seen her before, but for the moment couldn't put a name on her face.

But Thayu gaped and Nicha's face hardened.

The woman was in her late middle age, quite thickset, which was common for Coldi women of that age, and the friendliness of her face did not match Thayu and Nicha's reactions to her.

She said, "I see you are making good use of your host's hospitality."

She crossed the dining room to the table without being invited and sat opposite me.

Then I also knew who she was. Tayanu Palayi. She was Nicha and Thayu's mother.

I *had* seen her before, but only briefly, a long time ago, at Nations of Earth in Rotterdam where she used to be part of Asto's delegation, but had never spoken to her personally.

I wasn't sure whether to offer her any breakfast. We had mostly eaten all the good things, and the cook was making no sign of bringing out more food. At times like these, Coldi were painfully honest with each other. They offered food to friends and those whose favours they wanted to buy. Enemies and stickybeaks got nothing.

But to my human sensibilities, not offering her at least tea was rude.

I met Thayu's eyes across the table, and she shook her head ever so slightly. I hope this meant that she understood my dilemma, and did not want me to offer any food. The lines were clear. This was not a friend. I knew it. I still didn't like it.

She met my eyes and said in a prim voice, "One would think that, with his position of influence, Asha would clean up the mess around this place before letting his guests take possession of it."

The entire sentence rattled with accusatory pronouns, mixing the *loi* and *ani* forms in the same sentence. They were both pronoun sets that indicated the speaker's intention to ask for something from a person in a position of authority.

The sentence was a thing of grammatical beauty, to be honest, because people in Barresh and the *gamra* headquarters made far too little use of any of these intricate pronoun forms.

"We have been in the house since yesterday. It's *our* mess."

And I was not going to let her show me up, so I used the *zana* form that indicated mild inquisitive annoyance.

She flicked up her eyebrows. "Is that so? I had to hear through secondary channels that you were here. No one told me that you were visiting." Those were downright annoyed pronouns.

She looked at Nicha who stared back.

I never thought that she and her son had parted on good terms, and now I was certain of it.

She also very obviously ignored her daughter and looked at Ayshada, who sat on the floor in the corner placing coloured stones on a board with lines painted across its surface. It was a kind of counting game.

"There was a claim," she started.

Nicha interrupted her. "If the Azimi clan has a claim on me, I invite them to turn up here themselves," he said.

Oh, this was indeed about Ayshada, who looked up from his game and gave his father a wide-eyed, almost scared look. At meeting his grandmother's eyes, he pulled a face as if he was about to cry.

Nicha held out his hands, and he ran to his father, who pulled him onto his lap.

Tayanu said in a cool tone, "They thought it wise to send me, because of our relationship."

"What relationship?"

Another stare.

"Our dealings are finished," Nicha said, his tone cold.

"Oh, but are they?"

"Yes."

She snorted. Offended. I had to bite my tongue to keep from telling Nicha to quit it. We had quite enough enemies here. We didn't need him to provide us with any more.

"The young lady has expressed dissatisfaction with the way she was treated at the household, and asked me to help facilitate an agreement."

I said, "If the Azimi clan have a claim with me and the reception Xinanu received at my household, they can come here themselves. I have heard nothing from them, and I have checked the contract, and have not found any conditions I have breached."

"I haven't come here to discuss this with you." She met my eyes, the look in them defiant.

Veyada said, "I agree with him. If Xinanu Azimi has a claim against our household, I invite her to lodge it herself, in writing."

She gave Veyada a foul look. If she knew him well enough—and I was almost certain she did—she would know that he was a formidable lawyer and, with the addition of Mereeni, the pair was unbeatable.

And clearly Tayanu did *not* like Veyada. She might have hoped to be able to extort a concession out of me, but Veyada's presence made that unlikely.

"So be it, then." She made to get up from the table. "I was prepared to negotiate, but I see that I'm wasting my time. Expect communication."

She left the room.

Wasting her time, indeed. I watched her go from the security room near the door, walking down the path to a small craft next to ours. I doubted it was the last we'd seen of her or Xinanu. The upper echelons of Coldi society could not find enough dead horses to beat.

Not so long ago, I had found out that Nicha had paid out almost all his savings to Ayshada's mother to shut her up about the supposed bad treatment she had received at our house, which was entirely of her own making.

Put simply, Xinanu Azimi was a first-class drama queen, but now that she had a contract with Nicha requiring her silence, she couldn't use that avenue again.

Thayu had called her *eyli* which was one of those words that didn't see much use off Asto. The best translation I could think of was *gold-digger*, a woman who misused a man's desire for a child to screw him out of as much money as possible. Human gold-diggers were usually younger women of lesser social status. Coldi ones were professionals, and tended to be women from well-off families who were too lazy or dumb to take part in the concourse for a proper position and earn their own keep.

8

———————

"**YOU DID WELL,**" Veyada said.

The others had joined me in the security room, which wasn't quite big enough to hold so many people. Aside from Veyada and Mereeni, Isharu was there, as well as Deyu, Reida, Thayu and Nicha. And Sheydu and Naru. Anyu was squeezed in behind her, and Zyana, Sevayu and Leisha had to remain half in the hallway.

I was reminded once again that I must spend some time to talk to each of Sheydu's people. Security personnel were notoriously reserved. It had taken me ages to get to know Evi and Telaris, and I didn't want to repeat that failure with these people.

I asked, "Was there anything I missed? I didn't offend anyone by not offering her food?"

Veyada said, "Rest assured, none of us would have offered her anything. She is rude. She is wrong, and she knows it. She is just trying to abuse the fact that you're new to all this."

"I think it's more than that," Sheydu said.

One of the house kitchen staff came in to deliver tea, and Sheydu waited until the man had left before speaking again.

"This is typical Azimi clan plotting," she said. "They fear

they are losing control over part of the administration, so they're sending someone to extract promises from us that, no matter how innocent they seem, will tie us to them. Of course they won't come themselves. They tried with Ayshada's mother, but I think the woman was inept. She was good at creating drama, but poor at politics. They could have done so much more damage."

I'd spoken about this with my team before, and all seemed to agree that it was inevitable that Ayshada would, at some point, spend some time with his mother's clan, but hopefully not until he was older and understood the nuances. And most people agreed it wasn't necessarily a bad thing either. He was a member of the Azimi clan. He needed to become familiar with them.

Veyada said, "Tayanu's approach seems unusual, unless she has a scheme of her own. I think she is placing herself in the position of influence for her own purpose. I'm not even sure that the Azimi clan is involved with her presence at all, but she's just using it as excuse to come here."

"Then if she wants something from us wouldn't it be more productive to try to make friends?" I asked.

Sheydu snorted. "No, because none of us would trust her."

"So how does she think this strange visit is going to be beneficial to her?"

"That's the question."

"You don't think *she* might have ordered the *reychi*?"

"Highly unlikely. She's an opportunist, acting at a time she thinks we are vulnerable. She's in it for herself, not organised enough to plan a thought-through attack."

I looked again at Deyu, who held her head bent and was looking at the floor. I would have to speak to her about what she knew and get to the bottom of this.

It seemed that our association was suddenly being tested from all angles.

"Does anyone have anything else?"

Reida spoke up. "There is one thing I would like to say, if you don't mind."

He didn't normally say much in meetings like this. Being the youngest member of my association, and from the Outer Circle, he was easily intimidated.

"Feel free to speak freely, Reida," I said.

His cheeks coloured. "There are changes coming and, right here, we're in the middle of it. With increased rainfall, this valley is turning into valuable land. People can grow food. I think that's going to be really important."

Sheydu raised her eyebrows.

I asked, "So when people have agriculture businesses, do they own the land?"

Reida snorted. He glanced sideways at Isharu.

She said, "Nobody owns land. They can be allowed to use it. Technically, the Vonayi clan controls the use of land and buildings. In the city, they own the buildings and anyone who wants to live somewhere or use land has to apply to the Office of Lands, which is just an outpost of the Vonayi clan. But out here? The land doesn't have value to them. One patch of dust is pretty much the same as the next."

I said, "Except for this valley, which you, Reida, said your clan had given up control over."

"That's because they didn't want us near the army," Reida said.

"No, it's because they didn't want anyone near the source of the water that flows through the aquifers," Deyu said.

"That's what they said, but they don't want to admit that they're afraid of groups of people with new technology on their doorstep."

"It's about a safe water supply for the city," Deyu maintained.

They glared at each other.

Reida shrugged, defusing the tension. "It's all the same to them. They all live in the city anyway, and coming out here to check on contracts would mean they need to leave the city and come to the desert, and they're too good for that." Again, he glanced sideways at Isharu, who belonged to the Vonayi clan, and gave no sign of being either intrigued or offended by what he said. She was a security professional.

"What about those aquifers?" I asked Reida. "Those have to be more valuable than any other land."

"Most of the mushroom farmers use the land illegally," Thayu said. She had spent a fair bit of time spying in those aquifers. "They get away with it because it isn't technically land, because the law says land needs to be flat and a cliff isn't flat, obviously."

"Do they pay for the use?"

"Some of them do, but only to local administrators, who may not have any contract with the Vonayi clan and, if they don't, get to keep the payment, so it's a money-making scheme for them."

No wonder they weren't so keen to relinquish that control. "And those local administrators are which clan?"

"Mostly Talavi, from Eighth Circle."

"And the growers?"

"The mushroom growers are often poorly organised and they are from a number of different clans without a strong network between them, but the majority would be Omi."

That surprised me. "No Ezmi?"

Thayu shook her head. "The Ezmi clan is actually really powerful in the Outer Circle and they wouldn't let themselves be controlled by petty administrators. They're not farmers. They live in the tunnels, and their business is selling their finds and, increasingly, providing medical services, even to people from the higher ranks in the city. I've seen evidence of links between the Ezmi clan and the Palayi and Vonayi clans."

Reida lifted his chin.

This was significant. After hundreds of years at the edge of society, the Ezmi clan was climbing the ladder.

Deyu said, "So that just leaves the dumb Omi farmers who *are* controlled by petty administrators. That is just wrong, because they're not. The battle is about land and water, fertile land."

Reida snapped at her, "In case you hadn't noticed, I agree with you."

I said into the tense silence, "So, let's assume it's true that a power struggle is going on for control of this valley, how would we be involved enough to justify this attack?"

Thayu put her reader on the table. "We need to go back to this *doodle* that we were looking at before Tayanu came in."

She re-activated the projection of her last version of the schematic, with us in contact with the Ezmi and Omi clans and only distantly in contact with the clans of Inner Circle power, who were all tucked away and sheltered by the city's eight concentric zones.

"The struggle for land control is here." She pointed to the circle that represented us. "Domiri clan has an outpost in the desert by virtue of the army—which it can't use against our own people without creating a lot of trouble. The most powerful is the Palayi clan, but they have little contact with the contestants to take this valley, and the only clan that does have some control is Vonayi. But they're allied with the Ezmi clan—which doesn't do alliances very well, and which isn't terribly interested in agriculture. And someone in the Inner Circle has realised that this valley, and land like this, will play a major role in Athyl's future. I guess that most clans want a part of the action, and so they manufacture reasons to come here."

There were some nods around the room.

Her point was very well made.

Tayanu Palayi wasn't here because of potential claims against us by the Azimi clan over fictitious old-hat complaints by Xinanu against Nicha. She wanted to keep an argument going, so that she could keep visiting.

Hmmm. I wondered if she might have been more successful by simply feigning an interest in seeing her grandson. But no, that would stretch believability.

"Why concoct such elaborate reasoning for this attack?" Anyu said. She sounded irritated, but that was her normal state of mind. "The Ezmi clan is upset that we discovered their stash—"

"They're not Ezmi clan!" Reida said.

"I'll believe that when I see it. They're also upset that Rashanu Omi built this house without permit, and that she's cosying up to the Domiri clan."

Sheydu said, "We must keep it in our thoughts and keep our minds open to all possibilities. I will distribute this *doodle* to all of you and anyone who may have a need to understand. We will adjust it as we gain understanding."

More investigation was always good. If there was one thing I knew about the security training on Asto, it was that the watch and wait approach was very much favoured. They were told not to act until they were absolutely sure they had to. And more investigation would hopefully keep people from ripping off each other's heads.

Collecting people from all these different clans in my association seemed like an increasingly bad idea. I should have been like Sheydu, and only had members of the Palayi and Domiri clan in my group. Sheydu had always supported Reida and Deyu, and now even she was becoming hostile to them.

I'd thought I could defeat the established practices.I had been wrong.

The meeting broke up, and I followed the others into the hallway. Thayu went into our room, but I went to the veranda.

I should do some work, I should talk to people, but I couldn't face any of that right now.

Just as I was on the verge of being fully integrated into this world, everything came apart at the seams. My dreams of straddling two cultures, my ambitions to make a difference to the lives of people who had been dealt a poor hand of luck, were all falling into a heap.

You couldn't argue with biology. The *sheya* instinct was baked into these people and would resurface at a time of stress. I could do nothing about it. An association that contained both Sheydu and Reida and Deyu had no future. They belonged in three different groups. Sheydu had already split off, but the same would happen with the others, including my most trusted supporters. Veyada, Nicha . . . Thayu.

Maybe I should just give up. Tell Asha that I couldn't accept a position in the clan, and go home.

"Oh, here you are," Nicha said behind me. He came onto the veranda.

Moments ago, I'd thought I should have a talk to him about his mother and Xinanu and other things that now seemed irrelevant. Now he came to seek me out.

"You don't seem happy," he said.

"Nich', tell me honestly, do you think I'm making a terrible mistake?"

He smiled. "What is this about? Becoming a father? Yes, you will think it's a mistake, all the time. Get used to it. But then he smiles at me and comes to show me something or he does something silly, and it's all worth it."

"It's not about that."

His face sobered.

"Reida and Deyu have been disagreeing with each other a lot. I watched Deyu kill all those intruders. It was scary, but I think I understand. She's very angry about something and she's much too nice to talk about it. And now Sheydu starts hacking into Reida as well. Where is this going to end? I'm thinking I'm just stupid for trying to keep them all together. Reida belongs with his people. Look how proud he is of them. Sheydu is clearly sick of him. Maybe she thinks he's ungrateful. I don't know."

"Yes, you're making a mistake," Nicha said.

What? I had expected him to deny it.

"You're making the mistake I made for years. I wanted to fit in at Nations of Earth. I did everything. I made lots of friends, went out to parties. I got to know a lot of people quite well and it looked like I was accepted in the diplomatic set. Then Nations of Earth decided that Coldi people could not hold an Earth-based identification. I became an illegal and had to flee to Athens."

Of course I remembered him talking to me about this before. It had been a few years before I'd met him. Nicha had been aimlessly hanging around Athens for a while, waiting, while his mother still had the right papers to work at Nations of Earth in Rotterdam.

"I'm not sure I see the parallels."

"Don't you? I was partying and making friends, but I didn't really understand the concept of friends. When I went into hiding, they kept in contact, but they couldn't help me. I made friends with the expectation that they were my associates. That my relationship with them gave them status. And society on Earth doesn't work that way."

"It does, a little bit."

"Only a little bit. But see how you're now doing the same? Sheydu is a powerful associate, but she is not your friend. Deyu and Reida are associates, but they are not your foster children. They will be powerful allies, but don't have to be your family. In fact, they don't even have to like you. They don't have to like each other. There are plenty of examples of associations and *zhayma* pairs that are very loose. My father doesn't like Natanu very much. But he and she provide two stable halves of the second layer of Ezhya's prime association."

"So you think I worry about nothing?"

He met my eyes. "If Sheydu didn't want to be here, she wouldn't be."

That was true.

"She can be a little prickly, but if she thought there was no merit in being with us, she would have gone back to Ezhya when Mereeni took her place."

"But that was a while ago. She could have changed her mind."

"To the contrary. The fact that she went with her own association related to yours means that she strengthened her position. She finds it interesting. She sees potential."

She sure as hell wasn't acting like that at the moment. "Then what about Reida and Deyu?"

"That might be another story. There is no framework, no rule book for interactions between their clans, so they're still working it out, including who has the right to speak for the clan."

"So what *is* going on?"

He shrugged, "For what it's worth, I think the *reychi* were sent by some group within the Domiri clan who want to amuse themselves by making you feel nervous. *Reychi* are for influential people. Ezmi or Omi clan would not have access to them."

"And Azimi?"

Nicha leaned on the railing. "Look, I don't know what's got into her. After the whole affair with Xinanu, we're barely speaking, but she's still my mother. I doubt she's behind the attack."

"Last time I heard, you said she was sick."

"She got better." He shrugged. "I don't even know if she was all that sick or if it was just a game to get me to do something for her."

That statement was the centrepiece of the discussion. I understood. He felt *ashamed* to have been used by his mother.

"If she really wants to hang around us, why doesn't she just come to see Ayshada?"

"She's not like that."

No, I'd never heard any description of Tayanu Palayi that didn't include the word *ambitious*.

"Do you think there is a secret reason behind her visit?"

"Oh, yes." He met my eyes squarely. "Don't trust her. Not now, not in the future. She will pretend to be in trouble, appeal for sympathy, and the next thing, she drops you and is looking for the next victim to milk."

"She and Minke Kluysters would make a great pair."

And there I stopped. With that remark, I managed to scare myself. What if Minke Kluysters and his cronies had their claws in the disenfranchised elements of upper Coldi society? He'd asked me to arrange a meeting with Ezhya. I'd thought it was prudent to hold off on any promise that I had the power to arrange that. He didn't take no for an answer. He would simply worm his way up to where he wanted to be, using vulnerable people.

Well, shit.

A wave of frustration washed over me. Why were we stuck in this unlikely location? Why did we need to worry about whoever ended up owning this house and the surrounding land? Why was Ezhya playing games with me?

"Oh, there you are." Someone else came onto the veranda. Sheydu. "We need to talk."

Clearly.

Nicha quietly slunk away, leaving me and Sheydu alone on the veranda.

Sheydu was not known for beating about the bush. She started the conversation with, "When you look at the security scans, it's obvious where the attack comes from."

She pulled out her reader. With a touch of her finger, a recording played. It showed a vehicle stopping at the edge of the plateau. A group of people got out and made their way into the valley.

I frowned. "Is that—?"

But the next recording started. The group of people reached the area where the aircraft stood, and a few figures, presumably members of my team, ran out of the house, through the yard.

One of the attackers met with a member of my group. They faced each other briefly before a fight broke out. More people ran out of the house, and the person who had been challenged—Deyu, I assumed—went on a killing rampage.

"She was challenged," I said.

"Yes. She won."

"Why didn't she say anything?"

"Unfinished business? Fear of retaliation? We had a security debriefing. Deyu told us the attackers insulted her and her family and accused them of being traitors. It upset her greatly."

"So did she know who they were?"

"She said they were *reychi* and they were using a script. They might have had an insulting script for each of us, and it just happened to be Deyu they encountered first."

"Bad luck for them."

Sheydu snorted. "Yeah."

"Didn't that bug Reida found report back to Eighth Circle?"

"It did, but that doesn't necessarily mean anything. It could be a decoy, a deflection, and there are many clans in Eighth Circle." Including the majority of the ones in my doodle.

"What do you propose to do about this?" Because, being who we were, we couldn't let an attack of this severity slide.

"We're going on the counter-attack. But we need to know more about who they are. We're going to plant some bugs to listen in on the locality that Reida's bug reports back to."

Ah, that was the reason she came to me. With Sheydu there was always a reason. "You want me to come."

"I think you should come."

"What if I'd rather not? What if I preferred to take Thayu back to her father's house? I think she's been exposed to enough danger as it is."

"I doubt that's necessary."

"We've just been attacked."

"Yes, but even with our reduced state of vigilance they didn't even get close to the house."

True.

"We're taking a short trip, less than a day. We'll be in range all the time. The house will remain well protected."

"Who is coming?"

"Myself, Isharu, Veyada, Anyu, Leisha, Zyana and you. The others will stay here, and Asha will send additional people to protect the house."

Sheydu to set up the tech, Leisha to pilot the craft, Isharu because she was Vonayi and probably had knowledge about where we could place bugs. Zyana because . . . I didn't know him very well. He'd been one of those "grey, quiet" people Sheydu had introduced to my greater group.

"Am I needed for anything?"

"Yes. To talk to people if any want to talk."

"And where are we going?" I was still very unsure about this. "Inside Eighth Circle?"

"No. We're planting some bugs in the desert. We can't go into Eighth Circle without permits and a lot of guards. Because we'll be on the outside of the city, it should be easy. We can penetrate from outside without too much interference. We set up a couple of receivers on vantage points and let them report back to us. Once it's been set up the whole system runs on its own. We'll return home in the afternoon and we'll get a ping when something of interest comes in."

"When are you going?" I asked her.

"As soon as possible, but not before we're rested. Probably tomorrow morning. That's when Asha's people will be here. You don't need to take much, just your weapon. Wear comfortable clothing, temperature retaining suit and bring armour, but don't put it on."

I went back to our room and told Thayu about the trip. I asked if it was all right to go. "We'll go tomorrow morning and be back in the afternoon. Sheydu wants me to come because she says I might be needed to speak to people. I don't like it."

"You should go. If Sheydu thinks it's important, it will be important. You're here to settle your place in the Domiri clan and Asto society."

"In the desert? I'd prefer to stay with you."

"Don't worry about me. This child has made no signs of wanting to appear. It's bad enough if just one of us sits around here waiting."

9

———————

EVEN THAYU WANTED me to go, so there was nothing for it.

I did note that Sheydu hadn't nominated Deyu and Reida to come, and there was probably a reason for that.

In true security fashion, Sheydu prepared thoroughly for this expedition. First a time for departure was set, and everything else was planned back from that time. We would leave tomorrow morning, and a schedule that I obtained access to detailed all the things that needed to be done before we left. My tasks were limited, but the equipment needed to be prepared and calibrated.

After we had finished dinner, we carried everything inside the craft so it would be ready. Sheydu even posted Naru and Sevayu to stand guard in the parking area by the craft. Because you never knew. Oh no, she didn't trust any of this.

Before we went to sleep, I again asked Thayu whether she preferred me not to go, but she just laughed.

"You're going to plant a few bugs in the desert for half a day. Sheydu thinks there may be people whose stories you'd like to hear."

"I think she wanted to take me so I can provide a distraction."

"I think she'll want to show you something. It might even be the scenery. There is some spectacular country out that way. Just go with her and quit worrying."

Thayu was probably right and I should stop being silly. So I got ready.

Sheydu had told me to wear my temperature retaining suit. Not that I would have left the house without it. I still felt insecure about whether I could handle the climate. Out here in the desert, everyone wore it when they left the house.

I packed my gun and a canister with spare charges; a spare shirt and a towel, because you never knew when that would be useful; and, as a precaution, a face mask and a canister of cooling fluid. During my previous visit, wearing the mask had been a necessity, and I wasn't quite ready to go into the desert without it.

Even though I kept thinking I was forgetting something important, I slept well that night. The previous night's escapades had left me very tired.

It was before dawn when I was woken up by Sheydu coming into my room. She said nothing, so that Thayu didn't wake up, but gestured to the hallway.

I slipped out of bed, pulled on the suit and liner I had put out last night, and kissed Thayu on the head. She stirred briefly, but didn't wake up.

I picked up my pack from next to the door and went into the hallway. The housekeeper had put a small table with items of food in the security room. I grabbed a couple of mushroom dumplings and followed the others outside.

The sky was turning light purple-blue, with brown haze hanging over the horizon. As far as Athyl had seasons that were not hot and dry and hot and dryer, this was supposed to be the season in which storms were said to occur, with or without rain or dust, or both. At the moment, however, the weather was tranquil in that predawn time of the day.

A number of aircraft had arrived. Two of them stood next to ours, and at least one other at the top of the platform. The crew were coming down, meeting the others who waited in the front yard. Men and women in dark unmarked clothing, carrying between them crates of supplies of the military kind. I recognised the type of boxes from the stuff that Sheydu lugged around.

The promised military guards were here.

We all entered the aircraft. Being a pilot, Leisha took the controls, going through the motions in a professional manner.

I settled next to Isharu, who was looking at a map on her reader. Zyana sat on my other side. He appeared to be reading a brief. As always, he nodded politely to me, and went about his business, quietly and efficiently.

Once we were in the air, I unwrapped my breakfast. It was typical Coldi fare: three dumpling rolls of dough filled with a mixture of chopped mushrooms, noodles and other ingredients, held together with a sauce that became crisp when deep-fried. It was very messy to eat.

The craft followed the course of the creek. The rocky platform that provided the walls of the canyon was layered into dark grey and sand-coloured layers. At some time in the geological past it had been tilted on its side, and the dark rock stuck out as jagged peaks.

The very edges of the city were visible in the distance, a few buildings poking out of the haze.

But we weren't going to go in that direction.

Instead we flew in a parallel fashion to the outer reaches of the city. We left the creek behind. It wound lazily through the ever-narrowing canyon until it entered Eighth Circle.

After we crossed the plateau on the opposite side of the valley, we flew over another valley. This one was dry, but there were clear signs of habitation, with paths going through the sand and one area where tracks led into a cave.

The caves of course were not natural, but the remains of the ancient city of Aghyr.

Leisha landed the craft on top of the next ridge. It was a deserted place with hardened compacted soil, and already in full sunlight.

We all got out into the searing hot air. Sheydu and Isharu set up a box which they hemmed in between two rocks.

I remarked that this wasn't a very good hiding place, but Sheydu pointed out that the box included explosives. "Once we leave, we'll set an alarm and when someone comes near this thing, it will disintegrate."

Trust Sheydu to think of something like that.

We then left to set up the next listening point.

Now the craft flew over a landscape where human habitation was a lot more obvious. We crossed several bright green aquifers with settlements along the bottom of the cliffs.

"I thought we needed to place this thing away from habitation?" I asked.

"Wait and see," Sheydu said. Oh, she was enjoying this.

Once we had passed this area, we flew over a wall that people had built on top of a cliff to stop the drifting sand from clogging up the aquifer. I had heard about this.

Looking at the dusty landscape, it struck me how this was the oldest known human civilised settlement. Even on Earth, historians had been able to trace the oldest villages back thousands of years, but nothing came close to the fifty thousand years of Aghyr-Athyl, city built on the ruins of a city. It was like a Swiss cheese buried under a hard layer of stale bread, but the mice were still living in the holes. The tunnel network under the city was extensive.

Once we passed over the wall, a vast area of sand spread out as far as the eye could see. It disappeared into the hazy horizon.

"Whoa. I didn't know the sand was that close."

Veyada said, "It wasn't always like this. The sand moves all the time. It has been trying to invade the city for years. People just built this wall and they still have to shovel out all the sand. It never used to be so windy."

The climate of Athyl had gone through a lot of big changes even within my experience.

Very soon there was no sign of habitation anywhere in front of us and to the sides. The air was dusty, the sand was close to white, and glaring, and the sky was almost white as well. It had gotten quite windy, and the wind whipped up clouds of dust that made it even harder to see.

After we had gone a short distance, dark rocks began to poke out of the sand. First the occasional one, but they became more closely spaced as we went. Dark, jagged shapes covered the ground, some short, but many of them taller than a house. If the light hit them at a certain angle, the surface glittered.

"What are they?" I asked.

Veyada said, "This is the Crystal Wasteland. It used to cover a much bigger area, but much of it got buried by sand."

When the meteorite had hit, it had blasted so much searing air, it had melted all the sand into crystal. The covering dust had subsequently been blown away.

I gaped at the surreal landscape resembling the view of a field of broken glass seen through the eyes of a tiny insect.

In this area, the sandy ground was reduced to a few patches here and there. "Why does the sand have a different colour from the desert sand?"

"Does it?" Veyada said.

"Yes, over there." I pointed.

"Oh, that's not the sand. The Crystal Wasteland is a low area, and when it rains, water pools in between the rocks. It's a kind of moss."

That was astonishing.

The Crystal Wasteland, considered the most hostile area of

Asto, save perhaps the coast of the inland sea, was becoming green. That was a sign of how much things had changed.

We were flying much lower now. The ground was covered in so many glassy spikes that I hoped Leisha had a place in mind where we could land safely.

But through the front window I spotted a sharp ridge beyond which the world seemed to end in a mass of fluffy bluish haze.

The craft landed on a flat area. When Sheydu opened the door, a strange smell came into the cabin.

"What is that smell?"

Sheydu snorted. "I did realise your nose had become more sensitive. Have a look for yourself."

I stepped onto the rock.

Whoa, the weather had become oppressive and blustery all of a sudden. I hadn't noticed that the sky over the western horizon was not blue—I should have known that blue sky was not a thing on Asto—but leaden grey. That sure looked like bad weather.

Wind whipping at my hair, I walked to the edge of the cliff and looked out over the vast area of blue-grey haze. To the left and right of us, sheer cliffs descended into the mist. I couldn't even see the bottom. Ahead, the haze merged with the horizon.

"This is the impact crater, isn't it?" I asked Leisha, who stood gazing over the mist, his face into the wind.

Apart from the fact that I'd been told he was ex-military, I didn't know much else about him. The way he gazed over this site of ancient destruction, he seemed proud.

"All of Athyl fits inside this hole. Imagine if it would have fallen on the city."

As it was, this wasn't the biggest piece of the meteorite. That had fallen in the place where there was a shallow inland sea these days, an area of interconnected low-lying pools filled with water laced with poisonous salts. From orbit, all these pools had different colours, none of them blue.

If this fragment had fallen on the city, would the Coldi have the same technology today?

"How deep is the crater?"

"It varies. Very deep in some places."

"What's at the bottom?"

"No one really knows. The only people who have gone in have never come out. I used to come here a lot. This used to be where kids would take their battered up aircraft for skim racing. They would scoot over the gas all the way up to the point over there." He pointed. "The gas was much thicker, then When I was little, I wanted to be one of those heroic racers who makes a lot of money from appearance fees, but before I was old enough, a string of accidents resulted in the death of racers when they hit a patch of gas that was too thin to support their weight. Skim racing was always dangerous and illegal—not that we cared—but it became impossible. It has been a long time since the last race was held here."

The blue gas was sulphur hexafluoride, the heaviest and densest gas in existence. At a high concentration, it acted like water. It had been formed during or soon after the meteorite impact, and was the main reason that Asto had remained a hot world even when the surface had cooled down after the impact. But no new gas had been formed since the impact, and the greenhouse effects of the gas were said to last about fifty thousand years.

"I thought only kids from the Outer Circle took part in the races."

"Oh, no. We kids who wanted to fly were experts at sneaking out of the protection of wherever we lived to come watch the races. We formed groups that were about nothing else except finding the best excuses and providing alibis for each other on race days. We had groups of friends who were friends with kids in Eighth Circle so that we could roam the aircraft sales yards and parts warehouses in Eighth Circle. We never bought anything of course, but just the smell of an aviation workshop. . . ."

He took a deep breath, as if still smelling it. And somehow I felt like I could smell it, too.

"Our heroes—the older kids—took part. Sometimes they won, but there were all kinds of kids, young and old, trying to escape the notice of our parents, and avoiding the hiding we would get when they found out." He chuckled. "Recruiters from the military always visited the races. They picked off the young pilots who won and offered them places as fighter pilots. That was our ultimate hope, to be noticed by one of them."

"Is that how you entered the force?"

He laughed. "No. I was too young. I got in the regular way: I applied. I was always at the races, but not as pilot."

His eyes roamed the haze, as if he could still hear the whine of engines and the cheers of supporters.

"Are you sad that you could never become a racer?"

"I admit I would have liked doing it just once. But when I got old enough, there were horrible accidents because the mist was growing too thin. I wasn't keen enough to risk my life. I wanted to be a pilot, not a casualty."

When Sheydu had told me that Leisha was one of the best, I hadn't quite comprehended what that meant. But being a pilot was like being a negotiator: it was a way of life. For me, as diplomat, that involved keeping calm and listening. For a pilot, it involved safety over everything. It was all very well doing amazing things, but he wanted to go home at the end of the day.

And this realisation finally won me over.

"Sheydu says I should learn to fly and you should teach me."

"What do you say? Do you want to?"

I took in a breath. "I don't have much time, but I can see how it could be awfully handy to have our own aircraft that more than just one person could fly."

"Good then. First we choose the craft, then we can start lessons."

"After the ceremony."

Sheydu and Isharu were setting up their listening equipment. This setup took longer than the previous, because now that the chain—whatever that meant—was complete, both devices needed to be calibrated and tuned to each other so that they would send back the correct recordings. Zyana was holding up a little metal rod and the women called to him and he called back to move things or whatever. I couldn't claim to understand any of this tech.

While they were working, I climbed on top of a rock and looked around the countryside. It was a truly alien landscape, amazing to see.

I was starting to relax, kind of glad I'd come. No matter the reason Sheydu wanted me to come, this was worth seeing.

Veyada stood on a rock on the other side of the craft, looking around, weapons at the ready.

Sheydu and Isharu knelt on the ground where they were now covering their setup with rocks to hide it from view.

Anyu stood on a different vantage point with a scanner. Leisha was still with the craft, and appeared to be undertaking small maintenance.

There was nothing and no one here, so I was wondering why the alertness.

But then someone shouted a command. I thought the voice was Veyada's.

Sheydu rose from her work.

Both Leisha and Anyu took their weapons from their arm brackets.

I peered down the platform and finally saw the reason for their alertness: a group of people was walking up the slope that led to the crater rim. They were hard to make out, because their clothing blended in perfectly with the orange and pink hues of the rocks.

I went over to the craft, where Leisha was just closing a panel, his eye on the visitors.

"Who are they?" I asked.

He frowned. "I have no idea. Do they wear earrings?"

The people didn't walk very fast and were still too far away.

I guessed the first one was a woman, and out of the two people who walked behind her, at least one was a man but I wasn't sure about the other one.

Four more people were behind them, but they lingered back, giving the signal that they didn't intend to be threatening.

It was a typical association formation, so these were unlikely to be *zeyshi* who didn't "do" associations.

He continued, "They seem very formal. They're not Inner Circle, because those would have an aircraft close by. They're not Ezmi, because those would never walk in a formation like that."

He sounded puzzled. In his youth, he would have known this country well. It was a long time ago, and I didn't know how much of his knowledge was still current, but I took his puzzlement as a bad sign. Subconsciously, my hand strayed to my arm bracket where I carried my weapon.

Because I was at the head of my association, it was up to me to meet the newcomers, and hope that some sort of dominance situation would be established and there were no fights.

I went to stand at the top of what looked like a path down the outside slope of the crater rim. Sheydu and Isharu stood behind me. Anyu, Leisha, Zyana and Veyada waited behind them.

We were a complete association. *That* was one of the points of Sheydu's team selection.

This was my security team.

We waited.

Finally, the people were close enough that I could see their earrings. The stone was light blue. I didn't even know what clan that was.

Sheydu, next to me, said, "They're Talavi."

She said it with such a dark tone that it couldn't be good.

The Talavi clan, I remembered Deyu telling us, were the ones who extorted money from Omi mushroom farmers and didn't pass it on to authorities.

Zyana's expression chilled me. He held his hand on his weapon, and the expression in his eyes was hard. He was quite tall and slim for a Coldi person, and his eyes lacked much of the gold flecking and were very dark as result. He had a strong expressive mouth and chin, and honestly looked a little unusual.

At least all three people now bowed their heads as they approached me. So, at the very least, there wouldn't be a fight about dominance.

I stepped forward and touched the woman's shoulder. Her clothing was sturdy without being extravagant, and dusty from use.

"Well met," I said.

She launched directly into the conversation. "Forgive us for our incursion, but we were curious what you are doing here."

She was looking at my earlobes, but of course I'd handed in my earrings for Asha to give them back to me at the ceremony.

"We are doing some atmospheric tests for the Inner Circle," I said—the story we had agreed on. Weather tests, testing the atmosphere and humidity.

"I don't recall seeing a permission."

"I wasn't aware that we needed one."

"This has come into force recently. Too many people are moving into this area, and we need to keep track of who is doing what."

Behind me I could hear Zyana make small snorting noise. Veyada made a movement with his hand. I had no idea what it meant, and wasn't sure how to proceed.

We had good reception here so I opened the feeder signal to him.

This is Ezmi land. They have no authority here. Veyada said.

Interesting. "On whose authority do you act?" I asked.

"The Office of Lands."

Nonsense, Veyada let me know through the feeder.

"So what does the Office of Lands want us to do?"

"You have to apply for a permit to undertake any activity in this area."

Her face was prim.

"And what if I told you that we work for the Army base under orders of Asha Domiri? Certainly he would have a standing agreement with the Office of Lands that he can undertake whatever investigation necessary for military purposes?"

"I . . . don't know that any agreements of that kind exist." Her expression turned blank. She clearly didn't like talking about this.

"So, if we want a permit now to keep you happy, would we get one at the Office of Lands?"

"They don't give out permits that people can apply for."

"Then how do I get one? I would think Asha Domiri's word would suffice. We have people with us who are from the Vonayi clan, well connected with the Office of Lands. They can arrange this quickly."

"We're not the best people to talk about the process. We're investigating an instance of thievery in this area."

Ha, we were in the territory of deflection, but I could play along with it for a bit.

"What sort of thievery?"

"Aircraft have been stolen, and supplies."

"We've seen nothing, sorry." But as I said that, I knew it was probably a mistake. The woman had acknowledged me as a superior, so I should have said something a little bit more authoritarian. "We will just finish setting this up, and then we will be gone."

"I want you to take all your equipment with you. If there is any measuring to be done, it should be done under our authority."

Nothing more about permits.

"We are here under the orders of Asha Domiri. You have no business interfering in military matters. We will leave our equipment exactly where we want. Don't remove any of it. We will know."

The woman's face hardened. It looked for moment like she was weighing up the chances of taking on Sheydu, but must have decided against it, because she bowed and retreated.

No one spoke until the group had retreated all the way down the hill.

The wind had become squally and I thought I could hear the occasional growl of thunder. It could be something else, though. Even on Earth, thunder sounded very different in different places. It sounded much different in Barresh, too, and I wasn't sure what thunder on Asto sounded like.

Sheydu said, "Well, that's going to be trouble."

I asked, "Was that really what she wanted, for us to file some sort of request? Or was it about this thievery?"

"It's hard to say. It's unregulated out here, and I would be surprised if any of this was legal."

"What about looking for thieves?" I asked.

"That's the excuse they always give," Zyana said. "They're slippery characters."

"You have experience, obviously?"

"For a short period, as young man, I worked for the Third Circle guards."

Well, *that* was unexpected. The Third Circle guards were as close as Asto had to the Earth concept of *police.* I thought all of Sheydu's people came from the Inner and First Circle. I didn't even know there were Palayi in Third Circle, although I should have realised they were everywhere.

"What do you think this group were really after?" I asked him.

"They were curious. The Talavi clan is a collection of odd groups. They used to ply trade routes, but as more people had their own transport, their negotiating strength became less important. They're one of those clans where a lot of trouble originates because the youth has no clear path of what they should do with their lives."

"Like the Ezmi clan."

"Ezmi are stronger."

Veyada said, "Don't let Reida hear that. He won't stop bragging for days."

We all laughed.

Zyana continued, "As the Ezmi still claim to own the desert, Talavi like to think they still own the trade routes that go along the aquifers all the way to the mountains. They consider the farmers who live along the routes theirs to rule."

"Is this crater along a route?" I asked.

"There used to be a trade market at a tent settlement that used to lie at the bottom of the slope. But, fundamentally, Talavi clan don't belong in the Outer Circle. They're from Seventh or Eighth Circle and came out with the mushroom farmers when they ventured further into the aquifers. The ones out here are bloodsuckers. They live by charging rent, or collecting rent on the orders of others, like the Office of Lands, but more often than not, the money they collect goes straight into their own pockets. There are no official land use contracts outside Eighth Circle, that's why it's called the Outer Circle, because the land isn't worth anything. It's worthless desert."

Except the desert was slowly turning green, starting with the valleys.

We had finished our work and the equipment was successfully installed. Isharu and Sheydu checked by playing back some of the conversations it was already recording, conversations held in a building far from where we were, and which, Sheydu assured me, would be thoroughly analysed by her and the rest of the team back at the house.

It was time to go home.

The craft took off and we flew into the desert landscape.

The weather had turned blustery. The sky over the horizon

had taken on a dark blue hue. Since the sky on Asto was rarely blue, it could only be a massive thunderstorm.

A flashing lightning bolt confirmed this suspicion.

"Better hurry up," Sheydu said.

But Leisha kept glancing at his instruments.

Then he said, "What the. . . ?"

One of the warning lights was flashing yellow. I knew which one. "Doesn't that mean our charge is low?"

"It does. Those people? They came to teach us a lesson and drain our charge. Damn, how did they do that?"

10

LEISHA WENT INTO a frenzy of activity, calling for backup and giving our current location. He reported that reception was poor and, of course, this problem hit us while we were over the Crystal Wastelands.

Anyu, being a communications expert, helped him. Her voice remained calm and professional, but that made the situation all the more surreal.

Because the charge had drained so quickly, no one knew how long the remaining charge was going to last.

"The house is only on the next ridge," Veyada said.

"We're not going to make that," Sheydu said.

"No way," Leisha said. "I found a spot where we could possibly land. Can you see it to the right?"

Isharu peered out the window. "The weather is too bad. I can't see anything."

"I'm going down anyway."

He steered the craft sharply to the right. Two lights were flashing yellow on the control panel.

Anyu was still trying to establish contact with the house or the Exchange, but without much luck.

I wondered if the bad weather had anything to do with the lack of communication.

Then Isharu said, "I think I can see it."

"Is it big enough?"

She squinted into the greyness of the weather. "I can't see it very well. I don't know."

"Make your best guess. My instruments aren't accurate enough."

"Do we have a choice of places?" she asked. "Is there another option?"

"No. This is it."

The whole bank of yellow lights were flashing on the Control Panel before him.

I pushed myself back in my seat, gripping the armrest.

I didn't want to look where we were going but also didn't want to close my eyes.

The craft was dropping like a brick. My ears hurt from the change in pressure. The engine cut out, and all of Leisha's instruments went dark.

Oh, crap.

We were going to hit some horribly sharp rock and the craft would be torn to shreds and no one would find us. And Thayu—

The bottom of the craft clipped something with a clang, jolting us all around. Then we hit the sand with the right front of the craft. Anything that was not tied down flew through the cabin, while the craft slid along the ground for a short distance before coming to an abrupt halt.

For a moment, everything was silent.

"Everyone all right?" Leisha asked.

"That was not the best landing I have ever experienced," Sheydu said. "I think you forgot to use the downward jets."

"No power. They won't work."

Sheydu snorted. "You don't say."

She took a step. The craft rested on one wing and her movement threatened to tip it to the other wing.

"It looks like nothing has been too badly damaged," Leisha said. "But we have no power, and we will have to wait until the weather clears before we can charge our receiver."

"Let's get it set up before it gets dark," Veyada said.

While Leisha gave instructions on what he wanted done, Veyada pushed himself from the seat, half slid across the sloping floor in between our seats, and opened a door in the back of the cabin. Inside it were stored a number of things to be used in emergencies, including charging panels and the necessary wiring.

He collected a number of things, handed them to other people, and then slung a roll of panels and wire over his shoulder. When he opened the door, the wind tore around the cabin.

Veyada jumped out.

Others were also getting up, handing more equipment to Veyada, who stood knee-deep in a patch of sand, his hair whipped about by the wind.

I was disturbed by how dark the sky already was.

Leisha had explained that because of the unknown interference with the craft's electronics, he couldn't get an exact fix on our location, so he wanted some of us to place signal devices in prominent positions, so that we could create a virtual satellite dish that would enable communication with much weaker signals.

To my question whether it wouldn't be better to wait until we could get the charging stations up, he said, "We don't have enough power to fly, but we have enough to communicate. I'm going to see if I can locate the source of the trouble."

I followed them out the door.

Stepping out of the craft meant braving drifts of biting sand. The wind howled in between the rock spikes, making enough whistling and groaning noises for a whole zoo of demons. The sand stung my face and other exposed parts of my skin.

The combination of sand and dust made it hard to see past the first row of glassy, spiky rocks.

Leisha and Anyu had opened the engine panel on the side of

the craft. Veyada held up a sheet so that the sand wouldn't blow inside.

Isharu carried a bag of repeaters that she meant to place in elevated positions. I gestured at her that I would help her. Speaking would be a waste of breath for all the noise of the wind howling between the spikes of rock.

We waded through the drifting sand around the rock spikes. Isharu went first and I followed carrying a few bags with electronics, struggling to follow her broad back. The light was gloomy, but it was still too early for dusk. Thunder grumbled in the distance.

Isharu picked a rocky spike that sat at an angle. She gave her bag to me, took one device out and tucked it inside her suit.

She said something, but the wind whipped her words into unintelligible shards. However, she seemed keen to do the work necessary. From what I had seen, Isharu enjoyed outdoors activities.

She climbed up the rock. The surface was smooth, and she slipped several times before she reached the top.

She affixed the device to the rock and slid back down.

Then it was on to the next rock. I traced our presence on my reader.

After a few such climbs, she had collected a number of cuts from the sharp glassy edges. Some merely sliced the fabric of her suit, but one on her arm looked nasty, with a good caking of dust clinging to what I assumed to be a bleeding wound underneath.

When she had placed the last device, I led the way back to the craft.

Darkness had encroached even further. Unless the weather cleared up quickly, we wouldn't get out before sunset. I'd promised Thayu I'd be back before dark.

The first raindrops fell when we arrived at the craft, big fat drops that made little depressions in the dry sand.

I remembered rain on Asto.

It had such a high concentration of acid that it bit into stone and released a foul, suffocating smell. I had heard this depended on the substrate, but my memories didn't have the rationality of such analytical facts. I remembered the smell hitting me in the face like a wall. I remembered barely being able to breathe, and the burn of acid that lingered in my throat long after.

We clambered into the ship.

Leisha and Anyu had finished with the engine. The panel was shut, and the two of them sat in the two chairs at the controls, looking at schematics. Sheydu and Veyada sat at the back door with the familiar array of listening equipment.

When we were in, Isharu shut the door.

"Nothing works as it should," Sheydu grumbled.

"This area is a big communication black hole," Anyu said.

"I've placed all the relays," Isharu said. "As soon as the weather clears up, we can try to tap into a satellite."

"It's not going to be easy," Anyu said.

"No," Leisha agreed. "We have no idea what drained the charge, and can't guarantee it won't happen again as soon as we turn on the equipment."

If that happened, we were truly stuck.

We were out of view, and with our instruments misbehaving, wouldn't stand a chance of being noticed and found by a random craft that just happened to fly past us. If anyone wanted to do us ill, we wouldn't stand a chance against them, either.

We sat in the cabin.

Sheydu and Leisha were studying maps. At one point, Sheydu remarked that we weren't that far from the house. There was one more set of cliffs in between our position and the valley. Apparently the cliffs weren't far away, but in my foray outside, I had seen no sign of them. Without reliable tracking equipment, I was very hesitant to go out there and risk getting lost.

No one was going to go out in this weather. Braving the sharp spikes, climbing up the platform, down the other side, crossing the creek and climbing up to the house would be hard enough in ideal weather. Even Isharu had lost enthusiasm for going out there. In fact, she looked exhausted.

We had to wait until the storm blew over. But according to Leisha, storms like this had a habit of hanging around for at least a day.

We had nothing to eat, and only a little water.

Soon, the rain ran in rivulets down the craft's windows. The wind lashed sheets of rain into the side of the craft, occasionally making the floor shudder. Visibility outside became reduced to a few metres at most.

Leisha kept checking out the windows, walking from one to the other, running his hands along the window seals.

Coldi found rain scarier than the hard vacuum of outer space.

The sky went dark. The wind howled between the rocky spikes. The rain sheeted against the side of the craft. I'd lived in tropical Barresh for years, but I had rarely seen this much rain in my life.

For some reason, the satellite array Isharu and I had set up suddenly kicked into life.

Reida managed to connect to the weather scans, and brought up a three-dimensional projection of indistinct blobs of varying colours. Leisha just stared at the image.

"I know this area reasonably well, and I can't even tell what I'm looking at," he said.

Sheydu, Anyu and Isharu crowded at the back of Veyada's seat, blocking the projection from my view. They pointed at what they thought were geographical features, and discussed which parts were rain.

"What's that?" Isharu asked, pointing at an area that showed up white in the scan.

Leisha said, "I don't know. The air is too dense and the scan doesn't penetrate?"

Anyu looked over his shoulder. "No. It's water. The Crystal Wastelands are a depression. It's filling up with water."

Sheydu gave her a concerned look. Sheydu did *not* like water.

"Should we find shelter while we still can? I'm sure we can find a cave in the cliff face."

"The craft is designed to float," Leisha said. "It's much safer to stay inside."

Seeing my previous experience with rain on Asto, I thoroughly agreed with that. I pulled up my bag and checked the presence of the mask and air tank inside it. We might need them.

Veyada and Anyu kept a close eye on the white area, but even from my position, where I could only see the screen from an angle and in between people's backs, I could see that the white area was expanding rapidly.

Puddles formed on the ground around us.

And then—

"Whoa, what's that?" Sheydu was looking out the front window. The alarm in her voice was most uncharacteristic.

I peered into the murky semidarkness through the water lashing the outside of the window. Something out there was moving. Flashes of white came up and vanished.

"What is it?" Veyada said. "It's like the ground has come alive."

"Notice how much more water there is on the ground?" Isharu said.

I realised. "Oh, shit, it's a flash flood."

Coldi lacked the words to describe situations like this and I wasn't even sure that my literal translation made any sense, but it was clear enough a few seconds later when the frothing mass of water became visible.

"Strap yourself in!" called Leisha, while reaching to the side of the seat.

I dropped back in my seat, activating the seatbelt, which came out from the sides and slung itself around me.

By the sound of the zooming motors, the others were doing the same.

Then the water was upon us. It crashed into the craft. It

washed over the windows in a deluge of dark brown mud. It lifted the craft off the ground. It threw us into a rock. The craft bounced off and hit another rock. Frothing water churned past the window. The craft flipped upside down and then back up again. We banged into another rock.

I held my breath. Those rocks were sharp. I hoped none of them would pierce the hull.

Then we popped up on the surface. Most of the rock spikes were under a mass of brown, churning water. The wind whipped the surface into waves. The same wind also pushed the craft away from our landing location on the inland sea that had suddenly formed.

Crap, now the satellite repeater devices wouldn't even help us anymore.

And it was still raining heavily.

"Where are we drifting?" Anyu asked. The edge in her voice betrayed that she was also very unhappy about being this close to water.

"We'll probably be blown to a quiet spot, where we can wait out the storm." I had done quite a bit of sailing in my father's boat, including some hairy trips in bad weather where we had taken damage to the boat.

"We'll be far from our original location," Sheydu said.

"Yes, but we can set off an alarm, and we'll be easy to see."

"Easy to see for those we don't want to see us," Sheydu said, her voice dark.

"Let's just deal with that when it happens," I said.

Isharu pointed out the front window. "Look."

Then the landscape had opened up, and we were looking at a sheer cliff rising into the mist and rain.

Only it wasn't a real cliff.

The rock face showed compressed layers of brickwork and dust filling the spaces between them.

You could see where passages had been, the corridors and

rooms, whatever the people who built these structures used them for.

"Whoa."

We stared at the wall of ancient destruction in front of us, the stone wet and glistening with water. Here and there, little waterfalls tumbled down.

I could just about imagine the scale of this disaster that had wiped out an entire civilisation.

This had been where the world had ended. The crystal wastelands were a zone where the heat from the meteorite strike had been so intense that it had melted rock and reformed it into glass. Those rock spikes out there? They were all that remained of buildings of glass, metal and concrete. This was the edge of that zone. Thousands upon thousands upon thousands of people had died here. Their bodies were engrained in the dust. They had become part of the planet that raised them.

Seeing it like this, bobbing on the surface of a churning sea, made the sense of destruction more poignant.

"This is amazing," I said. "How many floors of buildings are under the ground?"

"No, look!"

Isharu pointed at a spot where the water met the cliff face. Her eyes were wide.

At the bottom of the cliff was a dark hole. It might have been there before or it could have formed under the pressure of the rising water level, but the water was escaping into the dark opening at great speed. Not only that, but all the water around us was rushing towards the hole, taking us with it, and we had no charge left in the engines to stop it.

11

THE **FLOW OF THE WATER** drew the craft towards the escape hole, then into the fast flowing area just outside it. Then into the opening.

Leisha had called for everyone to take to their seats and strap in again. I gripped the armrests. This was even scarier than coming down between those rock spikes. There were huge cavities inside these mountains.

We washed down a drop-off, a couple of metres into ink darkness. The craft fell sideways, crunched into the bottom, but bobbed back up. The water roared all around us Leisha attempted to light the outside lights, but before we could see if they worked, we were sucked into an underground maelstrom.

The craft bumped into the sides and obstacles in the stream.

I clutched the armrests of the seat.

If we got stuck, we'd be screwed. We wouldn't be able to get out until the entire lake had drained. We'd be fine inside the craft until the air ran out. And we had no spare fillings, and even the tanks used for Exchange travel only held enough for a number of hours. We could be stuck here for days.

Each time we scraped over rocks, I held my breath. But each time, the water pushed us over the obstacle.

Leisha switched on the emergency lights, but all they showed was rock walls rushing by, some made of rubble, some clearly artificial.

"Where is this going?" Veyada asked.

"With a bit of luck, we'll end up in the creek in the valley below the house," Sheydu said. But she didn't sound happy. She really didn't like water.

The craft got stuck on the creek bed. Sand scraped along the bottom.

"Well, that seems to be the end of it," Leisha said. "I don't know how we're going to get out of here."

The sound of water rushing past us was all-pervading. There was a lot of water, and it started pushing against the back of the craft.

"Don't get up yet," Leisha said.

The rush of water pushed the craft loose. We drifted a bit further, sand scraping the bottom.

Then the craft started to tilt.

In that moment of horrible silence, someone said, "Oh shit."

The craft flipped onto its side and fell, and fell—

Until we hit water with a bone-jarring crash. Metal creaked. Everything that was loose in the cabin flew around. The door to the emergency cabinet in the back flew open and a box with metal items fell out. They bounced through the cabin.

The craft sank into the black depths, and then bobbed back to the surface. It was pitch dark in the cabin, but you could hear water running off the roof.

I released a breath I didn't realise I'd been holding. Phew.

"Where are we?" Veyada asked in the dark. He sounded just as shaken as I felt.

Leisha said, "Some underground sea."

Coldi didn't have a recent word for "lake", because there had been no lakes for many years.

Leisha turned on the outside lights of the craft, allowing us to peer out the windows.

We were in a patch of calm water in an underground reservoir so big that it was impossible to see the sides. Admittedly, it was very dark in this cavern and the window was fogged up.

The main noise from outside was the roaring of the waterfall that we had just fallen over.

Leisha switched on the camera that now surrounded us with images as if we were outside.

"It's a big cavern," he said.

I peered past him, but could see very little.

"There's a light up there." He pointed.

Yes, I saw it, too—a tiny pinprick of yellow in the utter darkness above us to the left. I couldn't even guess how far away it was.

Leisha turned the camera to infrared. This cast a green haze over the image, but showed the warmer spots with greater clarity. I could now make out the walls and ceiling of the cavern, the vast amount of water—which was dark—the waterfall behind us, which dropped quite a distance. Had our ship come through the opening up there? It looked barely big enough.

The cavern wall stretched out quite a distance beyond the waterfall before curving back. The shape of the underground lake was long and fairly narrow, with the waterfall close to one of the ends.

A section in the wall opposite us was strangely smooth and curved inwards. A narrow strip of a different material ran from top to bottom.

Leisha said, "Interesting. Next to the light is a passage of sorts, leading away from the cavern, and a bit further along, there is a square opening. The light is on a kind of control panel." He pointed it out.

"Do you see people?" Veyada asked.

"No one."

By now, the craft's scanner had produced a three-dimensional image of the space. The square opening was at the very top of the smooth wall, the lip of it lower than the passage that led into the rock face.

The curving of the wall was peculiar. I could even see how it joined the natural rock wall. This wasn't something that had survived the meteorite strike. All the former buildings that made up this cave had been pancaked together. This was a new structure.

Then I realised. "It's a reservoir to collect water," I said. "That hole up there is the overflow. All this is artificial." It would hold a lot of water. The ceiling of the cavern was at least six floors above us.

Zyana took in a sharp breath. "Stockpiling water is illegal. People used to do it anyway, because out here, people used to survive by digging ever deeper into the soil for muddy wells. Water is the most sought-after resource. Water is survival. If you have water, you're rich."

"I'd hate to think how much a reservoir like this would be worth," Isharu said.

"A huge amount," Zyana said. "Or rather, it *used* to be worth a huge amount. Much less today, because there is water in the valley."

"A light just went on up there," Leisha said.

We all looked up.

"There is a walkway along the rock wall," Zyana said. "I've seen this sort of thing before. Some of the *zeyshi* warrens have wells where you can go a long way into the ground to find natural water."

"Is this a *zeyshi* construction?" I asked.

"Highly likely," Zyana said. "Although it may be quite old."

"Does anyone know it's here?"

"I can't see it on any of the maps," Leisha said.

"I can see someone up there," Veyada said.

It was true. A tiny backlit figure walked along the opening of the passage.

A stronger light came on.

Sheydu climbed on top of a bench of seats, reaching for the ceiling hatch. Because this was a craft that could fly into a vacuum for short distances, one hatch opened inwards and another outwards.

"Be careful," Veyada said.

But one didn't need to tell Sheydu those things. When she opened the outer hatch, the first thing she stuck outside was her gun.

She waited. All remained quiet.

"Can you still see them?" she asked Leisha.

The others studied the scan in silence, and then Zyana said, "There." He pointed. "They're letting down a basket or platform or some such on a rope. There is a person in it."

Sheydu went back to the front of the craft, where they were looking at the screen. I could see the person, too, a lighter figure on an infrared scan.

"Is there only one person?" Veyada asked.

Leisha said, "Seems so."

"There will be others," Sheydu said.

"The question is: will they be hostile?" I asked.

Zyana said, "If they were going to attack, they would already have done so."

"They're only sending one person. It's likely to be a trap," Sheydu said.

I said, "Even if it is, what else can we do? Wait until the water fills up so much that we get tossed over the top of that spillway over there?"

No, they didn't like that either.

I pushed myself up. "I'll go and meet this person to see if there is another way out of here. Veyada and Sheydu can be my guards."

I climbed up on the seat and pulled the ladder down from the recess inside the inner door. Then I peeked out.

Damn that night blindness. On Leisha's screen, the projection had included data from infrared radiation and rendered it visible to us. But out here, without that tool, I could barely see the roof of the craft, let alone the person coming down to us.

But I noticed the whining of a small engine, presumably the one letting the ropes down, over the constant rumble of the waterfall.

"We're lost," I said into the darkness. "We were affected by the storm, had engine trouble, water came up quickly and we were washed down here. Is there a way out of this cavern?"

A disembodied voice said, "Why should we believe your story?"

And damn the fact that male and female Coldi voices sounded so much alike.

"We come from the house in the valley. If you allow us to come closer, you can see our clan designations. We are Domiri and Palayi. I am the leader of the association. I am Aveya Domiri."

There was a small silence. Not the type of prying visitors this person expected, I thought.

"All we want is to return safely to our fellows. We can compensate you if we need to use your resources."

"We're not interested in money." The reply now came from closer by.

"What are you interested in?"

"We don't want any spies." People who would report them for stockpiling water.

"We have no ties with any locals. In fact, they stranded us in the wastelands before the storm."

Another small silence. Something bumped against the craft and a moment later, someone walked over the wings into the light.

A woman, I thought. I glanced at her ears, but she wore no earrings. Ezmi? "Is there a way out of here?"

"With the aircraft?" She sounded incredulous.

"Yes." I was not leaving it behind. Apart from the fact that it was Asha's, people who wanted ill could spy far too much from the craft's systems: all our identification numbers and travel details, all communication, all the scans we had made of the area, including the information about the listening bug and the depot of equipment waiting to be sold.

"We'd need some time. We need to bring winches."

"We have time. We can pay—"

"We're not interested in money—"

"—for your time. That's only fair and it's my word that I'm not interested in whatever business you're conducting here."

Another silence. From where I stood, her face was in the shadow.

Illegal business, obviously.

"Do you agree? Can I know your name?"

"Ilavu."

"Well met."

She did not respond. If she was Ezmi, she wouldn't have strong loyalty networks that required her to behave in a subservient manner. "How many of you in the craft?"

"There are four others." I hoped she wouldn't require them to come out, because that would expose Anyu and Isharu being in the hated Vonayi clan, and potentially they might know Zyana as member of the Third Circle guards.

"Come with me," she said.

I hesitated.

"We're not going far. We have an exit window up there and will need to use the cranes to get the craft up."

I followed her over the roof and wing of the aircraft to her metal basket. I gestured for Veyada and Sheydu to come with me.

She opened the side of the basket to let us in.

It was crowded, but we all fit.

She operated a mechanism on the side. A whining sound indicated that an engine sprang into life that hauled the basket up.

For a while we moved in complete darkness. Then we

reached the level of the opening. The light was not quite as bright as it had seemed from below, but at least I could see something here. Not that there was a great amount to see in the barren passage that led away from the cavern. It was quite a spacious affair, in contrast with most of the *zeyshi* warrens.

Was this a *zeyshi* warren? I had no idea. This side of the mountain ridge faced the valley where the house stood. Reida had said that there was an agreement that the Ezmi clan would not settle in this area.

Was Reida wrong? Had his contacts lied to him or did they simply not know about this? Or was this a different clan?

We were definitely above the level of the spillway, which was to the right, connected by a metal walkway attached to the rock wall. We were also close enough to the ceiling of the cavern that I could make out thick metal beams that ran along the rocky ceiling of the passage and then some distance into the cavern so that they hung over the water. From one beam hung a pulley taller than me, with thick metal wires. So did they bring in things over an underground river or did goods arrive up there and were then taken elsewhere across the underground river? Goods like retrieved ancient machinery or even goods smuggled into the desert from off-world?

Were these people the owners of the cavern under our house, and was it Asha's aim to have me bust a crime ring that was operating under his nose?

The light revealed a little extra information about Ilavu. She was in her middle age, with a fair bit of grey hair at the temples. She wore a plain, dark-coloured work suit. Out here, Ezmi of the *zeyshi* rogue groups usually wore a *shayka*.

Apart from the walkway to the spillway, the landing also contained a charging station. A number of canisters stood on a shelf, presumably containing charged pearls. The floor bore painted stripes which looked like landing guides for aircraft.

That was interesting. How did aircraft get here?

We walked through a dimly lit underground passage. There

were some doors on both sides, but they were shut. I was sure that Veyada and Sheydu behind me were doing their best to obtain as much information as possible.

The passage continued to be quite broad. The floor was bare except for a single white stripe down the middle. Clearly a guide for automated vehicles to follow.

We hadn't gone far when a warm, dry breeze hit my face.

The tunnel led outside. The white stripe was to guide aircraft. This was the way out of this cave.

The woman took us into an empty office, where she asked for our ID and scanned our cards. Both Veyada and Sheydu were on the record as having been part of Ezhya's bodyguard. My pass was temporary, to be replaced after the clan induction ceremony.

Her face showed no emotion while she processed the details. But when she said, "I'll have to speak to someone about this," she sounded annoyed.

Maybe she had hoped we were bluffing about our clan. Maybe she had wanted to get rid of us, citing that we were lying as reason to kill us.

She was done with the scanning, and told us to wait in an empty room, and locked the door as she went out.

Veyada brought out his reader. *I don't trust this,* he wrote on the screen.

Sheydu shook her head. Nope, she didn't trust it either. Neither did I. These people, whoever they were, did not want us here.

She pointed to her ear.

Yes, faint sounds of people talking drifted through the door.

She had also produced a scan of the hallway and adjacent rooms which she displayed on the screen. The picture was incomplete, with rooms dropping out of view where the scan had failed to penetrate, but it showed quite a large inhabited area. It also indicated electronic activity in a number of places, including a number of other chambers.

Someone had built an entire settlement inside this cliff.

Sheydu then called up the map that Asha had given us of this area and overlaid it with the scan. This map gave a much larger picture with much less detail, but because of the current scan, we could pinpoint where we were.

She pointed to a large hollow area—this was the lake. We had not recognised it previously. She pointed to the passage outside the door, which showed up clearly on Asha's map. Then she pointed at a spot where the passage ended, at the cliff face that was across the valley opposite the house. I remembered thinking that those dark holes on the cliff opposite the house could be caves.

I signalled, *wait*.

I pulled out my own reader and found the pictures I had taken of the view from the veranda.

We were then able to render a three-dimensional image from the picture and overlay it with both maps. And now I noticed what I had not given any thought to before: under an overhanging rock ledge in the cliff face was a dark shadow, and inside that shadow was an opening.

Sheydu motioned, *We can get out that way*.

Yes, but first we had to get the craft out of the water. I assumed Ilavu wanted it out of the water as well. I also assumed that she had contemplated just killing us and sinking the craft, but judged the risk too great, because she didn't want the attention a full-scale search from powerful people would bring.

Sheydu and Veyada continued to walk around the room scanning every part of the walls and ceiling.

Veyada would occasionally drop some remarks about Asha and how he would be wondering where we were. Sheydu then said that he was sure to be looking for us.

It was all bluff for the sake of scaring these people. They would be listening.

After a while, the door opened and Ilavu came back in the company of a man who also didn't wear traditional *zeyshi* clothing.

"We'll let you go. He will help you recover your aircraft," she said without introducing him.

They then took us back into the passage, away from the direction where I could definitely hear voices and other activity that indicated the presence of quite a number of people.

He walked at a quick pace, and didn't speak to us Both his arm brackets held guns, and a third gun hung on his belt.

A number of powerful lights had been turned on at the landing where the passage opened into the cavern. The light revealed just how big the lake was. You could fly an aircraft in there.

Hmmm, that made me wonder. . . .

Water was still pouring in from the inlet where we had fallen, a thundering waterfall that made the air humid and drowned out any sounds in the cavern.

There were a couple of other people at the landing, all armed. They all stood around, looking at our craft which floated below. None of them had yet made preparations to engage the beams and pulleys to haul us up.

"We will also need some recharges," I said.

"We will give you a canister," Ilavu said. "Just get into the basket and I will get it for you."

I was getting a very bad feeling about this.

"I would like to get it now." I looked past her to the charging station with a bank of charged canisters next to it.

"Just wait in the basket. I will get it now."

No, she wouldn't.

I reacted in a flash. I ran to the charging bay, grabbed two canisters and jumped over the edge of the passage, all before any of the armed people could react. It was a long way down to the water, and I hit it with a force that drove the air from my lungs.

Most Coldi hated water, most couldn't swim, so this was unexpected for them.

I made my way to the craft while Sheydu and Veyada

rappelled down the rope, and jumped the rest of the way into the water as well.

I could only imagine how much Sheydu hated this, but I had made her learn to swim, because one couldn't live in Barresh without being able to swim.

I reached the craft, where Isharu pulled me up. "Look after the others," I said as I climbed through the hatch and jumped down the ladder.

"I have charges."

I handed Leisha the canisters, and he ran to the interior recharge panel. While Veyada and Isharu piled in, I explained how we could get out through the passage.

Leisha dropped into the pilot's seat.

Sheydu was still at the top of the ladder, firing her gun. The sound of discharges mingled with shouting voices.

"Come inside and sit down!" Leisha shouted.

Sheydu pulled the outer hatch shut and dropped to the ground.

Leisha continued, "Everyone hold on. They're coming down. They're likely to fire at us." His hands went over the controls. "It's going to be tight and rough."

The engine fired. With much frothing of water, the craft lifted from the surface.

All kinds of alarms started beeping, indicating that the craft was too close to other objects and there was no clear path into the air. Leisha turned the alarms off one by one.

He steered over the water, first towards the far end of the lake. I could barely stand to watch because he was going so close to the cavern walls.

At the end of the lake, Leisha turned the craft sharply and went back in the other direction.

More people had come into the mouth of the opening. A flash of gunfire erupted. The charge zapped across the outside of the craft. Leisha had engaged the shield.

The craft made another sharp turn, and zoomed back to the far end of the cavern.

"What are you doing?" I asked Leisha.

"We need some speed to get through the tunnel and I need the engine at low capacity for most of it. I don't want the tunnel to collapse on top of us."

But even at gliding speed, the craft would still go down.

"Going in now. Hang on tight."

The craft turned so sharply that the metal groaned. Then Leisha gave the engine full blast before cutting it.

We shot into the passage.

People ran out of the way.

I held my breath. The opening was awfully narrow . . . the passage wasn't tall. We were gliding and were going to hit the floor soon. We were not going to make it. . . . The engine roared. Leisha had turned on the downward jets and we glided over the floor of the passage like a hovercraft, narrowly missing walls and people, blasting furniture aside.

The opening of the cavern loomed before us. When we came to the edge, the resistance of the jets fell away and we dropped like a stone, until Leisha switched on the main engine again.

Holy crap.

We tore away from the cliff face into our own valley.

In the time we had been inside, the sky had gone almost dark. It was still raining, but it had settled into a steady drizzle. The creek in the valley had turned into a frothing mass many times wider than it had been before.

The house was a beacon of warm light on the other side.

"That was the most ridiculous escape I've seen you make," Sheydu said to me.

"I liked it," Veyada said.

I asked Leisha, "Is that what they teach you in combat piloting?"

"No, but they teach you to make up stuff like this, without getting too many people killed."

I could forgive him for sounding pleased with himself.

"To be honest, you gave me the idea."

"Yeah," Sheydu said. "I keep telling him that he needs to learn to fly."

"He has already agreed to be a student."

While they discussed aircraft, all I could think was how much I wanted to be with Thayu.

12

———————

W E HAD MADE a miraculous escape. The house on the hill beckoned us like a safe haven, a surreal paradise with its warm glowing lights.

Nicha and Naru stood under the veranda watching us flying in.

When the craft landed, they came running down the path. It was still wet from the rain, and glistened in the lights from the house.

"What happened?" Nicha asked. "You are so late." His eyes widened when he looked at my sodden clothes. "You're in quite a state. You look like you went for a swim."

"I *did* go for a swim."

"Looks like you've sustained some damage." Naru ran her hand along the outer hull of the craft.

It had acquired quite a lot of scrapes but, overall, it was testimony to the structural strength of these small aircraft that our tumbles hadn't done more damage.

"It's a very long story," I said. "I hope there's food, because I'm hungry, and it will take quite a long time to tell."

"Yes, there's food. The cook wanted to know if you'd be here.

We hoped you would turn up, but we were worried, I admit." I could hear Thayu's worry through his words.

Thayu had come to the front door of the house.

I ran up the path and into her arms. She was soft, warm and dry, and I was wet and dirty. I probably stank.

"What happened?" Her voice was shaken. "You were late, but we didn't think anything of it until we couldn't contact you any more. Did you end up in the Crystal Wastelands?"

"That's only part of the story," I said. "It's quite something."

We went into the house, into the warm light and spacious dining room. The table was set for all of us. The heavenly smells that wafted in from the kitchen made my mouth water.

We sat around the table, and Ayshada greeted us with laughter and much squealing.

But a few people were missing.

"Where are Deyu and Reida?" I asked.

"Reida said he wanted to check something," Veyada said. He had run to his room to put on a dry shirt.

"Can't they ever stop working?" I got up from the table and went back to the security room. Sure enough, there they were, in front of one of the display screens.

"Come and have something to eat first. There will be time to work later. I can't have you fainting on the job."

"I want to check Ilavu's name against the register," Reida said. "They might take a little while to get back to us." This was the same name register in which I'd had to register my new name and we'd had to register our daughter's name, because each name was used only once.

"What do you think you'll find?"

He shrugged. "I didn't see what you saw in that cave, but if these people are from the Ezmi clan, the people I asked would have told me they were involved with something in this valley when I enquired about it."

And they had told him they had nothing to do with it.

"How likely would you say that the person asked was lying about it?"

"I trust them. I asked my mother as well. Everyone said there was no involvement."

"How about they didn't know about it?"

He shrugged again, looking uncomfortable. "It's always possible, but the reason I asked these people is because I trust them. If none of them knew about any activities of the clan in this valley, then either those activities weren't known to them, or there were no activities. No, don't ask me what I think. I don't know. It's all open. I don't like my clan being accused, but if they tried to kill us, then I want to know why and I want someone to be held responsible. Not me. I didn't do anything."

"I know you didn't."

"No, you don't know. Every time someone does something out here, it's always my clan that gets blamed for it. And you know what? They're usually right, because these people are *stupid*. I want to know: who did this? Why did they lie to me? Why can't they be honest with me? If they didn't lie to me, then who are these people? Did they send the *reychi* as well? I want to know."

His eyes were wide. From his reaction, it was clear that he was sure that these were people from his clan.

"Come and have some food first."

"No. I need to know this."

"You're having dinner now." I jerked my head at Deyu.

Between the two of us, we managed to drag Reida to the dining room, still protesting that he had to do so-and-so.

Before going in, I faced him.

"Look, I know you care a lot about your clan's reputation and your family, but the best thing you can do is to be a good example for how you think they should behave. Honesty always has the longest breath."

"I am honest. I just don't like when other people are not."

"Nothing you can do about that. We will find out. For now, come and have dinner."

We went into the room and we all sat down around the table, and we told the story of the things that happened since leaving the house in the morning. While a number of us told the story, I watched Thayu's face. She was looking more and more concerned.

"And when you left, you said you were just going to place some devices." Her voice was soft. I knew she'd much rather have been with us.

"Yes, I know," I said.

"I discovered something and I should have told you while you were still in range."

"You did? From here?" The thought that she might have left the house abhorred me.

"From the veranda. I asked the security for something to do, and they told me to make scans of the view in different wavelengths. While I was doing that, I found a rectangle in the mountain opposite that is much colder than the rest of the surrounding rock."

The door to the underground lake. "Where is it?"

She got up and slowly walked to the veranda. "It's a bit dark to see, but it's in that direction." She pointed upstream to the right. "It's a fairly large area."

"Yes that's where we came from, where the underground reservoir is."

"We never spotted any activity there. They're well shielded."

"They may have been there for a long time, and I wouldn't be surprised if they had another access to the cave."

Back at the table, Sheydu had again brought out my doodle on her screen.

Without taking her eyes off the image, she started, "We went to set some listening devices to spy on communication from the bug we discovered, and the information was going into a building in Eighth Circle. It's highly likely that the attackers came from or were sent by these people, who didn't like our discovery of their stash of equipment, even if we haven't quite found out where this cavern is and we don't know who is behind the monitoring of the valley. We were then chased off by people from the Talavi clan, who didn't want us there. We were on Outer Circle land at the time, and this is traditionally the territory of the Ezmi clan. Are the Ezmi clan in a relationship with the Talavi?"

She was looking at Reida.

He shrugged. "Not that I know of. Mostly, we don't like the Talavi, because of the role they play in exploiting the people who travel along the trade routes in the desert."

Sheydu nodded. "So what were these Talavi doing, and why didn't they want us to be present on land that they don't have control over?"

"The same reason they drained our charges."

"And that reason is?"

Of course no one knew the answer to that. It was all very frustrating and all we could do was finish our dinner and have some small talk about things that had happened at the house in our absence, which was surprisingly little. Ileyu was learning to walk, and she was holding herself around the edge of the table.

Halfway through dinner, Anyu came in and sat down at the table in a way that looked like she had something to say.

"Anything new?" I asked.

"It works," she said. "We have a link where we can listen to the people in Eighth Circle who own the bug that Reida found. The recordings are clear and all we can do is wait until someone says something to give away their identity or aims."

"How soon will we know?" I wasn't comfortable with the prospect of either being a sitting duck for future attacks, or drawing out a major conflict while we were in this vulnerable spot, with Thayu pregnant. I wanted answers.

Reida went back into the security room and came back with a result of his inquiry about the identity of Ilavu, frowning deeply.

"Anything unusual?"

"It says here that Ilavu Ezmi is a woman who lives on Origin Hill. Which means I might know her. Or I might know people who know her."

"And do you know her?"

"No. And every one of the people I asked about Ezmi involvement in the valley said there wasn't any."

"So, *someone* is lying," I said. Before Reida could protest, I added, "And because the replies from several people about the Ezmi clan's involvement all say the same thing, I'm not inclined to think the clan is lying."

"You're going to let them off?" Sheydu said. "Someone just made a targeted effort to kill you. I don't think we can leave that unchallenged."

"They weren't Ezmi clan," Reida said.

"The register says they were."

"They weren't!"

"We still don't know who they were," I said.

"Ezmi clan," Sheydu said.

"They were not!" Reida said. His cheeks had gone dark.

"We don't know," I said.

Nobody protested.

"So, what are we going to do now?" Nicha asked.

I had the beginnings of an idea, but I didn't know if it was going to work. "I think Sheydu is right and we can't let this go unchallenged."

Sheydu was professional enough not to make any "See, I told you so," comments.

"I also believe Reida's sources. But we can't solve this ourselves, so I propose to do something controversial."

"I know. You want to go and talk to everyone," Sheydu said. I didn't know if she meant it to be a joke or not. Sheydu didn't joke. She often disagreed with my methods.

She had been quite uncharacteristically argumentative with Reida. I didn't know what to make of that. I'd like to think she would go somewhere else if she felt we no longer kept her happy. I had even told Reida so, but all of a sudden I wondered. I was taking huge risks with a team that was already fragile.

So I took a step back. I'd wanted to barge in with my bold idea, but changed the phrasing of it.

"Talking to everyone might not be a bad idea—"

Sheydu gave a small snort.

"But it probably won't solve terribly much. In a way, we have already tried talking. By moving here, we've let it be known that we want to know who has interests in this valley. But no one has replied. We've been available for people to talk to us, but the only one who has come has been Tayanu Palayi. I think we might need to be a bit more blunt about it."

"Go to them?" Mereeni said.

"Yes, but we won't go empty-handed. Since Ilavu came up as belonging to the Ezmi clan, we'll assume she is responsible for everything that's happened so far and we'll visit them to bring them a writ, accusing them of attempting to kill us, not once, but twice. That should shake a few things up."

Sheydu, Anyu and Reida all spoke at once, in surprise, outrage and protest.

I continued, "I know it's a strong response, but Veyada has always said to me that writs can be used for many different things."

"To offend people," Nicha said. "What makes you think that upsetting a whole clan might be a good idea, when you don't even know whether they have anything to do with it?"

"We'll find out whether they do. If I send them a writ, it's up to them to prove that they didn't threaten us. Which means that they'll have to find out who did."

Nicha scoffed. "That's not going to work."

"To the contrary, it might," Veyada said.

"Yeah, I like it," Sheydu said.

"I would hate for something like that to happen to my clan,"

Deyu said. "They spend enough time on infighting as it is." The remark sounded like it came from the bottom of her heart.

I turned to Reida. "What do you think?"

"I'm not sure who you want to deliver it to. The clan has no leader."

"No, but we'll exploit that. We'll deliver it to someone who might be considered a leader by Inner Circle standards."

"Not *zeyshi?*"

"No, someone who presents themselves as compliant with society's rules. I want you to find someone who acts as administrative contact."

"That might be hard to find," Reida said.

But Deyu said, "There is an Ezmi clan office in Eighth Circle."

He glared at her. "No, there isn't."

"Yes, there is. Because every clan has to have an office in the city, and it can't be located in the Outer Circle, because that's not in the city."

Reida stared at her.

"It's true. I can show you."

I said, "Well then, that's where we'll take the writ."

Nicha said, "But, by the sound of things, they won't know much about the clan."

"That's the point. Force them to investigate. That's how we will use this writ. Let them show us how strong the groups of the Ezmi clan really are. Do they have the ability to find out the truth?"

"Hmmm," Veyada said. He thought for a bit and then he said, "It might work. Or it might backfire. Spectacularly."

"According to you, what is the risk?"

"Risks. There are many. It could spark a fight within the clan. It could spark a second secession from the city. We really don't want another Hedron."

"They could all go to Tamer," I said.

"Yes."

Shudder.

Veyada continued, "It could be that they will still protect the group in the cave. It could also be that the clan genuinely has nothing to do with it, and they will pry into another clan's business and upset them."

"Which clan?"

"Talavi would be one. They're not many, but they don't play nice. They have a lot of sophisticated weapons. It could get nasty."

"All right. What do you suggest as alternative?"

Sheydu answered for him. "Nothing. I like it. At this point, a lot of people will be hanging around to see if they can court your influence."

Asha had also said as much.

"You want to show them not to mess with you. You'll be like a young boy from a powerful family who is inducted into the clan. Everyone hangs around after the ceremony to see if they can worm themselves into one of the associations he will be forming. Only you are not a boy and you have far more immediate influence. There will be a lot more people hanging around, watching you. Make a strong response. We've been threatened after we told them who we are. Send a writ to a clan who never gets writs, and let them beat themselves out of the mess."

Isharu nodded. She obviously liked the idea.

Anyu liked it as well.

Nicha sighed, but he also nodded, his lips pressed together.

"I think it's dangerous," Thayu said. She wasn't usually this careful, unless she could foresee serious problems.

"But is there another option?" I asked.

"Other than just muddling along without clarity, probably not."

"Then I will do it, and let the future bring whatever it may."

I rose from the table, letting Veyada and Mereeni know that I would require their services when they finished eating.

I went to the security room and they came a bit later, after having put Ileyu to sleep. Together, we worked on a legal document, formally accusing the Ezmi clan of trying to kill us. In reparations, I demanded that the perpetrator be handed over to us to answer our questions about what the clan was doing with the underground lake, in a place where they repeatedly told us they were not active, and while stockpiling water was still illegal.

The document was firm without being threatening, but made it clear that we meant business.

The most important writs were hand-delivered, so we'd deliver it tomorrow. That gave us an opportunity to look at the Crystal Wasteland and what had caused our charge to drain so quickly again.

We went back to the living room but found it empty. Everyone appeared to have gone to bed already.

Just before Veyada and Mereeni were about to go up the stairs to their room, Veyada held me back.

"Just so that you realise this, I want to make it clear to you that this writ can have other consequences for Reida."

"Apart from accusing his clan?"

"In relation to accusing his clan. Because we have a member of the local Ezmi clan in our association, the fact that you are going over his head direct to the clan representatives will be considered a sign of Reida's disloyalty to them. So they will consider Reida a rogue." Asha had warned me that something similar might happen in the Omi clan and, in a way, it had.

"I thought he was already a rogue? I thought the Ezmi clan wasn't very tight-knit?"

"Many sections of it aren't. Some are likely to be governed by *sheya* networks. The Ezmi clan office that Deyu mentioned is likely to be staffed by people with the instinct. They will consider that Reida sides with us, and against them, when you, and not him, deliver the writ."

"Should we let him do it instead?"

"No, because it's your writ, and if he wanted to deliver it, he should have told us already."

I tried to think about what Reida had told me, and remembered how he'd been quite upset with his clan for threatening us. Poor Reida seemed to run into so many controversies.

"Should I go and talk to him?"

"It's your decision and he knows that." Veyada grabbed my upper arm and pulled me close. "You must appear strong, for the sake of all of us. I know you love talking, but just for once make a hard decision and stick by it. This is really important. All of us depend on it. I'm not sure you even realise how much."

13

———

WE WERE VERY MUCH on edge. Even though everyone was tired, I made sure that Sheydu had some guards posted to inform us of any activity coming out of the opening on the other side of the valley overnight.

Asha's people were reported to still be around, and Sheydu said they were in contact with our team, but they didn't come to the house, and I saw none of them.

Before going to bed, I made sure to shut all the windows. Thayu complained that it was stuffy in the room, but I was nervous that someone might try to climb through. Most of the members of our team were tired, and we had to guard both the aircraft and all sides of the house, which was very exposed.

In the past few days, our enemies, whoever they might be, had shown incredible creativity in getting through our defences, and although I trusted Sheydu's security team, I had no illusions that their surveillance would be watertight. Even so, I was so tired that I slept very well, and for once woke up to an orderly morning.

We had breakfast in the large dining room, where everyone

who was going to come with me to the Ezmi clan was getting ready.

Isharu reported that all had been quiet across the valley overnight. With the help of Asha's people, they had started to monitor a much larger area, but I suspected that any attackers had a supply route through the tunnels and could do whatever they wanted and we would be none the wiser.

I heard that, overnight, my team had obtained all permits to visit Eighth Circle, and that Asha's guards would be providing an extra level of security for us. In all, our party would comprise twenty-four, even though I would never see most of them. I thought it was overkill, but Sheydu was nervous about going into Eighth Circle, so I left it.

I finished breakfast and went to get dressed.

What did one wear when delivering overbearing ultimatums to groups of largely innocent people? Because I was not yet inducted into the Domiri clan, I couldn't wear any of their cere-monial outfits. I could also not wear of any of my official *gamra* clothing. *Gamra* blues would not go down well in the Outer Circle.

I eventually settled on a utilitarian dark body suit which gave a small hint that I might be involved with the army.

While I stood in front of the wardrobe, missing Eirani, who would always know which was the most appropriate outfit for any occasion, Thayu came in.

She laughed when she saw me in front of the mirror. "You're becoming as much a fusspot as Eirani is."

"It's important what I look like."

"Not in the Outer Circle, it isn't."

"So I could wear *gamra* blues?"

Her eyes widened.

Point made.

Thayu couldn't care less about what she wore. Right now, she had to wear a dress, which she hated, and she had to stay here, which she hated, too. Although she did love playing with

Ayshada and in between everything else that had gone on yesterday, Ayshada had proudly shown me the tracks and trains they had made in my absence. Thayu was committed not to waste any of his learning efforts on frivolous things. If she had anything to do with it, this girl of ours would become the best spy known to mankind.

I was so used to doing everything with her that she left a big empty spot by my side that I found hard to fill. Thayu didn't speak a lot, but she had lots of ways to communicate her feelings. I never realised how much I relied on her.

Overnight, Anyu and Zyana, who were both engineers, had cleaned out the craft's engine and made sure that everything was still working as it should. They had also stocked up on spare charged pearl canisters in case someone was going to pull tricks on us again.

"When we're anywhere near a parts supplier, I'd like to get a new antenna for the stability sensor," Anyu said, wiping her hands on a cloth. "I don't like returning the craft to Asha with damage."

"We can be glad that the damage isn't a whole lot worse," I said.

"That, we can."

We boarded the craft.

I was sure that when we left we were watched from across the valley. I remembered having this feeling even when we first came here. If all those chambers and passages in the mountainsides potentially contained people who were watching us, this valley was going to be very crowded indeed.

For a while, we flew over the desert. Leisha made a detour over the Crystal Wastelands where most of the raging ocean that had appeared yesterday had subsided into tranquil puddles.

I wondered if this meant that all the water was now in the underground reservoir. There would be enough water for an entire city for months.

I asked Leisha to keep a good watch on all the other vehicles in the area, but he noticed nothing out of place, and not much later we reached the first of the Outer Circle settlements.

It used to be that the Outer Circle was subject to abject poverty, and that people here would kill each other over a bite to eat or a bit of water. But even during my previous visit that was no longer the case. Not that anyone in this area was particularly rich, but small industries had sprung up, and some people had built substantial houses.

I was sure that this also had something to do with the illegal exchange operations by the Aghyrians, no matter how much *gamra* wanted to deny that those still happened. The second exchange was a genie that was not going back into the bottle. It would happen. It was up to us at *gamra* and my negotiations with Minke Kluysters and the Aghyrians to make sure not too much damage was inflicted.

Reida snorted. "This office in Eighth Circle is a farce. Most Ezmi can't even visit it."

"It's not about visiting. It's about representing the clan to other people," Deyu said.

"Other people have never been interested in the Ezmi."

"It's time they were. As you will have noticed, there is a lot of land here. The *zeyshi* can't expect to just sit on it and not allow anyone to do anything with it."

"No. They will just shove us aside, as they always have."

"Not if you are part of the conversation." Deyu spread her hands.

"No one will accept Ezmi clan as part of the conversation."

"Don't be stupid and stubborn. Your own mother is already doing this."

"What? She teaches *zeyshi* kids."

"She teaches them to be part of society, not to run away from it, like the *zeyshi* have always done. They just *want* people to say that they're hated, so they can go on living in their holes, making a nuisance of themselves."

"That's nonsense!" Reida got up abruptly, making the craft wobble.

Sheydu grabbed him by the arm. "Sit down. Stop bickering like children. I thought I taught you better than that."

Isharu was watching intently. The argument made them all uncomfortable, especially Sheydu's association. They were all in *zhayma* pairs from similar or the same clan. Their group encompassed only security people with a very narrow experience.

Because civilised Coldi society abhorred conflict. In fact, their entire society was structured so that conflict was contained and dealt with swiftly and on a small scale in a civilised, prescribed manner.

Despite the huge size of its army, Asto didn't wage wars. They delivered frighteningly powerful precision strikes with a very specific immediate aim.

It was exactly this tendency to avoid conflict that led to problems.

"Let them argue," I said. "It's a very important argument and one that has been brewing for a long time. Everyone has been complacent, going out of their way to avoid this argument. Two hundred years ago, when the living conditions in the Outer Circle became so bad that people could barely survive, the weakest and most marginalised of them broke off and went to Hedron, leaving a wound that hurts Asto to this day. We got warned not to mention Hedron in a room full of powerful people from Asto, because it could have been prevented. The current situation is potentially another Hedron. We have a group of resourceful, smart people with lots of money waiting at Tamer to take advantage. Some of them have already been here. It's vitally important that the position of everyone in the outer circles of society is settled."

But once we had become involved, Deyu and Reida each went to sit in a different seat row and didn't speak to each other for the rest of the flight.

I should do something about this if I got a chance, though I suspected that Reida wouldn't feel more secure until the matter of the writ was settled. Was he afraid that his mother had lied to him?

But one thing had made me interested. We didn't know much about Reida's family. He tended not to speak about them. But now the conversation with Deyu had revealed that his mother was a teacher of some kind. I knew he had *zeyshi* roots, and had assumed he'd come from one of their poor, often abusive and dysfunctional families, where he'd had to survive on the streets by stealing—since he was very good at that.

The airport in the Eighth Circle community where we landed was not big or highly advanced, but it was well organised, and sported a number of well-used and well-maintained craft. There was even a small maintenance shop, where Leisha indicated he was going to track down the antenna that he wanted to replace because it had broken in our tumble down the waterfall.

While he did this, Veyada led us into the settlement.

The street was paved with smooth tiles that look suspiciously like concrete. The buildings were neat.

Quite a lot of people were in the street, going about their daily business, shopping or meeting contacts over breakfast at the plethora of eating-houses.

And then I spotted something unusual: in the middle of the street, in front of a nondescript office, stood a large stone pot containing a sapling tree. I recognised the leaves as something very similar to the megon trees we had in Barresh. "I wonder where they got that?"

Deyu glanced at the building behind it. The door was unmarked, and didn't give anything of its purpose away, although it was obviously an office of some sort.

She said nothing, but then turned her attention back to the tree. "It looks like a megon tree. It is a bit different, though."

"It could be because it's growing in a different environment. Or could be because it is young."

"Or it could be because it is a different tree. Varieties of the megon tree were commonly found along the watercourses before the meteorite strike. They might have reconstructed the plants."

Again, I looked at the office, wondering what went on behind that door, but we had no time to investigate, and I had no reason to do so. I did make a note of the location on my reader, so that I could investigate it later.

The official office of the Ezmi clan was at the end of the same street. It was a fairly new building, with a light-filled open entrance that included a small garden. Again, I had a look at the plants that grew inside, and found that some of the species looked like they came from Barresh.

This time, Deyu agreed with me.

Entry was completely automated, and we had to scan our IDs and state our business to be allocated a person to see us.

Once inside the foyer, Reida was uneasy. He remained standing while we had been told to sit, and paced in front of the window. He still hadn't spoken to Deyu.

I might need to do some mending. Their relationship had always been atypical, much less emotionally involved than was common for *zhayma* pairs. I had assumed that it was because Reida's instinct wasn't very strong. But the last few days had shown me that there could be other factors.

After a short wait, a woman came to collect us from the waiting area. She took us to a brightly lit office that appeared to be just next to the waiting area and told us to wait a bit more.

I kept a close eye on Reida as the next woman came in, who introduced herself as an assistant to the clan leader.

"We asked to speak to the clan leader directly," I said. "It's a matter of importance."

"I'll have a look at it first."

This was not how Coldi people normally did business. This was how people on Earth did business. This woman didn't have the *sheya* instinct; I could feel it.

I wondered what that meant for the importance of the office. Surely, if the clan wanted to play nicely with others, they'd employ people with the instinct who wouldn't offend other clan officials?

She took our carefully prepared document with an unemotional expression, read it, and put it down. There was not a shred of emotion on her face.

"Why do you think we're involved with this threat to your lives? How did you come to this conclusion? Because it happened in the Outer Circle, we're the guilty party? Many different clans live there."

Reida glanced at me as if to say, *See?*

"We ran ID checks on the people who threatened us and they came back as belonging to your clan."

"They don't. That's a lie."

"Then I want to see proof of that. As far as I could tell, they're *zeyshi*."

"Did they display any sign of this? Did they wear *shaykas*?"

"They wore no clan designation. Their leader told us her name. It's down in the register as an Ezmi name. We were on Ezmi territory in the Outer Circle."

"No, you were not. The Ezmi clan sticks to the agreement about the Twin Valley. We have stuck to our agreement to leave the valley in return for Origin Hill. We've suffered for it, too. The problem is with the name Ilavu, which has been used a number of times. The register seems to be unable to delete it from its administration. It pops up under various clans depending on the time you're looking. I don't know this woman that you met, but Ilavu she's not. She is also not part of our clan. We have no control over these people. You can't hold us accountable for their actions. Not like this." She gestured at the writ document. "I'm not about to accept culpability where we have none."

"Then prove it, and I'll be happy. All the details are in the attached document. You can go and find those people yourself. They've ensconced themselves at the top of a very large illegal water reservoir. We entered it by accident, and they were prepared to kill us in order to preserve their secret, I guess because they are well aware that stockpiling water is illegal."

While I spoke, it was as if a light went on in her face. Yes, she knew what I was talking about. It was telling that she no longer denied involvement.

I rose from my seat. We left the room in complete silence.

"That was interesting," Veyada said when we had left the building.

"She knew," I said. "She wasn't going to admit it. She would have been laughing in my face if she had half a chance. That office is a joke. They don't respect any of the Inner Circle customs."

"The question is: are they going to be able to do anything about it? Make these people apologise, give up their underground lake—"

"Which has lost much of its value," Deyu said. "They've thought for years that they were sitting on riches, but now it starts raining and their treasure is worth nothing, besides still being illegal. Wouldn't you be just a little annoyed about that?"

Since neither of the youngsters had been with us in the cave, they had nothing more to add.

"So, what's next?" Sheydu asked.

"We should give her a short chance to change her mind, and if she doesn't, we should take out a second writ on behalf of another one of our other clans. We can send her as many writs as we have clans."

"You want to put further pressure on her?" She seemed surprised.

"Surely there is a way I can do that?"

"There is, but why? That will only lead to trouble She was disturbed enough with this one."

"We can disturb her some more until she comes forward with the information we need, or proof that the Ezmi clan really didn't have anything to do with it. It's up to them to provide evidence. That's the rules."

"Yes, but you don't want to use the rules to increase conflict."

To be honest, I wanted to do exactly that. Because we needed to see where the conflict was in order to solve it. We needed the parties in the open, stating their positions. "Do you remember the first time I was here, and we were hosted in Taysha Palayi's apartment? It became clear that he was trying to get us out of the way while obstructing events with ridiculous claims."

"I remember, yes, although I probably don't remember the details of it."

"It was the first time you explained the process of issuing writs to me. I knew what they were, of course, but you were explaining that it was within my right to send Taysha a writ. Then I asked if that was what you and Sheydu would do, and you said, 'No, if it happened to us, we'd just go in and shoot him.' Or similar words. It's that rule I want to evoke, that sometimes the rules make no sense and you have to get to the heart of the matter very quickly and decisively, and sometimes it means making the problem worse just so that you can see what the problem is."

"Well. . . ." Veyada scratched his head. "You have a better memory than I do. Also, if you want to bypass established legal procedure, you might figure out how not to get yourself killed once you return to the Inner Circle. Out here" —he spread his hands— "anything could happen. These are not associates of ours."

"Yet they are. They're Reida's people. Reida has networks in the Outer Circle that will feed into our association. I can't help if those people are not the ones the Ezmi clan office approves of, but that is their problem. I don't like this defensive woman. She just uses excuses. She's just going to keep denying involvement. She might not even give us any leads."

I turned to Reida. "Do you know anyone we could talk to?"

Veyada warned, "You know you're talking about upsetting the structure of the clan?"

"Everyone tells me the Ezmi clan has no structure. I simply want to talk to someone more informative and cooperative."

I hated disagreeing with Veyada. I wanted to tell him to trust me and that it would all be fine, but the truth was I didn't know that either. I was making this up as we went. It might all go badly.

14

———————

REIDA HAD NEVER been keen to talk about his family. Hearing from Deyu that his mother ran some sort of school made me wonder why.

"I need you now," I said. "I need you to introduce me to some influential people in the clan."

He looked down. "I don't know."

"Your family still lives there, don't they?"

"They do, but you're my family now."

"Could we visit them or someone else you think might be able to talk to us about the clan, land ownership or plans for land use?"

"The Ezmi clan have nothing to do with the valley." He sounded defensive.

"I know. I want to talk about their visions for the future in general."

That seemed to surprise him. "But the Ezmi clan doesn't—"

"I know. It has no leadership. It doesn't do loyalty networks, people don't have the *sheya* instinct. Yet somehow the clan managed to send a group of outcasts to a dark, hostile world and, within the space of a hundred years, turn it into one of the most powerful industrial worlds with the highest wealth per inhabitant. So can we please get past the excuses that we should *not* talk to the Ezmi clan? Their members live in this area, if not in our valley. They have an interest in who uses the land if it becomes fertile, even if they continue to live in their caves, do they not?"

Reida met my eyes, but said nothing. I didn't like putting him under pressure like this, but oh, I hated how he was always so evasive about his family. Other people from the clan, *zeyshi* or not, often shared that attitude. It was probably baked into them from birth. Right now, it did no one any good.

I continued, "I want to talk to a person you respect, who may not be the ultimate leader you profess not to have, but who is a leader in the community. And I want to talk to this person about positive things. And since we're here, close to the city, I'm asking you to take us there."

Reida blew out a breath. "I can take you to Origin Hill. You can talk to some people. You would find my family interesting. I wouldn't mind if you met them. Just . . . I don't want to take anyone else." The latter in a low voice.

He glanced sideways at the others. So . . . he was ashamed of his family in front of other Coldi?

"Arrange it. I will take whoever I think necessary for our safety. You can make suggestions about who you think is suitable."

He nodded.

"Deyu?"

"Not Deyu. No one on Origin Hill will talk to us if she is there. Veyada can come. Sheydu can come."

Interesting. He chose the most senior trusted people, eschewing those who were actually employed to guard us.

I allowed him some time to arrange the visit and I slowly walked back to the craft behind him.

Reida had always been hesitant to talk about his family. I knew about Deyu that she used to drive trains and her father had a furniture business in Eighth Circle and that he was politically active on a local scale. I knew next to nothing about Reida, except that his family was of *zeyshi* descent, or at least some of them, but I didn't know how much they were involved and whether they lived in the desert or had moved to the Outer Circle settlements. I had no idea why Reida was so coy about them and didn't know what to expect. That his father was a wanted man on the run?

It would be interesting.

At the aircraft, I asked Leisha to let people in the house know we were going into the city. I didn't want Thayu to feel worried.

Because we had crossed the Crystal Wasteland, Leisha had to use the Exchange, because there was no direct reception in the direction of the house. He said he'd spoken to Isharu who would relay the message to all concerned.

From the plateau it was only a short distance to the Outer Circle. Flying over the landscape, it was easy to spot the numerous winding tracks worn by thousands of young feet on their way to the crater rim for the skim racing. But even some of those tracks were now disappearing under a layer of drifting sand.

The Outer Circle didn't have a well-developed main airport, because it didn't have the train network of the Eighth Circle and relied much more on air transport, so there were many smaller landing fields. The one closest to Origin Hill consisted of a patch of compacted dirt, marked with a couple of white-painted rocks. A handful of clapped-out aircraft sat in one corner, some in such a state that I was sure that they hadn't moved in a long time. Compared to those, our craft looked positively new, although I was sure it was a military workhorse a number of years old.

There was no security and no fence. People just walked in and out without regard for their own safety or that of others.

Reida, Veyada, Sheydu and I ventured into the settlement, a

jumble of blocky houses painted white. Because the proper boundary of the city was still a distance away, people had been able to build as haphazardly as they wanted. The area was mostly flat, baked soil, with a hill of dark rock poking out from the plain. Origin Hill, ancient as humanity itself. Houses and other forms of shelter occupied every bit of the flanks that weren't too steep to build on, allowing the residents to look over the surrounding countryside.

The road zigzagged up the hillside, flanked on both sides by rickety shacks and increasingly sturdy buildings. It was quite busy in the street. A track that carried small trolleys moved constantly up and down the hill. Some of the trolleys contained a single seat and there would be an old man, or a woman with a young child, sitting on it, being carried up or down.

People in the street gave us strange looks. I presumed few people from outside came here.

While we walked slowly up the road, Reida told us stories and memories of the people who lived there. We passed several shops where he said he had worked at some time. All were work-shops where electronic equipment was being fixed or put together.

"Where do these shops get all this?" I asked him.

"This is where, many years ago, people found the first pieces of Aghyrian technology that were still recognisable enough to use. There has always been a town here, even before the disaster. In those days, it was known as Pakkatish."

One of the oldest settlements in all of humanity.

I squinted into the mid-afternoon sunlight filtered through a haze of cloud. I tried to imagine the top of the hill with a magnificent marble temple, which was said to have stood here— a temple of sorts, at least, probably made from a stone other than marble. These days, the hill was occupied by a jumble of blocky houses and shops.

Reida continued, "You ask where the technology comes

from. When our people became outcasts and went in search of better places to live, they came to this hill, which used to have several caves. Sheltering in the caves, they came across many things that told them they had found something important, even if they knew nothing of it. Remnants of old buildings, artworks that were broken but still showed how beautiful they would have been in the past, books, wall carvings. They worked hard to understand the language and the culture."

These days, information about the Aghyrian language was openly available, but that hadn't always been so.

"Then they dug deeper and found a lot of technology. Much of it was damaged beyond repair, but the deeper they dug, the more they found and the more complete it was. These people were digging very deep for wells. Days and days of digging by hand for a muddy puddle. So they cleaned and fiddled with it until they understood how it worked. Then they sold it to the city. That was how they survived. It is also why the Inner Circle could build the Exchange. It was not because of their work. It was because of ours. They bought everything we could find. In the beginning, that was easy. Now, it has become very hard, so we create our own technology. We fix things; we make them better. That's what we do. When I started working in the workshops here, I discovered that I was quite good at it, and my bosses would always give me the difficult jobs."

We kept climbing and climbing. When I looked down the hillside, I could see the airport and in the distance the hazy depths of the crater. I could see the place where we had set up the listening equipment. Listening not to these people, but to Eighth Circle.

I could not see anyone near the craft, but I was sure that the other members of the team would be inside.

To the other side, the city stretched towards the horizon. We were too far from the Inner Circle for us to be able to see the magnificent domed buildings, but I thought I could see the giant platform of the official airport in third circle. I could definitely see the train lines, which crisscrossed the jumble of buildings like silver lines. Sometimes you could see the glimmer of a train as it moved in and out of the sunlight.

"Nice view," I said.

"It gets better at night," Reida said. "On a clear night you can see the entire city."

Yes, I could imagine.

We were almost at the flat top of the hill, where once the temple would have stood, when Reida turned into a laneway on the low side of the road.

A solid-looking wall ran along the street, with a porch and a gate.

"Is this it?" I asked.

"If anyone's here." He sounded nervous.

He opened the gate and pushed it inwards. We entered a covered courtyard where benches and tables and chairs stood in small groups.

The sound of voices drifted from inside the building on the other side. Children's voices.

"I think we're in luck," Reida said.

"What is this building? It looks like a school."

"It is a school, of sorts."

Veyada and Sheydu seemed to have an unspoken agreement with Reida that they would wait here. They each found seats at the tables.

Reida preceded me into the building, into the hallway with, on both sides, open doors that led to large rooms with more tables and chairs. Some rooms were empty, others were occupied by small groups of children of varying ages. Each group had an accompanying adult, and all groups were taking part in lessons. But instead of reading and writing, these children were learning how to put together electronics.

Someone squealed, and a woman rushed out of a doorway to the right. She ran into Reida and flung her arms about her him.

"You came back! You're back, you're back!" She danced around him. She wore the traditional *zeyshi* garment called a *shayka* that consisted of a long piece of fabric wrapped around the body to form a loose pantsuit that was held together with a broad embroidered belt.

"I never said I wouldn't be back," Reida said, disentangling himself from her grip.

She turned around and saw me.

She was probably a few years younger than Reida. Her hair was tied back in a ponytail, but it was curly, like Mereeni's.

"This is my new boss," Reida said to her, and to me, "This is my sister."

Then another young woman came into the hallway and the whole process was repeated.

This woman was even younger, but dressed similarly in a *shayka*.

"Let me guess. Another sister?"

Reida nodded, but he did not meet my eyes.

A woman spoke in another room, and then came into the hallway.

"Reida." She rushed down, and swept him up in a hug. She was older, probably Reida's mother.

"I'm so glad you came. Your brother was just asking about you because he'd heard you were here. Oh." The latter when she saw me. Her eyes went wide.

"It's all right," Reida said.

He turned to me, his cheeks coloured. "This is my family. My mother Jeetari and my sisters. This is the man I work for, Cory Wilson."

Significantly, he didn't mention my new Domiri name. Because it was not yet official? More likely because he thought it would bring negative reactions.

Reida's mother and his sisters greeted me with a brief folding together of their hands. The *zeyshi* didn't do subordinate greetings.

I was quite puzzled. Reida had one brother and two sisters, which was highly irregular, because every woman was only allowed to have two children. I might have thought that two of them would be foster children if they didn't all look very much alike. They were real brothers and sisters.

"Come in, you must have some tea," Jeetari said.

She preceded us further into the building, where we came out into a big bright room. A window and balcony ran along the entire far side, offering a magnificent view over the city.

I understood Reida's comment about the view being better at night. He only needed to sit on his balcony to see it.

"Reida tells us that he now works for you," his mother said. She was thin and wiry, like the other *zeyshi* women I had met.

"He does," I said. "He has done very well, and I am happy with his work."

Reida still wouldn't look at me. I didn't understand his behaviour. I didn't think there was anything to be ashamed about.

"What do you do here?" I asked.

"Our children do not have access to education," Jeetari said. "When we ask for education, The Second Circle sends us teachers that teach them useless things about the Inner Circle and the history of the city. Those things are for rich children to learn. Our children need work. They need to know how equipment works and how to fix a range of devices. That is why we set up this school."

All along the walls of the room hung schematic charts with explanations that were mostly in Coldi except for the technical terms, which were written in colloquial Aghyrian script. I was amazed that someone on Asto still used it.

The walls themselves were artworks, too, painted white with intricate patterns drawn into the cement and then traced in golden yellow. At the top of each wall panel was a line of formal Aghyrian characters: the hieroglyph-like images that I also knew from the caves near Barresh. Aghyrians loved to draw on walls.

The panels were reading charts, for young children to learn to read.

"This is a very good project," I said.

"We try to provide the children with stable education," Jeetari said.

"Have there been no more raids then?" Reida asked.

"Oh, yes. They come every so often. We usually get notified and we can move all the children out and send them home and pack away the things before they get here. There are advantages to being on the top of this hill."

I asked, "Who are they?"

"Third Circle guards, checking for illegal items."

"Like what?"

"Imports, unofficial teaching materials, signs that we're running a school."

"I don't understand. Why is a school illegal?"

"The Inner Circle will never tell us whether it is legal or not. There is no rule banning schools, but they dislike that we take matters into our own hands. They like us stupid. They like to blame us for crime. They like to blame us when things go wrong. They like to say that we are too stupid to have a say over what happens to this part of the city. They already know this is wrong. Some of our people provide services that they themselves use. We discovered all the technology. We are learning how to use it. I'm not afraid of those people. They should be afraid of us."

Third Circle raids? By people like we had in our association, like Zyana? Inner Circle threats and deception? By the contacts of Sheydu and Veyada?

Was this the same mega-city that Ezhya ruled, in what had seemed to me a reasonably fair manner? I knew that the Outer Circle hadn't always been treated well, but hadn't all that changed recently?

But no, Jeetari and her daughters assured me that the latest raid had not been long ago.

"They go for the shops, too, and make up excuses to demand

to see the books and then demand payment for protection. Many shop owners keep two sets of books—one for raids, the other for real."

Reida was nodding.

My head was reeling. No one had ever said anything about this.

After the ubiquitous *manazhu* had been served, she took me on a tour through the complex, where I also met Reida's older brother, teaching a bunch of adolescents. Both his sisters were also involved in teaching. In this, they followed the self-guided teaching methods of old, handed down through the ancient books of the *negari* wise women of Pakkatish.

I found out the school had over three hundred pupils of all ages. They also taught traditional things like reading and writing, but did that mostly at night so they could include adults in the lessons.

The complex at the top of the hill was huge and sprawling. The family occupied the top floor.

To my questions about what she saw as the future of the Ezmi clan, Jeetari said it all depended on what would happen when more people came into the desert with the more frequent rainfall.

"Already, the water trade has died completely. Those people are not happy. The water luggers were usually young men. I have some of them in my classes." They had no interest in farming or establishing themselves as landowners. "We'll build workshops and specialised factories to supply technology. We're not interested in digging in the dirt."

While Reida had been touchy about the clan having given up access to the valley in exchange for this hill, his mother clearly thought the hill was the far better deal, especially since more children learned about the historic value of Pakkatish and the temple that used to stand in the place now taken up by the school.

She said, "We want to teach, because knowledge is peace. We are happy to welcome new people, because to grow is to thrive."

"Would you be happy to work and speak with people from other clans?"

She laughed. "If they would lower themselves to come out here and be fair and polite, maybe. But I can't see that happening."

The afternoon was wearing on, so we said goodbye. Jeetari invited us to come back again, and to let her know in advance if we wanted to speak to other people in the clan, of which there were many. In addition to the three hundred students and their families, the school community also included thousands of ex-students and people who supported the school.

"And *zeyshi?*" I asked.

"The children's fathers are *zeyshi*. Those people tend to want to go their own way. I know some of them, for sure, but they will come or stay away on their own terms."

Then we left, picking up Veyada and Sheydu in the courtyard.

"I don't understand," I said to Reida when we walked back down the hill. "Why did you never tell us that your family runs this amazing school?"

"It's not like you think it is at all."

"What do you mean? Your family does great work. They're very well connected."

"We're always in hiding. I saw you looking strangely at my sisters. They're illegals in our own home. Only my brother and I can ever register and travel and have formal education, or do anything at all. My mother is always afraid she'll lose my sisters one day, because they're illegal. I've heard you and Thayu talk about how she is only allowed to have one more child all the time, and here I am from a family with four children. We can't do anything. My mother wants to help children, but the first thing that is going to happen is when she becomes more prominent, she will be punished for it, and my two sisters will be taken away. That's the fear she lives with every day."

"Even in these modern times?"

"Yes. Because that is the way it has always been. Whenever the inner circles need a distraction, or they need to blame someone, they find something that we have done wrong, and they punish us much harder than is justified. Especially because my mother is a modern-day *negari*. I keep thinking that one day someone will turn up and take me away from my position with you, because of what I am. And my family has given up so much for me to have this opportunity."

"No one will do such thing," I said.

"You don't know these people."

"I have a direct line to Ezhya," I said. "What more influence could you wish for?"

"It's not Ezhya that we should be worried about. He sits there in the Inner Circle and does his things. He doesn't know about any of this. It's the people in the middle, the second and third circles, who send out raiding parties so they can justify their existence."

"Then that has to stop. We have plenty of protection. I don't want any more of this kind of holding back information from you. I think the school is wonderful. You should be proud of it, and you should be proud of your family."

I put my hand on his shoulder. "We will make sure that your family can be proud of you."

He didn't look convinced, but some ideas were starting to form in my mind.

It had been a very interesting trip. Reida's family was nothing like I had expected them to be. Somehow even I had subscribed to this notion that the Outer Circle Ezmi were desperately poor, unemployable people with few skills, no money and no pride. How wrong I had been.

We arrived back at the aircraft not much later.

I asked if anything had happened in our absence, but was informed that things had been pretty boring.

Leisha was going through all the checks. We sat down and Deyu shut the door. I presumed there was no news from the house, because otherwise someone would have given it to us. Time to go home.

"Did you learn something?" Sheydu asked me.

"I did. Not what I expected, but I definitely did."

15

———————

THAYU STOOD ON the veranda as we came up the path to the house.

"We delivered it," I said to her. "We can only wait."

"What about the second trip you took?"

"I had an idea. I don't know if it's going to work." I'd tell her about Reida's family later, when we were alone.

I thought she sensed that something was off, but Thayu was very much a wait-and-see person, and to be honest she had different things on her mind.

We went inside and I was about to go into our room to get dressed in something more comfortable when Deyu said to me, "I'd like to say a few things to you, if I can."

Reida gave her a sideways glance. I wasn't sure that they had repaired their relationship as much as I'd liked. Although she had said nothing, she might have felt passed over when Reida wouldn't let her come to see his family.

"Only if Reida can listen, too."

She glanced at him and the two faced each other for a while. Neither of them wore feeders a lot, because they didn't like it and didn't seem to need it to understand one another.

I was afraid that the relationship would fracture, but Deyu, being Deyu the gentle giant, said, "All right then. If he can listen to my point of view for once."

I took Deyu and Reida to the veranda. With the lingering clouds overhead, the view was dulled by shade.

Being mid-morning, the cliffs on the opposite side of the valley were in the light, but I couldn't see the reservoir wall or the opening that I knew to be there.

I leaned against the veranda facing both the youngsters. Deyu glanced sideways at her partner, and he stood back with his arms crossed over his chest.

Clearly she preferred him not to be here. I was wondering if I was doing the right thing, preventing the flow of things, because associations changed all the time. Was I just hindering its natural progression? Deyu and Reida had always been a strange pairing and I had only heard vague stories of how it had come about. Apparently Deyu had challenged him after Nicha had already chosen Reida.

"I just want to make sure that we understand each other," I said. "I have found your presence beneficial to our group and I would like it to continue. If you have any grievances with each other, I would like you to discuss them to see if we can resolve them."

"You're changing the subject," Deyu said. "Everyone has been changing the subject on me ever since we got here. We talk about the higher ranked clans and we talk about the Ezmi clan and how they are all victims of this or the cause of this or whatever. We don't talk about my people and the people who do all the work and get no recognition for it."

Yes, Asha had mentioned Deyu's clan, but I hadn't seen a reason that we needed to consider them. "If there is anything about your clan that you want to tell me, you know that I am always open to listen to it."

"Even the way you're saying that is wrong."

"What do you mean?"

"I mean that it implies that we just have our problems ready to be expressed to anyone who asks. If it were that simple, why would we wait to hang around in case someone asks?"

I noticed that she was trembling. It was a major thing to challenge a superior.

"Just take it easy."

"I don't want to take it easy any more. This is what the Omi have done all our lives, taking it easy. Being quiet, not saying anything, not upsetting anyone, so that we can continue to do the work that everyone needs to have done. Every now and then someone comes up to us professing to want to make our lives better—they want us happy because they want us to do more work—and asks this question: are you happy? And the people who get asked these questions don't have the words to reply that whenever decisions are made, no one ever talks to Omi clan. The Omi clan provides the food that they eat at their gatherings. They make the furniture that they sit on, they design and build the buildings where the gatherings are held and drive the trains that people use to get to the gatherings. And yet no one asks us to come to the table. No one asks whether we would like to own our land, whether we see business opportunities that we'd like to exploit but we can't, and no one asks our opinion on whether maybe it might be a better idea to build a commercial centre somewhere else."

"I am listening now."

"People talk about the Ezmi clan, because they make noise, they create trouble, and because they make pretty gadgets."

"You're just jealous," Reida said.

"And you're just arrogant."

"Let her speak, Reida. You're not being helpful."

Deyu took in a deep breath. She was still trembling. "The other day, we even talked about the Talavi clan and their stupid vigilante teams that go around the mushroom farms to demand payment they are not allowed to charge. It's illegal. Everyone knows that, but rarely does anyone do anything about it. Why? Because the Omi clan does the work regardless. Why? Because we've learned there is no point in raising issues unless you're willing to go to war with the very culture that feeds you. They can extort us, they can lock us up, because we are frightened for our families and we will do the work anyway."

A glance passed between her and Reida. He was smart enough to keep quiet.

"But if you and all of these powerful people think that the Omi clan are just stupid, then why do you think our leader built this house?"

"I don't think you're stupid. I think you're one of the smartest young people I've met. I just need some help understanding what is going on. Do you know anything about this woman?"

"Rashanu is our clan leader, and by numbers, that makes her one of the most powerful people on Asto. I don't know her personally, but she has become quite well-known because of her actions. She is a bit like me. She is not very rich but she knows a lot of people who can do things for her. She figured that since no one officially owns any land out here, she would claim some of her own and for her own people."

"And where are those people then?" I asked.

"That is the question, isn't it?" Reida said.

"Would you just stop it with snarky remarks?" She snapped at him.

Reida didn't give up. "But it's true, isn't it? If the Omi clan are doing anything, where are they? Why are they not here?"

"I would rather ask another question," Deyu said. "I would like to know why we have been placed in this house and why you think that is 'not doing anything'. They built this house, according to an old, significant design. They have been in contact with Asha because otherwise he wouldn't have known it was available, and they agreed that we could use it. I would call that being very active."

And there was that feeling again. At some level, there had to be a connection between Rashanu and Asha.

I thought of Asha's austere home in the army base, of how he lived with a grumpy housekeeper and a number of extremely straight-faced military people. There was no fun and relaxation visible. From my experience with high-ranked Coldi people, a lot of their business revolved around relaxation.

What if—just if—Asha had a connection with Rashanu, because she was clearly an intelligent, forward-thinking woman?

She would have told them about issues that faced the clan. The oppression by illegal rent demands from the Talavi. The fact that they were hemmed in by the crowded Seventh and Eighth Circle walls, and that they couldn't expand their businesses as they wanted.

And he couldn't talk about it to anyone. If he were to be seen talking to the leader of the Omi clan, all kinds of questions would be raised, because it was outside his loyalty networks.

So he sent us. And he did not let us know what was going on. He hoped that we would sort it out ourselves.

How typically Coldi.

"Just to clarify: your people have an interest in this valley?"

"Who wouldn't have? They are farmers. There is going to be a lot of farmland opened up around here. Of course they want some of the action, especially since the Ezmi clan are not farmers, and have no interest in the land other than to see it as a buffer to keep everyone else away."

"That's not true," Reida said.

"It is true. It is how you deal with other people. You are so full of your own victim status that you can't ever see that everyone else is moving forward without you. And then you talk about me being jealous. It is you who are jealous."

I held up my hands. "Please, no arguing. Why do you think both of you are in my association?"

They both glared at each other, as if they were wondering that very thing.

"I appreciate both of you very much, because you bring aspects to my association that makes it one of the few groups, if not the only group, able to deal with this type of situation. We need all the clans of this area in a discussion about what they want and how to achieve it. We want to stop another section of society breaking off like Hedron. We want negotiation."

They eyed each other. I didn't know if this was what they had expected. Maybe they had expected me to tell them to start packing their bags.

Reida said, "You've sent a writ to my clan. Is that negotiation?"

"It was an attempt at negotiation, but, as I half-suspected, it was delivered to the wrong address. The Ezmi clan office has no say over the clan. I wanted to make sure. I wanted to look like we'd done the conventional thing. We can involve your mother instead. She is well connected and respected."

"Are you crazy? We will lose my sisters."

"No, you won't. I've already said so."

"I already said that's determined by what the self-righteous administrators want, not by what Ezhya says."

"What Ezhya says should be final, but in case it is not, I'm sure your sisters will be safe in Barresh until all is sorted out."

Reida still didn't give up. "They won't sort it out because it sets a bad precedent. Other people will argue that they can have larger families, too."

"When you educate the women, they rarely want many children. Besides, now that the desert is becoming green again, those restrictions will probably be relaxed a lot. Athyl may even *want* extra people to farm all that new land, before someone comes in and does it for them."

That finally seemed to win him over.

I explained that since she had clear plans for the school, Jeetari was a better representative of the Ezmi clan than the designated "leader," whoever that was. And because Rashanu had plans for the valley—plans that involved the house—the two women should speak to each other. And maybe the Ezmi people who lived at the underground lake could be involved as well, because the water could still be valuable to any farmers who moved into the valley. And then the Talavi should be invited, because otherwise they'd feel left out and would create trouble.

Both Reida and Deyu seemed hesitant about my suggestion. It was not how things had traditionally been in the Outer Circle, they said.

"Would you say things were good?"

No, neither of them thought things were good. Change was coming and it was necessary. But what I suggested was very . . . radical.

"Breaking associations into tiny little bits and rebuilding them from the ground," Deyu said.

"And rebuilding them without the Inner Circle," Reida said.

"Yes." Deyu's expression was horrified. "It might upset everything, right up to Inner Circle."

"Not if there is a connection between the Inner Circle and the things that are happening out here. That connection is us."

"A loyalty network that holds most of the Outer Circle and that links back straight to the Inner Circle? I've never heard of anything like that."

"Doesn't Amarru on Earth work in exactly the same way? She has an association that's full of Palayi clan who live in Athens as well as Zhori clan people, all the way down to the mafia. And then she has a direct link to Ezhya."

"This is Athyl. It's not another world."

"But it might work."

Their expressions told me they weren't so sure about it.

"I hold you two responsible for keeping your two clans informed. You are our link. I want Ezmi, Omi and Talavi people talking to each other about their involvement in the Twin Valley. Tell me what you think we should be doing. Think about it, and let me know when you've reached a conclusion."

I didn't expect an immediate reply, but Deyu said, "We have visited his clan twice already. Now what about we visit mine before you become part of the Domiri clan and we can't go into Eighth Circle without bringing hundreds of guards?"

I began, "We need to—"

"No, we don't need anyone. Just me and you and Reida. We'll get Leisha to drop us at the border station. A train goes to my part of the city. No one in Eighth Circle has guards. You don't need them."

"Sheydu won't like it."

"No, but she doesn't understand. Has she ever been anywhere in Eighth Circle that's not an authority office? No, don't answer that. She hasn't. She can't, not without taking a lot of guards and then leaving behind a ripple of people wondering and gossiping about what she's doing there and maybe something is going on, someone has done something bad. People would be stalking her, and that's why she'd need the guards, because some people might even decide that she doesn't belong there, because she's so clearly from the Inner Circle. No matter what she says, and no matter how much I appreciate what she has done for me, she does *not* understand. You still have a chance to understand, and you can visit, until you join the Domiri clan and have to take all the guards, too."

Reida nodded.

"Just me and you two?"

Even in Barresh, I rarely went out without an armed companion or two, or three.

"Yes."

"And what are we going to do there?"

"Talk to my father."

Who, I remembered, was politically active, and a moderate, whatever that meant.

As I had expected, Sheydu disagreed with this trip. Very much so.

"This is why we're here: to protect you. Not send you off into Eighth Circle by yourself and get into all kinds of strife."

"We're just going to talk to someone."

"That's what they all say: 'just' this, 'only' that. That's what we said when we went to put out our listening devices. And instead our lives were threatened. Where would you have been if you'd been alone in that craft in the cave?"

"I wouldn't have been there at all."

It hadn't been my idea to set listening bugs.

"I can't allow you to go into Eighth Circle by yourself."

"Reida and Deyu will be with me."

"That place is a danger trap."

"Have you been there a lot?"

She glared at me, her nostrils flaring. I knew she had not.

"I will be with two people who know this part of the city well and can help me avoid trouble. You trained them. You've been happy for me to go into Barresh with them—"

"That's different."

"Is it so different?"

"If you're in Barresh and something goes wrong, we can come to help. If you're in Eighth Circle, we'd need to get in extra people and apply for permits to come in. We'd have to submit a plan of our movements. We can't just come to help. No, I don't like this at all. It would be stupid. I don't know whose idea this was."

Deyu's obviously, but I was beginning to see a thread through these conversations. Deyu was right. I needed to do this.

Yet, walking back to our room, I felt terrible. I didn't like disagreeing with Sheydu. I respected her judgement because it had served her well.

Thayu sat by the window in the easy chair, with her feet up on the windowsill.

Being Thayu, she wouldn't lower herself to an activity like knitting baby socks, and she was looking at security documents on her reader, which she had balanced on top of her rounded belly.

I told her about what Deyu had said, and our plan for a trip.

"I bet Sheydu doesn't like that," she said.

"No. But what do you think?"

She put the reader on the table next to her. "I discovered something yesterday. You know the bug that Reida discovered?"

"The one we went to investigate and then got stuck in the Crystal Wastelands?"

"Yes. It goes to a building in Eighth Circle."

"Yes, I know that."

"The building is a half-commercial, half-residential structure. The top floor contains a huge apartment with a number of balconies, and the bug sits on one of those. You can hear a lot of people talking, but one of the sets of conversations comes from a nearby apartment: one that belongs to Rashanu Omi."

"So she uses the bug to keep an eye on her own house? What about the cave with equipment?"

"This is where it gets complicated. It's a repeater bug. We've seen the surveillance images, but other sources also use it. One of those comes from the army base."

Holy crap. "Don't tell me: your father."

"How do you know?"

"I don't. I was guessing. But I was thinking that he clearly knows and respects Rashanu because otherwise why would she have lent him the house for us? And. . . ." My mind was racing. "When he first took me here, only one room contained any furniture at all, the one upstairs that Veyada and Mereeni are using. It contained a bed with no bedding and some chairs. The kitchen also held a few things."

Thayu and I met each other's eyes. We didn't need to say it. This house might be a historical project, but it was also something else: a love nest.

Holy crap, holy crap, holy crap.

And now I understood: I *had* to go to speak to the Omi clan —if not to Rashanu, at least to Deyu's father. It was the reason Asha had put us here. He *wanted* it.

I went upstairs to the room Deyu and Reida shared on the side of the house that overlooked the entrance.

Deyu sat on her bed studying and Reida lay on the ground, surrounded by bits of electronics.

"What are you doing?" I asked him.

"Something I'm going to give to Sheydu. She wants to keep an eye on us, so I took one of the flying spybots from your world and put an extra bracket for another charge so it will fly further for longer. Then she can follow us if she wants."

I sat down next to him and put my hand on his shoulder. He looked up, his dark eyes questioning.

"It's not your fault that Sheydu is angry. It's mine. I don't want you to take any responsibility for that, but it's wonderful that you're doing this."

He shrugged. "Well, she's been teaching me lots of things, so I thought it was only fair."

"I'm sure she will appreciate it."

At times I underestimated how much he considered Sheydu his living goddess.

"We're going?" Deyu asked.

"Yes, we're going tomorrow. I'll ask Leisha to drop us at the border station as you suggested. Then it's on to your people to hear what they have to say."

I wasn't quite ready to share what Thayu had found out.

We discussed the trip for a bit. Deyu said she'd check if there were any problems we might run into. Her father always worked at the factory, she said, and we only needed to go there to speak with him.

Then I asked if she thought any of the others could come.

"Honestly? No. Even if they wanted, it would be risky."

"I'm not sure I understand why people like Sheydu almost seem to be afraid to go into Eighth Circle. Why do they think they need so many guards? Is it because they feel afraid?"

"No. They actually need them."

"To protect themselves from what?"

"To protect their associations."

"Right. Now I'm confused. I thought these people were at

the top of their associations and the instinct took care of meeting strangers in the street."

"It does, but the instinct only goes so far. Ezhya has two people under him: the *zhayma* pair Natanu and Asha. Each of them have two people, and each of those another two. And then he has other associations, for his security, for education, for the army and so on. They're vast networks that spread out from the Inner Circle, always outwards, to First Circle, Second Circle, Third Circle."

"I know." Of course I knew. I'd been living this life for many years.

"I don't think you do. This is about what happens at the very edges of these vast associations, when the instinct is no longer strong enough to maintain the network all the way back to the Inner Circle. You know about the Ezmi clan and their weak instinct, but for every one of us, there is a point where there are so many people in between us and our leaders in the Inner Circle that the connection is lost. Athyl has become so large that this happens in Seventh or Eighth Circle for most people. So if you live in Seventh or Eight Circle, you no longer have a direct network that includes people like Sheydu. If Sheydu walked the street alone in Eighth Circle, people in the street would react to her strongly. Her dominance is very strong, and most people would feel subordinate, but quite a few would challenge her. They'd challenge her minor associates first, but people in Eighth Circle work with their hands and many are physically strong. They might beat Sheydu's minor associates. They would upset her association. They might even beat Sheydu herself. That gets awfully messy."

Yes, I could see that.

"But what about. . . ?" I was going to say, *What about Ezhya*, but I could see the problem. The big, huge, looming problem. Ezhya couldn't go into Eighth Circle, which was Athyl's largest population group. He'd be challenged with every step he took.

Likely, if he came, he'd be challenged by almost everyone. It would only take one successful challenger to upset all of Asto's stable society.

Deyu must have seen the horror in my eyes. She nodded.

Reida nodded, too.

And I was somehow expected to solve this issue for Ezhya because he couldn't do it himself? That was impossible.

16

———————

I N THE MORNING at the breakfast table, Sheydu informed us that there had been activity on the platform on the other side of the valley overnight.

Anyu showed me a couple of vid clips with lights moving against a dark background. In one, I could just make out a human figure leaving a vehicle.

The vehicles were still there, Anyu said, but the people appeared to have disappeared.

I asked, "Do you think there is a passage that goes into the ground and that links up with the community at the lake?"

"We have no evidence for that. They could be the same people or a different, unrelated group. They could be a team performing maintenance on the relay stations up there."

"Asha would be able to tell you if that's the case," Thayu said. "They have a pretty good system of recording who is doing what maintenance where."

Sheydu said she'd check.

Then Deyu said, "If they were doing maintenance, why would they camp up there during the day?"

That was a very good question, and one that made the maintenance crew option less likely.

"We could just go over and have a look," Reida said.

This was followed by an uneasy silence. Seeing what Deyu had told me yesterday, I fully understood why. I'd always known that the *sheya* instinct created strong pillars in society that were unwilling to interact with each other for fear of sparking conflict. But most of my team were so far out of their comfort zone in this valley, in the territory of clans they had no affiliations with, that they feared running into pretty much anyone.

So Reida and Deyu could go over there and check it out, but it might be a problem for almost everyone else, unless they took a large team with a display of force, and that could also create trouble.

We'd deal with it when we came back from our unusual visit.

I told them to keep an eye on what was happening, and let us know if there were significant developments. In turn, Sheydu and Anyu told us to be careful.

Reida offered Sheydu the drone he had made.

"So that you can keep an eye on us," he said.

She gave him a rare smile. Like this, she looked disturbingly motherly, and I could almost believe that she had once given birth to a child, rather than having acquired Veyada at an age where he'd been past all the childish behaviour.

She put Reida's concoction on the table next to her. "I will keep it right here with me. Why don't we use it to have a look at what's happening on the platform up there?"

"That should work," Reida said. He sounded almost disappointed that he got to miss out on this.

We finished breakfast and got ready to go. I asked Thayu if she was all right.

"What do you mean? There is nothing wrong with me. Anyu just gave me a whole bunch of scans to analyse and I will sit here and do it. The ceremony is only two days away." And I was sure she planned to give birth as soon as we came home from that.

We were cutting it very close if we wanted to get a handle on what was happening in the valley. What's more, I realised that something might well blow up.

"It might get dangerous here. How about you go to your father's house?"

"That's not necessary. I'll be fine right here."

But she was not doing a good job of hiding her apprehension. She could read the signs. She thought something was up, too. The difficulty was, none of us knew what shape the problem would take. The second difficulty was that it involved clans we had no authority over.

It was time to go. Leisha came into the room wearing his flight suit, and Deyu, Reida and I went with him. Of course he would not go alone, taking his *zhayma* Naru with him.

The flight to the station was short, and none of us said much.

The view out the window showed the increasingly dense population.

Leisha dropped us at the border train station's air pad. It was a small but well-paved airfield that, unlike the other Outer Circle airports, had some security measures in place. It wasn't big and he couldn't stay to wait for us, so he said he'd wait at a nearby bigger facility.

The station was massive, and there was a lot of building activity going on, with sections being cordoned off and new above-ground lines being built.

"They're expanding the lines into the Outer Circle," Deyu said, her eyes wide.

"There never used to be trains outside Eighth Circle?" I asked.

"No. The city ended there, according to everyone, and people who lived out there were just rabble."

Clearly, that was no longer the case.

"The Outer Circle is the fastest-growing population in Athyl," Reida said.

Looking at all this activity, I believed him.

The train lines *still* ended here, for the time being, but the station consisted of several levels of platforms from where many sleek single-carriage vehicles departed at the same time, and it had been designed—by Omi builders, I assumed—to accommodate new lines leaving the city.

Under the guidance of Deyu, who continued to marvel at the changes made, we found the right platform and got on a train.

The vast train network of Athyl, and especially Eighth Circle, consisted of single-rail tracks elevated over the roofs of houses, often ones of several storeys. I'd heard about the section in Seventh Circle where the trains connected a number of high-rise buildings well above the ground with "hanging tracks" where vehicles were propelled by little more than gravity and momentum.

But even Deyu, who had driven those trains, was surprised with the amount of expansion and new construction.

"Where is all this coming from?" she asked, looking out the window as the buildings slid by.

"Well," Reida said. And then he hesitated. "There has been talk that people from outside have been trying to get people from Eighth Circle and the Outer Circle to buy into their projects. Some of the people are very keen to do this, because they have been promised benefit to themselves. But I don't trust it. Because I know who these people are, having worked for you." He glanced up at me, holding his hands on his knees.

"It's that old divide again, isn't it?" Some of the *zeyshi* and others in the Outer Circle were closely allied with the Aghyrians from the ship, who had either settled in Barresh or had gone on to Tamer, and were now in negotiations with a number of rogue worlds to start a second exchange. And I could barely even believe that it was happening, but it was inevitable and would have happened anyway.

Reida said, "I think the Inner Circle was asking for it. Either a lot of people get fed up and leave like what happened with Hedron, or someone else moves in."

"People with a lot of money." People like the Aghyrians and

their technology that had taken them outside the galaxy, people like Jasper Carlson with his data gathering, people like Minke Kluysters with his money. "So, those people are already here with their plans?"

"It's only what I heard," he said.

"It's a bit more than that," Deyu said. "The producers have been promised customers. They have been promised that they will be able to sell their products. The problem with a lot of people living in Eighth Circle is that they want to produce things, but the people in their communities are too poor to buy those things, so they can never make proper things. Like my father. He has a furniture business. He makes furniture that is very poor and he knows it and hates it. The materials he has to use are so poor that they deteriorate in the heat. He knows how to make good furniture, but he can't sell it, because all of the people who buy his furniture are too poor to do so. It's very frustrating. So when someone comes along and promises them a market for their goods, then they are going to be interested, aren't they? Up until now, there hasn't really been a lot of opportunity for these people to export their products, because they all have to go through most of the city's circles just to get to the airport. They have to pay many fees for freight to be taken through the city just because they are from Eighth Circle. And if someone offers them an alternative, they will grab it with both hands."

"Have you heard about any concrete plans?"

She shook her head. "A lot of it is probably just rumour or wishful thinking, but I have heard that some people are planning to build another exchange in the Outer Circle, so that all the people from inner circles can then pay fees to them to use their airport."

"I've heard that some of my friends have been offered jobs," Reida added. "But that nothing has gone ahead yet. People are waiting. They want this, and now they're getting angry that it's not happening fast enough."

The two of them were almost talking to each other as if I wasn't there, in the way they used to do when they first arrived at my household.

Living with a number of Inner Circle people had changed them, too. It had made them cautious and less open. But in these trips with just me and them, they had opened up a lot. They had shown me their role models and told me the real issues that went on in the communities they'd left behind to work for me.

The best I could do by them was to let them speak.

We got off at the station, and the first thing that struck me was how huge it was. I had been told many times that the bulk of the population of Athyl lived in the Eighth Circle, but somehow I had found it hard to realise what that looked like until I got here. The station hall, of which Deyu told me there were many just at this station alone, was cavernous. She told me that many train lines, such as the ones that she used to drive, went from place to place inside the Eighth Circle, without ever crossing circle boundaries. The trains ferried people and produce. A whole level was dedicated to merchandise. Vehicles delivered crates at the entrance, which were automatically scanned and automatically transferred to the correct platforms where, according to Deyu, no people worked except those in the control room.

"Driving trains in there is dead boring; you wouldn't believe it. You have to sit there while the machines unload the freight, and you're not even allowed to get off, not even to pee."

We went from the station hall into a huge square surrounded by tall buildings that dwarfed the structure of the station. They might not have been as extravagant as the constructions in the inner circles, but they were much bigger and much more functional. Multiple walkways connected the buildings at higher levels.

In the square, a couple of passages disappeared into the ground, and Deyu told me entire villages lay underneath, where people lived in all the old underground Aghyrian passages that were safe enough.

We had only gone a short distance before I lost track of where I was. I knew that the Exchange—and my reader—would have an answer to that, but without electronic assistance, I would be helpless.

Deyu had lived with her father and her two brothers. While people in Asto each got the right to have two children, rights for extra children—obtained from those who forfeited their right— were put in a lottery and Deyu's father had won an extra spot.

But when we got to the spacious building with light-filled apartments, neither her father nor her two brothers were home.

"We can try the factory, but he's not usually there at this time of day. He goes in early in the morning, to make sure all his workers have what they need."

"What does he do the rest of the day?"

"People visit him here and they talk through deals."

I had assumed the business to be a large workshop with a factory floor where carpenters sawed, hammered and sanded. But of course the people in Eighth Circle couldn't afford expensive wood, so I'd expected a factory floor with people putting synthetic pieces together. Kind of quaint and old-fashioned.

I hadn't expected "workshop" to mean a building three floors high, with a huge factory floor. People not only sat in a clean room designing furniture, but, on the other side of the glass, machines produced the resin, heated it, made moulds and poured the resin in, stacked it into drying rooms, took it out after hardening, sanded off the rough edges and assembled the items. Tables, chairs, shelves, all individually designed, rolled off the assembly line and were neatly stored away in storage compartments. All without human intervention.

On the second floor, machines made soft furniture: beds, couches with cushions. Carpets, curtains, each individually designed. Deyu told me that her father's people would visit customers in their houses to design everything for them.

To my comment that I'd thought that these people were not well off, she said that they weren't well off. They couldn't afford many things that people in the inner circles had, domestic staff being one. So they spent their money on home improvements.

The top floor of the warehouse was all about technology in the home: gadgets that opened doors, operated windows, regulated temperature, that could drop or lift sections of the floor to create tables, beds and sitting nooks that the Coldi so loved in small apartments. Foldable stairs, foldable tables, pop-up kitchen benches.

This was not at all what I had imagined when Deyu spoke about cheap furniture.

We entered a section of the building with smaller rooms. The door to the office at the end was open, and inside a man sat at a desk. He was middle-aged, with greying hair tied in a neat ponytail. He was well dressed in a dark tunic and loose trousers, both with tiny embroidered stars. He wore ornate golden earrings with the lime green stone of the Omi clan, and a number of rings on his fingers.

The office contained a bank of electronics to monitor and control the factory.

During my many and long interactions with Coldi people, I had heard a lot of things about Eighth Circle and the people who lived there. I had been made to believe by my contacts—none from any lower than Third Circle—that they were poor and not interested in bettering their lives. The elites didn't speak about them much other than that they sometimes caused trouble, and then they only spoke about who they would send to fix it.

Everything, every picture I had formed in my mind of people in Eighth Circle was wrong. They were not poor, they were not dumb, they were not hungry or struggling. They had their own society.

By the look of things, Deyu's father was an influential and

wealthy man. And probably frustrated as hell at being constrained by his social status to living in Eighth Circle.

When we entered, he got up. "My daughter!" He rushed to the door and I witnessed a truly affectionate hug between Deyu and her father.

Whatever picture I had formed in my mind about Deyu's family was also wrong. She had been painted to me as someone from a struggling family, who was desperate to get out.

Deyu might have been desperate for better opportunities, but definitely not desperate in the sense of trying to survive.

"My daughter, my daughter. I didn't know whether I would ever see you again, working for all those—"

He hesitated and looked at me, frowning at my earlobes, which were empty, because Asha had my earrings.

"This is the leader of my association that I have told you about. His name will be Aveya Domiri," Deyu said. Then she turned to me. "This is my father, Narisha Omi."

The man performed a subservient greeting, but I could feel that he didn't really want to do this.

I touched his shoulder as was required, and then told him to look up. "As you can probably see, I am not from this culture. I understand it pretty well, and although Asha Domiri has accepted me into his clan, I am also quite capable of seeing the plight of other people."

"I have heard a lot about you."

"Have you?"

"Yes, out here we read the new services that come out of Tamer. They give us a lot of the news that the regular channels don't. We heard about your visit there and how the People's Exchange will go ahead."

A feeling of cold crept through me. It was as I thought. The Tamer Collective had a lot of influence here already. "The People's Exchange" was even an apt name for the alternate Exchange that might eventually be set up, that would be cheaper, allow for encryption of communication and travel to non-*gamra* worlds.

All of a sudden, I'd felt like the ground had shifted under me, and I was now allied with the bad guys.

But I needed to keep the conversation on the topic we had come to discuss: the clan's plans for the future, in particular in relation to the house and the Twin Valley. "We're staying in the house that your clan leader built."

"I heard that. It's a historic and significant place."

Everything I understood told me that Coldi people didn't care much for history, but clearly that was wrong as well.

"Do you know why it was built?"

"Because it's a historic place, because we have owned the plans for a long time, because other people have wanted those plans because they wanted to build the house, but only so that they could keep people out of the valley."

I ignored all the barbs he laid in that response, too. "What is the Omi clan's plan for the valley?"

He narrowed his eyes. "Have you ever been hungry? I don't mean what you feel when coming to the table after a long day of work, but knowing that your kitchen is empty and your pots will only hold enough food to feed your children, and that the food you have is poor and monotonous."

"No, I haven't."

"I haven't felt that, either, but my parents spoke of it often, and for many people here, that memory is closer than they want to admit. In fact, my children are the result of the opening of the agriculture halls. Smart people worked out how to grow food efficiently inside buildings, and suddenly, people no longer needed to go hungry because we were no longer at the end of the long line of imported food. I didn't want to put children in a world where they needed to suffer. But suffering hunger always remains a threat. It affects everyone."

He gestured out the window that looked out into the factory hall where a number of people controlled machines.

"Do you think I could run a factory like this with people who are hungry? Who, no matter how well I pay them, can't find enough food to buy?"

"But people aren't hungry." This line of discussion puzzled me. What did he want to say?

"No, that's the point. But things can easily go bad again. We don't have enough space to grow crops. The warehouses are good, but bad things can happen. Diseases flourish so much better in a crop grown in a hall than ones grown in a field, or even ones grown from hanging racks in the aquifers. Our relationships with other worlds that grow our food for us can change. We know how quickly things can go wrong."

"So you want a stake in the land use of the valley?" It was about agriculture, as Reida had hinted.

"We have the people with the knowledge. We have the money. We have asked the Office of Lands often enough if we can use the land. They always bring up excuses why we can't. Because of the army base, because of the Ezmi clan, because they can't guarantee our safety. But the funny thing is, they make no effort to make the valley safe. It doesn't need to be made safe. It doesn't need their Talavi puppets hanging around acting like they own the place and extorting money from us. No one owns the valley. The Inner Circle doesn't think it's important enough to settle the land use question. But they have never been hungry."

"Have you tried going to them?"

It was on the tip of my tongue to talk about the apparent relationship between Asha and Rashanu and that the Omi clan could get their information through her.

Narisha snorted. "Why should they talk to me? I have no connection with any of them. The Inner Circle doesn't want to see us as people. They think they control us, and they don't see our problems. So we have to do something for them to take notice of us. We built the house. That makes them take notice."

"I think you're wrong. I think people are taking notice. Do

you think I would be here if I didn't want to know what you thought?"

He gave me wary look. "You're Domiri, and those people have no interest in us."

"I took your daughter and her Ezmi friend in. My association contains all manner of people that are not traditional. Yes, Asha probably sent me to the house for a reason. But he hasn't provided me with instructions on what that reason is, so I'm doing whatever I please. They may not like hearing what you have to tell them, but here I am, asking about it anyway. If you have anything to say, any wishes or plans that could be helped by the Inner Circle, I suggest you mention them to me now."

After some hesitation, he started telling us the story of extortion and intimidation by people professing to act for the Office of Lands. I had to question him pretty hard to find that most of these people were from a faction in the Omi clan who wanted all the local businesses to move out of the city. They wanted to start a new city outside in the desert, where they could do whatever they pleased. They drew their inspiration from the Ezmi clan's escape to Hedron.

"Only they wouldn't need to go to another world, they said. I said it was the most stupid thing I have ever heard, because why did they think no one from the inner circles was going to come after them? Why ever did they think that people who had successful businesses in the city were going to leave everything and go out there?"

"So you think it's a bad idea?"

"I don't think so, but I think they're too impatient. I don't want to start a war, I want to keep my business."

"And your business is doing as well as you want it to?"

"That has nothing to do with that. No, it isn't. But a lot would have to happen before I would take part in such a ridiculous scheme."

"Do you know which people they are?"

"I would rather not give names that could end up in the

wrong hands. I don't agree with them, but I don't wish them harm."

"How well developed are their plans?"

"I am not answering that question, because I don't know."

But I could hear the answer in his voice. I could also hear the stress. "If you're keen to stay here, what have you done to protect yourself from the threats?"

"I had to get rid of all the workers that have anything to do with this breakaway group. They even managed to get Talavi bloodsuckers to work for them, that's how far they've sunk. You can't trust anyone anymore. This is why I am in the factory, and why some of my friends are working for me."

"If you want, I can put you into contact with some people who may be able to help you find employees."

"I don't want any people from the inner circles here. That would mean nothing but trouble for me. I might as well put a big flashing light on my head saying *traitor*."

"They wouldn't be from the Inner Circle." I was looking at Reida, hoping he might understand that I was talking about his contacts. "I can ask people from other parts of the city." His mother and her school would be happy to assist. She trained people in technology.

He gave a low hiss. "We haven't solved this issue for years. I don't expect someone from the inner circles to blow in and solve it for us."

"And you still don't want to leave the city?"

"Of course not. We were here first. I worked very hard to set all this up. I will stay where I am, and if I can prevent my people doing stupid things, like turning themselves into *zeyshi*, then I will."

I felt we had got as much out of him as possible, thanked him for seeing us, and then led Deyu and Reida back outside after saying goodbyes.

Deyu said, "I'm sorry about that. My father has very strong political views. He doesn't find it easy to trust people. There are reasons for this, but explaining all of them would be boring."

"To the contrary. I think it was very enlightening."

"Was it?" She frowned.

"Yes. I understand why the Ezmi clan is so possessive of the valley. *They* signed that they wouldn't settle there, and they now feel that if ever it becomes acceptable to live in the valley, they should be given first priority."

"But they're not farmers," Deyu said.

"Everything can be learned," Reida said in a tone that imitated Sheydu.

We laughed.

I continued, "Meanwhile, we have the Talavi clan, which is seeing a large—and illegal—source of income slip from their grip and is trying to do something about it by being hyperaggressive with threats and collecting rent. This was probably why they came to see us at the crater rim. They couldn't work out who we were. They found we weren't anyone they could intimidate, and so they helpfully drained our charges."

"But we still don't understand how they did it," Reida said.

"My guess: with some clever devices bought from the people your mother trains."

Reida's cheeks coloured.

We had arrived at the station and stood a moment in silence on the platform while we waited.

Between the three of us, we had just worked out what was likely going on: the Ezmi clan thought they owned the desert. The Omi clan wanted a piece of it. The Talavi clan did some of the dirty work, probably for both clans.

I had never felt closer to these two young people.

In that moment, a young girl came up to us. She was part of a group of young people who stood further down the platform, giggling to each other.

The girl wore a factory uniform and lime green, Omi, earrings.

"Can I help you?" I asked.

She performed the most subservient greeting I'd ever seen. "Are you really the one they now call Aveya Domiri?"

"I am." I was puzzled. How did she know this?

"I just . . . me and my friends. . . ." She glanced at the group of giggling girls. "We wanted to say how much we thank you."

Whatever for? "Well, thank you very much, but I'm not sure—"

"We thank you for listening to us and taking us seriously. We're all cheering for you. Me and my friends and all the others at the factory. I will tell them that you were here and they will be so excited."

But then it clicked with me. Narisha had said that they all got their news from Tamer. They had watched reports where I had been the voice of the disenfranchised people, countering the established powers.

She said, "We will make things better. We're ready to work hard. If you tell us to work, we will work. When there is a challenge, you will win."

Then she left again, bowing profusely, and I was left with a cold feeling.

There was no challenge of this part of society against the established order, or, heaven forbid, of me against the Inner Circle or Ezhya.

This was not a fight.

It *couldn't* be a fight.

I desperately wanted it not to be a fight.

17

———

BY THE TIME we had returned to the busy airfield at the border station, the sky was once again dark over the desert. A pink haze hung over the horizon, signifying whipped up dust.

"I hope we can get home safely this time," I said as we walked to the craft.

While we had been away, Leisha and Naru had taken the craft to a less busy airfield where they had cleaned it up.

Gone were the dust and muddy footprints in the cabin. Gone were the scuffmarks on the outside. Leisha had also replaced the broken antenna, but I would never have noticed if he hadn't told me.

I asked if more bad weather was coming, and Naru said it was. A thunderstorm was rolling over the desert, whipping up a cloud of dust to herald its arrival.

No one said much on the flight back. I was sure I wasn't the only one who expected the engine to cut out any moment.

Leisha avoided the Crystal Wastelands, "To show you different scenery."

Yeah. Right.

But we reached the Twin Valley safely at the time the first

raindrops fell. The air held that distinctive wet stone smell that had once almost killed us in Athyl, but I'd been told such a strong release of poisonous vapours wasn't common anymore.

We found everyone around the table for the late afternoon snacks. Asha's cook kept a traditional schedule.

Nobody said anything about it, but the relief that our trip had been uneventful was obvious.

Over steaming cups of *manazhu* and savoury bites, I told everyone what I had seen and learned.

When describing the technologically advanced factory and the huge vastness of the place, most members of my team were silent. Few if any of them had been inside the heart of the Eighth Circle recently, if ever.

Their expressions were uneasy, especially when I told them of the Omi clan's plans to leave the city and start their own communities.

Nicha remarked that this would bring them into conflict with the Ezmi clan. They debated whether "Ilavu" was from the Ezmi or Omi clan, or someone else altogether. No one knew for sure.

We'd had no response to the writ.

"I fear that sending a writ to the Ezmi clan might only have made the conflict worse," I said. "We need to get these people to talk to each other rather than turning them into enemies. Is there a way we can retract it?"

Veyada's expression told me that there probably wasn't.

"What *is* the best way to go forward?" I asked them. "I would like to talk to them, but to be honest, it can wait until after the ceremony." I still wanted to read up on the procedures—I'd done this before, but couldn't remember much of it—and on the people who were likely to be there, and who—according to Asha —were likely to try to get my ear. And then there was the question whether it was my place to lead these negotiations anyway, being an outsider with no strong connection to the valley.

For a change, most of my team agreed that avoiding conflict

was best. We'd done a lot of investigating already, and there was not much more we could do.

At night, in our room, I told Thayu more about the amazing difference between what I thought Eighth Circle was like and reality.

"It is, isn't it?" Thayu had been there, clearly.

"Those people seem so keen to educate themselves, because they see it as a way to increase their chances of getting a good position. To them, it has been a great frustration that they can't get enough business and that there doesn't seem to be quite enough to do for all of them."

"That's why the population limits were instated," Thayu said. "There can never be more than a certain number of people in Eight Circle, which means that they'll have a job, they all have a home, and there are enough resources to feed all of them. That was the idea."

But over the years, the rigid control had gone by the wayside.

"It seems that they are very keen to feed themselves. It also seems that they want to work harder than what has so far been possible. They want better businesses and they are making some strange choices to make that possible. Deyu's father said that if they leave the city, they will become like *zeyshi*."

Thayu didn't reply. She often thought for a long time before she said anything.

I continued into the silence, "But the reason I wanted to talk to you about it is that I feel the problem is much bigger than just who can grow crops in this valley. It's turning into a class war being fed from other worlds. The Aghyrians may have given up trying to get control of the whole planet, but they certainly will not stop trying to get control of a certain part of it."

"That has always been the case."

"Maybe, and that's why I am asking you. Do you think I should involve your father or Ezhya? Don't you think it strange that Ezhya hasn't contacted me at all? I'm supposed to be working for him and the last time I spoke to him was a long time ago."

And that conversation had been really strange, in which he had attempted to assess me for how much I had really changed as a result of my fertility treatment that made me compatible with Coldi genes.

Since that time all my communication with Ezhya had been written.

And now that I had been here for a number of days, he hadn't even made an effort to contact me, apart from that very lame welcome message that Thayu said he'd only sent because he knew I would have expected it. You know, like a silly human.

I was reasonably sure that he was invited to the ceremony, but that was still two days away, and if things were going at the speed they were now, a major conflict might blow up by then.

"I don't think my father will be in a position to do anything about either the Ezmi or Omi clans. The army is not meant to control internal matters. The army exists to protect our home from invaders."

And the army did some very strange things out in deep space that no one was supposed to know about. "But what about Ezhya? Wouldn't he be interested if there was a rebellion in part of his city?"

"He would be. I'm sure he's watching."

Well, great, but that didn't help me a lot. I was like a goldfish in a fish bowl. They were all sitting around the table watching how I handled myself.

Just the thing high-ranking Coldi people loved to do.

If just once, like fucking *once*, people would tell me what was going on . . . nah, scratch that. If that ever happened, I'd die of shock.

We went to bed quite early. I wasn't sure what we were going to do tomorrow. Today hadn't led to any major discoveries that needed acting on, and I hoped to finally have some time to look into things that I would need to do for the ceremony and people I would need to speak to who would be there.

I must have been really tired, because I slept like a log.

Unusually, Thayu woke me up instead of the other way around. I was so sleepy that I wanted to go straight back to sleep.

"Get up," she said.

My heart jumped. Was it time for the birth? She said it would be after the ceremony.

"What's going on?"

I sat up and became aware of a low-level hissing noise. "What's that sound?"

"Oh. It's raining."

She turned on a light and by the faint glow, I could see that she was dressed in outdoor clothes, not the type I would expect her to wear if she was about to give birth. Unless we needed to go to the hospital. But Coldi women rarely did. And I would probably know about it if that was necessary.

"Have a look outside."

I stumbled across the room to the window. At first I could see very little, but then I noticed that there were lights at the bottom of the valley. Rather a lot of them.

"What's going on down there?"

The lights moved in rows.

The door to the room opened and Nicha said, "Did you see that?"

"I'm seeing it right now, even if I'm unsure what I'm looking at. How long has this been going on?"

"Sheydu says since midnight."

"Did anyone trip the alarm again?"

"They're too far away for the perimeter alarm."

"What are they doing?"

"Just moving through the valley as far as I can see."

"They're not coming up here?"

"No. They're not paying any attention to us at all."

Whoever was down there had to know that the house was here.

I rubbed my eyes. Damn. I'd been sleeping so nicely. "What are you doing about it?"

"We're going to have a look. Do you want to come?"

Both Thayu and I said yes at same time, and then I said, "You're staying here."

"I agree with that," Sheydu said from the hallway. "Something is going on out there, and it's likely to be dangerous. They're quite likely not to be keen on us watching."

Thayu grumbled something about being bored. "It's dark. No one can see us anyway. If they really didn't want us to see them, they should have stayed away. Of course they know we'll see them. I'm sick of waiting and doing nothing."

I wished she could come with me, because to be honest I was getting quite sick of doing everything by myself. Sheydu's conviction about how things needed to be done got on my nerves a bit. Yes, she was older than me, but her experience, while valuable, was also very narrow.

I told Thayu, "Open your feeder and I'll send you images. That's the next best thing to being there."

"I don't want to sit in this room." She let herself fall back in the pillows dramatically, spreading her hands. I went over to her, and stroked her face. "Not long now, and you'll be able to do anything you like."

I pulled on some clothes and went into the hallway, leaving Thayu in the room looking grumpy.

I felt for her. I really did. I knew how much she wanted to be part of the action, but there was nothing I could do about it.

A few of us were going down. Besides myself, there was Deyu, Reida, Sheydu, Isharu and Anyu.

While we waited for everyone to get ready, there was some speculation about what was going on in the valley, but no one had seen any more than I had. *Vehicles moving in a line through the valley*. That was all we knew.

Sheydu went through the checklist.

Take guns.

Take explosives.

Body armour.

Helmets, visors.

Water—for washing out acid or poison.

Emergency rations—if we got stuck.

She inspected each of us thoroughly, walking around me twice before snorting. "You must be learning."

In Sheydu's language, that was a compliment. She had nothing to criticise.

Meanwhile, the rain had become heavier, rivulets pouring from the sloping roof. At some point, someone in Athyl would have to make provisions and design houses with gutters. The original, Aghyrian, design would probably have included those.

We set off, ducking under the dripping water and tromping down the path.

It was dark, my eyes were still used to the light, and the infrared view didn't help much, because everything it was supposed to show was cold in this weather, and because the visor kept fogging up on the inside. The only thing I could do was follow the person in front of me, who happened to be Deyu.

Progress down the hillside was slow, since no one wanted to make a light. Also because the fine dirt that held the loose gravel got slippery with the rain.

Anyu walked at the front. She was going down the steep path without slipping. I wondered what sort of technology she carried. Deyu in front of me did not carry any. She slipped several times, once hitting me with her arm and taking me down with her. I didn't need her help for my other two unceremonious slides on my backside. The water seeped through my suit. I had to wipe my hands on my stomach, the only part of the suit that wasn't yet covered in mud.

As we got closer to the valley floor, details of what was happening became easier to see. The lights we had seen from above were attached to vehicles moving slowly backwards and forwards across the valley floor in a neat formation. Because they were electrically charged vehicles, there was no noise except for the sound of sand being moved and clunking and thunking that I couldn't place.

We stopped before we got too close, half-sheltered behind a large rock.

"What *are* they doing?" Isharu asked.

We peered into the rain. Water was running from my hair down into the back of my suit.

The headlights from the vehicles reflected in the shards of rain teeming down. One closest to us came first. The vehicle next to it was slightly behind and backlit its neighbour. It was a blocky thing, lumbering and heavy. It left behind an area of disturbed ground, steaming with warm moisture when hit by the rain.

As the first vehicle moved past us, it hit something with a clunk. A rock rolled over the disturbed earth.

They were clearing the land of rocks.

There were at least ten of these vehicles, and they were systematically sweeping the valley floor for big rocks, combing through the top of the soil.

Behind them was another row of vehicles that were all moving in a line. What was the bet that those were ploughs?

"They're making the land ready for agriculture," I said.

"Where did they all come from so quickly?" Isharu asked.

Another piece fell into place in my mind. "Those are the vehicles we saw when Reida found the bug. They were waiting in a cavern under the house." Someone had stockpiled these machines ready to go when the conditions were right.

Not only that, but they had set up a camp at the base of the cliff on the other side of the valley. The rain had eased a bit and I could see the light and temporary shelters and people moving around.

They had not just started using the land. They had occupied the valley.

Were they of the same group as the ones who hid in the cliffs opposite the house?

There was no one to ask. Sheydu said that the people probably communicated, but she couldn't pick up any transmissions on her equipment. She didn't want to disturb our people in the security room who were likely listening.

We debated going up to these people and talking to them, but Sheydu didn't like that. There were a lot more of them than there were of us, and we didn't know if the vehicles were armed. No point in turning them hostile before we knew who they were and what they were doing.

So my team collected all the imagery and scans Sheydu wanted to use, and then there was nothing else we could do except to go back to the house and report on what we had found.

At least it had stopped raining.

On the way up, we got a message from the house that the relay and surveillance bugs had reported what I'd already suspected: the cavern was empty. All the vehicles we'd seen in there were working the soil in the valley.

The members of my team were not familiar with large-scale agriculture. They'd visited Earth and had seen crops. Even in Barresh, where almost every crop grew in water, agriculture was something that happened in other people's lives, in other places, like in Bendara on the Mirani side of the border. But no one ever went there. I had to explain to them how people grew crops in New Zealand, by turning the soil and planting seed and spreading straw to make sure that not too many weeds grew.

And as I was talking, partially out of breath because we were making our way back up the hill, I remembered vague reports from many years back, about "those chans" attending agricultural colleges.

A number of years ago, I'd found out about plans—by the

largely Earth-based Zhori clan—to grow plants from Asto in parts of Africa. I'd assumed those Coldi people in the agricultural colleges were Zhori from Greece and Egypt.

But what if I'd been wrong? What if some of them were Omi from Athyl?

Were we witnessing the great exodus of the Omi clan from the city that Narisha had told me about only yesterday?

By the time we came back to the house, wet and extremely muddy, a faint glimmer of daylight already coloured the horizon.

The others were all awake, aware of all the goings on in the valley, which still continued unabated and were clearly audible from the veranda.

"Are they really removing all the rocks?" Thayu said, leaning on the veranda.

From up here, the straight lines in the freshly turned soil made a neat pattern, and left no doubt in my mind about what they were doing. A few people in a smaller vehicle were driving across the freshly turned soil, picking up all the rocks and depositing them on the sides. "They need to clear the fields before they can use the land."

True to our team's dedication, Naru had produced a map of the valley with all the activities filled in. She sent that to all our readers and explained to me what they'd observed so far. "The area they've treated goes quite a way back to where they've fenced off the valley. They've left a space on either side of the creek, and left roads in between the fields. They've set up a village of sorts on the other side of the canyon. It's a temporary camp with demountable shacks. We've counted at least forty people there."

"Any idea of who they are?"

"We will have to go and check later. I believe Isharu is working on securing an invitation."

We had breakfast, but most people ate at the veranda, from where we watched the spectacle unfold. The rows of agricultural machines tracked backwards and forwards over the valley floor. After all the rain, the soil was rich and moist, and after the first pass of ploughs had done their work, other machines moved in.

"I wonder what they're growing?" I asked no one in particular. I didn't expect anyone to be able to answer that question. Not much had grown on these soils before. They would have had to do some research.

Yes, there had been Coldi people in Barresh looking for remnants of Aghyrians plants to re-introduce. Had there also been Coldi people at Mars University in Pavonis studying how people from Earth made Mars soil ready to grow plants?

I didn't think this was a hastily planned venture. And then I remembered seeing the tree in a pot outside an office in Eighth Circle. Was that a sign to those who could read such signs that this was a place where people who wanted to re-vegetate the valley lived?

Word came from the security room that Isharu had established contact. She came to notify me herself.

"They seem quite open to a visit," she said. "Their leader was aware of our presence, and called us their security."

"I hope they were joking," Sheydu said. "I don't intend to be anyone's security but our own."

"Yes, of course," I said. But I was thinking of yesterday's occurrence at the station, when those girls came to fawn on us. The Tamer Collective had been putting out news that painted us —me—as representing their interests. The Tamer Collective news services were clearly very popular in sections of the outer circles. I could do something with that. These people might not have much time for the inner circles, but they might just respect me enough to take some of my suggestions, such as not to create conflict and work with each other, to make local networks that included all affected clans.

"Let's visit them. Arrange it, Isharu."

Later in the morning, a few of us went into our newly cleaned aircraft. It was no more than a short glide across the valley, and I debated going on foot, but the aircraft was the only way of transport we had that would take us out of anywhere quickly.

Leisha searched for a channel to warn the settlement that we were coming, but couldn't locate one. They weren't expecting air traffic just yet.

Leisha did however listen in to communication from the city that spoke about the happenings in the valley, and that indicated that some craft were to come and pay them a visit shortly.

I wanted to be there first, because I expected trouble to erupt when the authorities showed up.

"Let's just go quickly. We won't do any negotiating, but with a bit of luck we can establish a relationship."

My group included Deyu, because I thought it most likely that the farmers were Omi, as well as Reida, because they might be Ezmi, as well as Veyada, because he was a lawyer and Sheydu because her presence with all her weapons would show that we meant business, so that we had all our bases covered.

Nobody said much during this short glide across the valley.

The people who had set up the camp were well organised. The temporary shelters were set in rows, a neat road wound between them, and it led to an empty space that was clearly for aircraft to arrive.

When our craft landed there, two people came out of a nearby structure. It was not a tent, and it was not a house exactly, but looked very much like a prefabricated shelter. I was impressed with their level of organisation.

I went first, followed by Sheydu and Veyada. Deyu and Reida walked behind them.

At this time of day, the cliff face was in full glaring sunlight. All the rain from the past days had gone and the sky was as clear as it was ever going to get: a glaring white with hints of pale purple above and a soft peach-coloured haze at the horizon. This made the sand and the rocks very glittery.

The inhabitants of the camp wore sturdy work clothing and heavy boots for work. I could only see the colour of the stone in their earrings once they came closer. As I had expected, they were from the Omi clan.

"Well met," I said.

There was no response, but both people, a man and a woman, came forward.

I was alarmed by this. Normally, in situations like this where neither group knew the other, Coldi would revert to comforting structures of power. There would be one leader and a layer of two people underneath. There would not be two equal people meeting a group of unknown people.

I had often feared that the weakness of the *sheya* instinct would spread out from the Ezmi clan, and this was clear evidence that it was happening.

But no, both of them made subservient greetings to me.

Well, that was. . . .

I glanced sideways at Veyada, but his face showed no emotion.

These people . . . considered themselves a *zhayma* pair . . . under me? I didn't even know them. I started, "I'm—"

The man completed, "The one who will be known as Aveya Domiri, our best hope for a fair, prosperous life."

What the. . . ?

At the time when I was first introduced in Coldi culture, Amarru in Athens had given me a poignant lecture about Coldi networks, especially because some Coldi people professed to having a *sheya* reaction to me. Her words came to me, in her usual dark voice. *And sometimes it can be that people you don't know come up to you and want to be in your association. You may not know them, but they always know you.*

Do not show them surprise. Do not reject them. Do not say anything to them except expressions of thanks, and that you will always keep their best interests at heart. Because if you're a leader of an association, you'll be responsible for them, and they will look up to you. If ever you lose that respect . . . that's when people get killed.

I'd been in my late twenties, had just been faced with a somewhat disturbing reaction of a Coldi man to me prompting Amarru's stern lecture, and I had been terrified by her words.

Because Coldi leadership was determined by *instinct* and could move in ways that made absolutely no rational sense.

Except it did.

The Tamer Collective had spread the news that I was these people's voice. So I treated them with respect as I'd been advised all those years ago.

Their names were Olinu and Remiya Omi. They belonged to a radical group in the Omi clan who believed they needed to seize land before people sat down to talk, because otherwise the Omi clan would miss out.

They sold their businesses in Eighth Circle to start a farm.

"We're taking our fate into our own hands. The inner circles refuse to give us permission to use this land, but they don't have plans for it, either. They just want us to disappear. The Talavi act like they own the rights to give out land use permits, and want to charge us huge fees just to leave the city. You defeated the Talavi. Your presence gives us hope."

Wait—the people who lived in the mountain with the lake were Talavi? Now that could make sense. They might want to force farmers to pay for the water they had squirrelled away as a last-ditch attempt to control a situation that was fast getting out of hand. It might even explain the Talavi's attempts to get rid of us: strand us in the Crystal Wastelands and let the rest of the team do the cleaning up.

I had to tread carefully. "I visited Eighth Circle and heard about your plans, but I had expected you to negotiate with the authorities."

"They will never negotiate. They don't understand the things we can do. They don't talk to us. They only give orders."

"So are you expecting any formal trouble?"

I looked around the camp, but could see no evidence of heavy weaponry although I was sure some of it had to be there.

"This area is so large it is indefensible. We hope that by showing what can be done, defence will not be necessary."

"How long have you been working on this?"

"Many years now."

And a lot of those ideas they had were clearly borrowed from Earth.

"Have you had any help from outside?"

"We don't need any help. We have bought all this equipment fairly. We have worked for all of it and have built a lot of it ourselves."

"What are you growing?"

"We've performed a number of trials. The best crops are not the ones that we are planting today. We need to grow some crops to prepare the soil first."

There were all kinds of insinuations, barbs and evasions in that statement.

They weren't saying what they were growing, because the plant material had been imported illegally. Maybe they were afraid that other people would copy them. Maybe they were not saying what they were growing because they wanted to circumvent rules that I didn't yet know about.

They showed us around the camp, where I was introduced to a number of families. All of them came from the Seventh and Eighth Circles, families who used to have businesses.

Reida knew some of them. Deyu knew others. Several times, I witnessed people pledging allegiance to them. My own, Reida's and Deyu's networks were growing explosively.

We were treated like royalty. It was disturbing, because it made an utter mess of loyalty networks I'd already developed, all of them with people from inner circles. Was it even possible to count Omi workers and *zeyshi* as one's associates as well as Inner Circle people? Whatever happened to the vast tree of networks that always flowed from the top down? This one went from the bottom up.

18

I**T WAS STRANGELY RELAXING,** seeing all this planned, well organised activity.

I relayed what we had seen to Thayu when we came back.

We were sitting on the veranda, overlooking the valley where a couple of machines were going back and forth over the fields, which were starting to resemble crop fields with a patchwork of different colours as the turned soil dried out. They had rolled out a huge robotic installation that crawled over the field and sprayed water. Like Earth's irrigation installations—if I was still wondering where these people had acquired the ideas, skills and materials.

These quiet, industrious workers had outsmarted everyone. For years, people on Earth had been worried about technology, like weapons, coming in from Asto, but nobody had worried much about technology going out. We'd just been slightly bemused by some Coldi businesspeople having a penchant for collecting rubbishy plastic figurines.

But this was something different altogether. And it was happening right under our noses. Should I tell Asha?

I asked Thayu, and she said he probably already knew.

"It would be nice if he spoke to me about it. He or, better still, Ezhya. They've been far too quiet. It's like they don't care."

"They care."

"Then why aren't they talking to me?"

I hated to let my frustration show. I'd worked with the Asto Inner Circle for many years, and I *knew* that most of the time they favoured this hands-off approach. I *knew* that a fact would be revealed at some time and I'd understand everything, and I even felt I was on the cusp of that understanding. But if it was true what Deyu had said about the Inner Circle not being privy to Eighth Circle dealings, I would have thought they'd jump on the first chance they got to lift a corner of the blanket.

Apparently not.

So I decided to do what I'd always done: prepare a report for Ezhya in a similar way I had done about Earth's referendum and about the Pretoria Cartel and about our trip to Tamer.

Something was very odd about it. I was talking about my employers' own world, while my employers appeared to be avoiding me.

When I finished, I went to the communication room, and asked for contact with Ezhya on the off-chance that he would accommodate me.

But I heard that he was busy. I could only get onto a junior administrator in his office. It was so frustrating. I couldn't very well shout: Look, I am solving problems in your back yard, can you at least acknowledge that I exist? But meanwhile I had a strong feeling that I was being stonewalled, and I couldn't, for the life of me, understand why. After all, this man paid for most of my expenses at *gamra*. It was baffling. So I just sent him the report.

Asha, however, was more accommodating. He was both in his office and happy to see me, if I could come to the military settlement, which was only across the valley. I would see him at the ceremony tomorrow, but there might not be a chance for me to speak privately to him until much later.

I took the chance and chose Deyu and Reida to go with me.

As we sat in the craft, with Leisha at the controls, it struck me that the two youngsters had both gone through a lot in the past few days. It seemed to have strengthened Deyu while having shaken Reida's confidence. He'd been convinced that I'd judge his mother for having two illegal children, and I had praised her instead. So where did that leave him? A member of a rogue clan, who were being obstructionist by trying to hang onto the only thing they had: the vast desert outside the city. A desert that was turning into useful land.

On top of that, he was still convinced that his clan had been responsible for trying to kill us when we discovered their lake.

Deyu, however, was all self-righteous pride. The Omi clan *was* clawing itself out of disadvantage in different ways, but did she have to be so smug about it?

I didn't know where this relationship was going, but I hoped we'd survive this trip with our association intact.

After the spacious rooms of the house, the dark and dreary army base felt cramped. A stiff military officer directed me to meet Asha in his private office while Deyu and Reida waited outside.

Like so many in this part of the building, the room was airless and dark, with a tiny window that overlooked the court-yard where small craft took off and landed, bringing supplies or visitors and endless amounts of gritty dust.

Asha was looking at a map projected on the table in front of him. I didn't recognise any of the features displayed in the projection. He used his stylus to draw lines between dots in the projection, and marked them with scrawled symbols.

He appeared not to have noticed me. His demeanour was strangely relaxed as he studied the image before him and moved one of the lines.

The moment he saw me, it was like a chill went through him. He shut down the projection, got up and came to the door.

We shared a super-awkward moment where neither of us

knew what we were supposed to do. Had I just seen him do something that he would have preferred to remain private?

That brought my apprehension back. Should I ask him about his relationship with Rashanu Omi? Could I ask him for direct help?

Being a purist, I knew he considered me as having no current status on Asto, which meant he wasn't supposed to instinctively feel where I belonged in the clan and his associations. But I saw in his eyes that he knew, and that he was calculating which of his associates to move elsewhere to make place for me.

He gestured at the seat opposite him. "How is the house?" he asked, in a most uncharacteristic display of chattiness.

"It's very comfortable. We've had a great view just recently." And in the same no-nonsense way he usually displayed, I launched straight into the goings-on in the valley. He listened quietly, in his usual deadpan face that made it impossible to guess what was going on in his head.

When I'd finished, he just nodded. "I think that is a fair assessment. We've seen their overnight movements in scans."

And then he said nothing.

"Doesn't it concern you?"

"It does."

"Wouldn't it concern Ezhya?"

"I'm sure it does."

And again, he said nothing for a while.

This was the second-highest ranking person in Coldi society. Surely, he would have a lot to say about unauthorised invasions—theft—of territory, no matter how opportunistic? "Are you going to do anything about it?"

"I can't do anything about it. This is not my task. I command the Armed Forces, and they will not be used on our own citizens."

"Wouldn't you talk to them?" But as I said that, I realised: these people didn't talk, they ordered. They had probably already ordered, down the line, for illegal activities to stop. The people in Eighth Circle were pretty much a law onto themselves, as far removed from the leadership as they were.

I was determined to give these people a voice.

"They're Omi clan. We know that there are other people hiding inside the mountain, above a vast illegal supply of water. We're not sure of the clan affiliation of those people. They need to come out so that we can all come to an agreement. If they're Talavi clan, we need to find out how they can be settled in a way so that they don't resort to their game of extortion. If they're Ezmi clan, they probably have little interest in agriculture, but those people do have some interesting educational initiatives that I think are worthy of support."

"Then support them."

I frowned at him. "Me? I don't think it's my place to—"

"Will they respect me when I go there? Don't bother answering that. We both know the answer. Those two rascals of yours standing outside the door don't have any time for me."

"They listen to me, and they behave themselves as decent citizens."

He pointed directly at me. "*That* is the important part."

This conversation was getting beyond weird.

He repeated, in case I hadn't understood the first time, "They listen to you, so tell them what to do, and what not to do."

Er—okaaayyy. "Any suggestions?"

"I trust you. Ezhya trusts you to sort this out. Just *don't* let it spill over into Sixth Circle."

Like that. Set the boundaries. Don't touch Sixth Circle, where our authority still holds. You sort it out.

Holy, holy crap.

And then, as he was wont to do, he did an about turn and changed the subject.

"Let's discuss clan matters." He turned the projection back on. "The ceremony."

I forced my rattled mind to change gears.

The ceremony would take place in one of the complex's covered courtyards. I would sit at the front with everyone else who was joining the clan, most of them twelve- and thirteen-year-old kids.

"I encourage you to make note of who else joins the clan on the same day, because this may be important later on. The guests have all been invited. There will be a great number of people attending."

"Does that include Ezhya?"

"It's a clan matter."

"That means he is not going to be there?" Could he just stop being mysterious about it?

"As far as I know, he has been invited. All the leaders of other clans receive invitations as a matter of routine, but it's up to him whether he decides to take up the invitation."

That meant Rashanu was going to be there? But I resisted the temptation to ask. "Then explain to me why he hasn't been in contact with me yet. I work for him, but he hasn't contacted me once since I arrived here, and I barely spoke to him before."

"He's very busy."

"He was never too busy to visit me previously."

"Yes, well, it is not my task to say what he needs to spend his time on."

"Of course not but, being his second, I would have expected you to know at least the reasons."

"He is busy."

And I clearly wasn't going to get anywhere else with him. I didn't understand why there was this coyness about Ezhya's motives, but I would probably find out at some inopportune time and it would be something I had never thought about. He wasn't going to tell me, and I would look stupid asking.

We returned to the house not much wiser than we had come.

I convened everyone in our living room to discuss an action plan.

By now it was afternoon, and the sunlight was beating down

on the valley outside. Humid haze hung over the fields where people in smaller machines were looking across. With the humidity it seemed even hotter than before.

I looked around the circle of faces in the living room. My own association was used to these meetings, but Sheycu's people looked a bit bewildered.

I started, "We find ourselves in a precarious situation. There are at least two, possibly three groups of people who are trying to gain control over this valley: the Omi farmers; the people at the lake, who may be Ezmi or Talavi; and the Ezmi clan, which ceded control over the valley to the army. The Inner Circle admits to having no control over any of them. We are on our own."

I looked around and saw all the solemn faces. All of these people still listened to me unconditionally.

Solve it, Asha had said. I brought out the doodle we had adapted several times.

I rearranged our association to cut in at the top of the Omi clan, possibly only outclassed by Rashanu herself. The Tamer Collective's newsfeeds had made us heroes in the eyes of most of them.

We didn't know what the Ezmi clan—possibly holed up in the mountain opposite, if those were Ezmi, and under threat from our writ—was going to do.

I suggested we should try to bring all parties to a negotiation, even though I knew writs and posturing was the preferred style.

I explained about the situation and the deep divisions in society as I saw them. I spoke about what I learned in Eighth Circle, where most of them had admitted to me they couldn't come without a big contingent of guards. I spoke to them of what Deyu's father told me and how most people of the Omi clan supported them and us.

I continued, "So I ask you, with all your honesty, what do you believe we should do, what do you believe the outcome will be if we don't do anything, and what could we possibly do to stop any bad outcomes."

For a moment of tense silence everyone stared at the projection on the floor. It showed two systems. Regular society with Asha and Ezhya at the top. And this kind of rogue band of people—a substantial number of them, but none with a high status—under Rashanu. And the Ezmi off to the side.

Then Isharu said, "If we do nothing, the entire society will fracture and there will be a lot of fighting, a lot of deaths. Omi clan is very big and the Ezmi clan is smart and has technology. They could wage a war that I am not so sure that anyone in the Inner Circle will survive."

That was a surprisingly honest admission from someone who had a lot riding on the fact that the Inner Circle would survive.

Sheydu said, "I agree with her. People in the Inner Circle would never see it coming. I didn't until you took me out and made me see." She looked at me, and it was one of those very rare moments where Sheydu displayed gratitude to anyone.

I said, "Asha and Ezhya don't want anything to do with this problem. They are not talking. They are not listening to anything I say. They brush off concerns or plainly ignore them."

"They want to listen," Veyada said. "I don't believe for one moment that they don't want to, but they realise that their help will only make matters worse."

"So what have we got here? Civil war?"

"If that description satisfies your needs for answers, yes."

A chill crept over me. "So they've ceded the situation to me, and us. I am sorry to have put you in this situation."

"Are you kidding? I am happy to be in the situation," Reida said. "Because if anyone can do something, you can."

The others agreed with him, even Sheydu's association who had not been with me for very long.

And then Sheydu rose and stood with the head bent down and palms back.

She knew how much I hated it when people did this to me,

especially people I knew well. But at this moment it seemed utterly appropriate.

I rose, and everyone else in the room did the same, including the cook who had just come in to ask if we wanted some lunch or tea or whatever she was offering. They all stopped and stood with their heads bowed.

They wanted me to solve this immovable situation that had their leaders stumped and unable to solve themselves.

There was nothing left for me to do except use the war cry. "Ichumiya ata."

And as one, they all replied, "Ichumiya ata."

It shook me deep into my heart, deeper than I ever thought something like this would do. These people trusted me with their lives. They wanted me to help solve this situation so that thousands of people would not get killed and their beloved civilisation wouldn't fracture and be thrown into war.

I let that solemn moment linger for a while before I sat down.

"All right. We're a small unit, and we have to solve this without too much fighting, because we would never win. We need to form a plan." Making plans was what my association did. Especially Sheydu was very keen on plans.

I suggested we start by shoring up our relationship with the people in the Omi camp on the other side of the valley, and that we involve the people inside the lake, who might want to sell their water to the farmers. I suggested we needed to find out who these people camping on top of the platform were and whether they had an interest or involvement with the valley.

I suggested that we ask them to call a meeting of all of their people, and give me the opportunity to talk to them.

"They may not be interested in talking," Isharu said.

"They had better be, because they can't fight everyone else."

"It could be that the people we met are not the leaders, and that the people who lead this organisation consider themselves above you," Veyada said.

"There is a small chance of that," Nicha said. "Although I'm not sure who inside the Eighth Circle would be considered of higher ranking."

"Maybe some rogue elements from the higher clans were involved," Veyada said.

That was always a risk.

We drew up lists of things we absolutely had to do—establish a permanent link with the settlers in the valley below, establish the loyalty of all of them. Make a list of their names and their contacts in the city.

We discussed the issues—the Office of Lands and their view of this occupation of the land, the Ezmi clan, the military base.

It was a comforting checklist of all the issues that needed to be addressed. I should contact Rashanu Omi and involve her so she could extend her network.

I should also contact Jeetari and make sure the students from the school got involved as well, even if only to safeguard against a major conflict breaking out between the Omi and Ezmi clans.

I was again moved by how much these people, all of them from different walks of life, supported each other and the common goal of our very unique association.

In the middle of the meeting, Anyu got up.

A light flashed on the security panel. I knew that in the light of the activity in the valley, my team had tightened our perimeter so that they would now be warned if someone arrived at the bottom of the path that led to the house.

Anyu switched off the alarm and went to the veranda.

She came back a moment later. "There is a child coming up the path."

We all filed out of the room.

Child was a very loose description for the girl of maybe thirteen or fourteen who was clambering up the hillside at decent speed. Knowing how steep that hill was, the hurry in her step was clear to see. Had something happened?

It would still be a while before she arrived, so Anyu and

Isharu went back into the security room and Anyu came to get me not much later.

"It looks like our settlers have visitors," she said.

I stared at the grainy, much-enlarged image on Isharu's screen. I could barely make out the makeshift shelters, but it seemed a few vehicles had arrived where our craft had landed earlier today.

"Who are they?"

Neither of the two women knew.

Meanwhile, the girl arrived at the house panting and out of breath. The others were talking to her on the veranda.

Veyada's voice was clearly audible. "He's inside."

They all came in the direction of the main door. Sheydu would never allow a stranger to enter the security room, so I went back to the veranda.

"Child" definitely didn't apply to this girl. She had to have been inducted in the clan because she wore the lime green Omi earrings. Her clothing was simple and dusty from fieldwork.

She dropped into a subservient greeting as soon as she saw me. "You must help us. A group of people came into our village. They have guns and they're holding my parents and other people. They want us to leave or they say they will flood the valley."

I glanced sideways at Sheydu.

We knew the people who could do this.

19

———————

THE GIRL'S NAME was Tiyu and we talked to her on the veranda. I told the cook to give her some food, which she refused initially, but then changed her mind.

While she ate, she told us that her father, her sister, her mother, mother's sister and two cousins were all in the camp. She had never left Eighth Circle until she and her relatives got on a truck in the middle of the night and drove through the desert.

That made me suspect that they came from the part of the city closest to the valley, the part where the aquifers cut through the stone, where the mushroom farmers worked. This was not close to where Deyu came from.

She could only tell me the name of the district, which meant nothing to me, and I didn't want to disturb Deyu, who had gone inside and was doing something in the hallway under the direction of Sheydu.

I asked Tiyu to describe the attackers and where she thought they had come from. Definitely in trucks from the city, I was told.

Were they people from the Omi clan or another clan?

Oh no, she said, they were Talavi. Hadn't we heard about it?

"Heard what?" I asked her.

"It's a long time ago now, but the Talavi took over the *zeyshi* warren at the underground lake. The Ezmi are still sore about it, and they're bickering over what to do. Some say they should take it back, and the self-righteous ones say that they signed the agreement not to be involved in the valley, so they shouldn't."

She was unaware that we had one of those "self-righteous" Ezmi people with us.

When I asked Reida if his investigations with his clan had told him anything about this, he said that everyone had only strenuously denied having any involvement with the valley.

"Do you think any of them knew and were lying to you?"

Ezmi, especially *zeyshi*, were notoriously hard to pin down. They were proud people, and the loss of such a major site would have been a sore point that might have elicited a "don't mention the war" reaction.

When I put this to Reida, his reaction was uneasy. "I hate that they would lie to me. They're not making it any easier for themselves."

He conceded that a Talavi victory over the underground lake would have been a major coup against his clan, especially if it had been a few decades ago.

"Not so much now, though," he said, eying the neatly ploughed fields in the valley.

But slowly, bit by bit, we were able to put the situation together.

The army base had been established in a strategic position to ensure the safety of a major source of water for the mega-city. The army had made bargains with the *zeyshi* tribes to make sure that the valley remained empty of camps. The lake probably predated the agreements and had been a major source of *zeyshi* wealth, and had lain undeclared and undiscovered for many years. At some point, it had come into Talavi possession.

I put to Reida whether he thought his clan might have sold

the lake to the Talavi when they realised that its value would be reduced to zero because of increasing rainfall.

Reida said he didn't know, but the expression on his face told me that this theory was well worth investigating, as it could explain why the Ezmi clan had never said anything about the lake recently.

At any rate, the Talavi clan, now having realised their asset was worthless, were getting desperate.

Now that Omi farmers were in the valley, the Talavi were at risk of discovery. Worse, when Omi mushroom farmers started speaking to authorities, their previous extortion of fees for land use would come out. So they came into the valley to shut the Omi farmers up, preferably before authorities arrived.

Tiyu had come to us for help, and we should do something, if we had the resources.

I went inside to check with Sheydu. By the look of things, she had already decided that some operation was imminent.

All the boxes in the security room and those against the back wall of their bedroom were opened and all the weapons and explosives had been unpacked. The armour, the stands, the rocket launchers, the ammunition, the charging panels, the masks. Everything was lined up in the hallway.

I found Sheydu in the corner of the bedroom, explaining to Leisha how a particular weapon should be set up.

She turned around when I came in.

"We're going?" I asked.

"If you give the orders," she said. Which she clearly thought I should. "We're pressed for time. The attackers have called for some friends to help them. There are also some convoys of overland groups on their way; some may be *zeyshi*. Rashanu has recruited help for their clanspeople. This is going to get very ugly very quickly unless we step in and establish a truce."

"Negotiations," I said.

"That's your thing. A truce will do for me."

"What do we need?"

Sheydu walked me through extensive preparations she and her team had already made.

I realised: they had been prepared for this type of conflict from the moment we came here.

Anyu and Isharu had obtained what security called a group profile, detailing all the members in a team or group, in this case the Omi settlers in the valley, their communication handles and lines they communicated with.

I'd seen Sheydu make these in Barresh sometimes, but never in this much detail. Isharu had seriously high clearance with the Exchange and could get things that even Thayu couldn't get her hands on.

The profile showed that the Omi settlers had communicated mostly amongst themselves, although one conversation had been logged to that same address that we had investigated earlier, which we now knew to be Rashanu's home.

Thayu was standing back in the hallway, leaning against the wall with her arms crossed and resting on her stomach. She didn't ask any questions, but watched Sheydu's actions with an intense look.

"We'll be in the valley," I said softly to her.

"There is a conflict going on down there. Shouldn't you go with more people?"

"We're going now so that we won't need more people. The Omi in Eighth Circle have been notified, but it will take them some time to get here."

"Please," she said, and then she hesitated while Naru walked past with a crate of electronic detonators and other equipment. "Please, be careful."

Her tone was different. She sounded fragile. I knew she hadn't slept well in the past few days, complaining that she found it hard to get comfortable.

"Are you all right?" She *had* said that our daughter wouldn't be born before the ceremony. I had imagined we'd be lazing about and relaxing until then, and maybe prepare for some meetings before or after the ceremony.

"I'm fine." But the confident tone from earlier days had gone.

"I would be very happy if you went to—"

"That's not necessary."

An uneasy silence followed. Why was she so stubborn? As if going to her father's house would be conceding defeat.

"We'll be back soon." I touched her forehead with mine. Her skin was dry and warm, where I was sweaty from wearing that armour.

Sheydu declared that we were all loaded up, so we all got into the aircraft.

I offered Tiyu the chance to stay safe inside the house, but she wanted to be with her family.

Thayu was going to stay with Isharu and the two of them would man the communication hub.

Sheydu rattled off a checklist: weapons—she had passed me another, heavier, gun—canisters with charged pearls, emergency beacon.

The door shut.

"She doesn't look happy," Nicha said about his sister.

I let out a sigh. "I wish she'd go to her father's house and we'd meet there for the ceremony tomorrow."

"That's not like her. She'll want to be involved until the very end."

He was right about that. It was just Thayu being Thayu, and being cranky that keeping up was not easy for her right now.

The craft lifted off and glided down the hill.

A few machines still sat in the field, but none were moving. Tracks across the freshly ploughed field indicated where the operators had rushed back to the settlement.

Our plan was to first survey the area. We flew over the platform behind the house and then on to the other side of the valley, finding the small camp still in place at the top of the cliffs opposite the house. There were only three tents and two vehicles. When we flew over, a single person came to have a look.

The security room had kept an eye on these people overnight, but judged they were unrelated to the Talavi people at the underground lake or the Omi in the valley.

Leisha then flew over the Omi settlement at the base of the cliff and we got a closer look at the siege situation which was in a camp further down the valley. A couple of tents were surrounded by agricultural vehicles and a couple of trucks with open cabins.

The people Tiyu identified as having attacked the settlers had brought a number of rough terrain vehicles with large wheels. Several of them were standing in a line around a portion of the camp. They looked up when we flew over. One or two pointed weapons, but they knew we were out of range.

"Those are the bad people," Tiyu said. She sat on the seat next to me, her eyes wide. I doubted she had ever flown in an aircraft.

We flew over again.

Sheydu counted nineteen people in the camp who hadn't been there on our previous visit. Their vehicles didn't use detectable electronic communication that my team could spy on. Any personal devices were likewise silent.

"They'll be using *zeyshi* sign language," Reida said. This was widely used in the Outer Circle.

We had planned for this. Thayu knew it well and she would "see" through my visor and would tell me anything that was communicated between the members of the group.

When we flew over a third time, Leisha transmitted a message to the occupiers that we were coming to talk.

We received no reply, but we observed no signs that the occupiers planned to defend their position against us.

Leisha landed the craft out of range of their weapons in a freshly ploughed field behind the area where the vehicles stood, in such a way that anyone coming from within the settlement couldn't use the trucks for shelter without first crossing an exposed area. He kept the engines running in case of trouble.

We got out, sinking into the loose soil. The faintest haze of green from the growth of thousands of little plants already hung over the ground.

We had a lot of equipment. Veyada and Deyu stood at the cargo door to the craft handing everyone their packs as we walked past. I shouldered mine. It contained shell-proof blankets to throw over groups of people. Oof, that thing was heavy. At least my team no longer made any special considerations for my physical weakness.

There were a lot of us, since Thayu and Isharu were the only ones left at the house, together with the two children minded by the cook.

In facing the occupiers, we had decided that we wouldn't stick to convention where the highest-ranking people—in this case me—would walk at the front. I was near the front of the group, but Deyu, Reida and Mereeni walked in front of us, because they belonged to the clans involved in this conflict. Sheydu and Anyu walked on either side, protecting the other three. Tiyu walked bravely next to Deyu, but I was ready to snatch her to safety at the first sign of trouble.

Veyada, wearing a white shirt to indicate his status as lawyer, walked next to me. All the others followed close behind.

Sheydu informed us through the feeders that people were moving in the camp, using the tents and trucks to hide themselves from our view. We were doing the same, but we had backup about their movement from Thayu and Isharu at the house.

A couple of crates stood next to a truck, as if the driver had been interrupted while unloading it.

We were three-quarters of the way to the first tents when we could no longer play our mutual game of remaining out of sight. All that remained between us and the tents was a patch of exposed dirt.

Three people came out from between two shelters, and a moment later another three. They were armed, wearing cloths around their heads to disguise their faces.

For a moment, we just looked at each other. Sunlight beat down from directly overhead. A hot, humid breeze ruffled clothing.

I was hot inside the helmet. The visor didn't display any information about the line of figures waiting for us, and the temptation to take it off was great, but Thayu was watching them with me. We kept walking slowly.

The other people didn't move.

"We come to talk," I said. "I am Aveya Domiri. I have an interest in keeping the peace in this valley. Come here to meet our diverse group with people from many clans."

One of the people gave a sign.

"They say to wait, but be careful," Thayu said in my helmet.

Slowly, they stepped forward, one step, and then another.

We waited.

The breeze blew dust around my feet. A drop of sweat ran down my back. Another tickled in my neck, but wiping it would mean letting go of my gun.

Slowly, very slowly, they came closer. Close enough to see the whites of their eyes. Close enough to hear their breathing.

There were six of them, while a few other people poked their faces out of the tents in the Omi camp.

Tiyu tensed. "Mam and sis."

It was the first time I'd heard a Coldi person describe their family like this. Nicha and Thayu called their father by his name, as if he were merely an acquaintance.

"We are here to talk," I repeated.

One of the people had stopped in front of Mereeni. She was a thin, wiry woman with a cloth around her head that showed only her eyes. The skin around the eyes was pale and wrinkled.

Mereeni was not as formidable as Deyu, but, having been in the Hedron Guards, as with most women at Hedron, she bore the initiation scars on her upper arms, and while she normally wore garments with sleeves, she was only wearing a singlet today. One that clearly advertised her status as a new mother, because Coldi women's breasts vanished unless they were pregnant or had a young child.

Mereeni looked magnificent. Her curly hair hung loose over her shoulders.

"So. What are you doing here?" the woman asked. "Foreigner."

"I am a member of this association." Mereeni's Hedron accent stood out clearly.

"Meddling in our business? Spying on us? Laughing at us?"

"I'm not seeing anyone laugh," Sheydu said.

I asked, "I would like to know what *you* are doing here. Trying to finish what you couldn't when you had us caught inside the mountain?"

She frowned at me, but I saw a disturbed, calculating expression in her eyes. I shifted my right elbow slightly, the sign that we would use to warn each other of potential danger.

But nothing happened.

There had been nineteen attackers. I hoped Sheydu knew where the other thirteen were.

"We're here to negotiate, because once the Omi reinforcements are here, you'll be gone."

"Once our reinforcements are here, *they* will be gone."

Another tense silence.

Then I asked, "Why? Why this attack on people who have done nothing against you?"

"They disguise themselves as farmers, but they are thieves. They've taken our land."

"It's no one's land," said a clear voice.

Some of the Omi settlers had also come closer.

I recognised Olinu and Remiya from our previous visit. In addition, another four of the occupiers had come forward.

Olinu continued, "We checked very carefully which land is

under valid land use contracts. We took care not to run foul of existing claims."

"You have no right to take this land by force."

"We're not taking the land by force. We only want to use it."

"You have no right to do that."

Olinu said, "So you lock up the water and threaten anyone who discovers it with violence?"

"This is our valley."

At the same time as Reida said, "No, it is not," Veyada said. "By law, it's no one's land. The Office of Lands and, by proxy, the Vonayi clan gives permits to use it. If anyone had applied, which they have not, they would have been told that this area is important for the safety of the city, and land use permits can't be given out easily."

"The Vonayi clan are stuck up elites who don't even know what the Second Circle looks like."

"Why then do we have two of them with us?" I said. "We have a lawyer and two Vonayi representatives. We can solve your disputes right now."

The woman gaped at us. They were outclassed and outbluffed.

She made a small sign, which Thayu told me meant to surrender.

"Just like that? I don't believe it."

"No, don't believe it," Thayu said. "They'll likely pull some trick."

Sheydu and her team went around and divested the group of their weapons. The captives stood quietly while the pile of illegal weapons grew.

I told them to take the cloths off their heads. The people underneath were unfamiliar to me and my team, although I wondered if one of them had been in the group of Talavi who had come to meet us at the crater rim.

While we were rounding up the group, Isharu contacted their clan leader, a brash young man called Yita, and informed him that we would be transferring the writ from the Ezmi clan to the Talavi clan.

We were helped by the Omi farmers, whom I instructed not to harm the prisoners. We wanted to negotiate a land use agreement, not fight.

At this point the group camped out on the top of the platform contacted Isharu, stating themselves to be Ezmi, demanding to be part of any talks regarding land use.

Recognising that I might not get another opportunity to have people from all three clans talking to each other, I told Isharu to send them down into the valley.

It was quite amazing that all of this had gone without conflict. I had expected so much worse.

The Omi farmers wanted assurances from me that I wasn't going to hand them over to groups who would force them to return to the city.

The Ezmi arrived at the site not much later. There were only three of them, but they wore *shaykas* and made a proud picture against the dusty and bedraggled other groups.

The leader was a muscled woman with not a gram of fat on her. When she moved, you could see muscles rippling under her skin.

Both her upper arms were encircled by black tattoos, forming a circle of geometric shapes. Reida had these as well.

Olinu said, loud enough for everyone to hear, "We're not going to agree to a different kind of bloodsucker latching onto us."

I said, "I'll make sure you get a fair deal."

"I don't believe it. Once other clans are involved, they tend to ignore us."

Reida had come forward. "Look at him." He gestured at Nicha. "He's Palayi, and so is he, and she." He gestured at Veyada and Sheydu. Then he gestured at Anyu. "She's Vonayi. Our leader is Domiri. My *zhayma* is Omi, we have a child in the household who is Azimi, and we have another Ezmi from Hedron. If we can get along, then you should be ashamed of yourself that you're still not talking. Because you all want the same things: to be safe, to have enough food, to have freedom and to flourish. And there is no reason why you shouldn't be able to do that in this vast area."

I went to stand next to him, and so did Deyu, and one by one, all the others in my and Sheydu's associations.

And then something extraordinary happened: the wiry woman who was the Ezmi leader bowed her head and let her hands fall away from her weapons so that the palms faced backwards.

I thought *zeyshi* didn't do subservience.

But obviously some did, like Reida.

What if the reason a subservient reaction was triggered had to do with the strength of the leader's *sheya* instinct, and had much less to do with the subordinate party's instinct?

Reida was a strong leader. His mother was a strong leader. She needed to be involved in these negotiations. She needed to be assured that she wouldn't be punished for having four children.

Olinu reluctantly agreed to be part of a negotiation.

Then we were left to figure out what to do with the nineteen captives. I didn't want to take them up to the house, but I figured it was likely we'd need to transfer them to the army base. What did one do with people who had to face justice?

Then a whooshing sound echoed through the valley. I peered in the distance against the glare.

It sounded like—no, it *was* an aircraft. I spotted it. Two. Three. Rapidly coming closer. None of them were Asha's very distinctive army-owned craft.

"Who are they?" I asked.

Sheydu's face was dark. "Trouble."

What was more, a convoy of vehicles approached through the valley.

20

T HERE WAS A SHOUT.

While we weren't looking, a couple of the Talavi prisoners had made a run for one of the vehicles. The Omi farmers chased after them, but they had already reached the truck.

The truck was moving before the door was even shut. They took off in the direction away from the oncoming convoy.

Meanwhile the dust clouds thrown up by the approaching convoy had come closer, and the three aircraft roared over the valley at low altitude.

"Come with me!" Olinu shouted.

Most of us piled into a vehicle. I got into the cabin with Olinu, and most of my team got in the tray at the back with the weapons.

Leisha and Anyu were taking the aircraft. I tossed up telling them not to move. Another aircraft might draw unwanted attention from these aggressive-looking craft. But one didn't tell a pilot to leave his aircraft, so I hoped we'd be fine.

"We'll wait at a sheltered spot," Leisha said via the feeder.

That made me feel a bit better.

"Who are all these people?" I asked Olinu behind the controls.

She didn't reply, but she followed the craft with the escapees while keeping her eye on the aircraft which tore down the valley at low altitude. They were not the type that the military used. Asha had made it pretty clear that the military didn't interfere in local matters. It was not the military's style to intimidate their own citizens.

For now, they were only flying over the valley. Surveying, scanning.

The vehicle in front of us threw up so much dust that I lost sight of the craft.

"Crap, we lost them," Olinu said.

I really wished she would keep her eyes on where we were going. The truck hit a patch of deep sand and spun its caterpillar wheels in the effort to get out.

"No, there they are," Deyu said.

She pointed.

We had come out of the dust and I could see them, too, little specks just above the horizon, fast coming in our direction from down the creek.

I glanced at Nicha next to me. His face reflected what I felt: why were we out here in the open chasing this truck which not only drove recklessly, but which was probably in contact with the aircraft? We should find shelter.

"What's going on?" Thayu's voice sounded in my head. It pained me to hear her so stressed.

"Who are these aircraft?"

"Privately owned. We don't know who's in them."

What was the bet they were the Talavi backup? And the convoy I could see rumbling through the valley behind us? They were probably Omi backup.

We kept going at full speed, following the dust cloud of the vehicle in front, but their truck was a faster vehicle and they were gaining on us.

Where were we going?

The craft flew over. Three of them, dark shapes in the sky.

Then a sound echoed through the valley. It was like a sharp crack of lightning followed by thunder, but different, much closer and much more ominous.

"I didn't like the sound of that," I said.

My team in the back didn't like it much either. Sheydu and Veyada had set up the rocket launcher on the roof of the cabin. Sheydu was following the craft through the weapon's visor, her hand on the control panel.

"Look, there!" Olinu said.

She pointed ahead and to the left.

At first I didn't notice anything. We'd just hit a sandy patch and the vehicles ahead of us were creating too much dust. Then we hit a stretch of rocky ground and left the dust clouds behind.

Another dust cloud had formed, further up the valley. Its roiling front spread outwards over the ploughed fields.

There had been a rock fall.

No, an entire part of the cliff face had come down. That wasn't at the spot. . . . I grew cold.

"No," Olinu said. "No, that can't be. No."

I knew: she was afraid for the makeshift village. It was at the bottom of that cliff.

We lunged into the dust cloud. It became hard to see where the road was.

In the back of the vehicle, Sheydu had covered the rocket launcher with its carry bag to keep the dust out.

We slowed and slowed. Olinu tried to contact the others but there was no reply. Somewhere above us, beyond the dust that blocked our view, the aircraft roared over the valley again.

Olinu stopped the vehicle.

The trucks in front of us had also stopped, and people were running across the sand.

Nicha opened the door to the cabin. A waft of gritty, dust-laden air came in.

I could still hear the aircraft overhead. I wanted to yell at him not to go out. I wanted to know that Thayu was safe, all alone with Isharu in the house that sat oh-so-visibly on the rocky knoll jutting into the valley.

All around us, people came out of vehicles and were running towards a heap of rubble. Olinu got out as well. Most of my team went with her, running to the pile of rubble ahead.

I couldn't see any of the temporary buildings. If they were all covered by rocks. . . .

"Prepare the craft for an emergency take-off," I said to Leisha.

"Definitely."

I followed Nicha.

Sheydu and Veyada had uncovered the gun again. They were not leaving the vehicle.

A number of large boulders had fallen onto the road ahead. Someone screamed, the voice high and shrill. A child?

I thought of Tiyu.

Then we reached the first of the fallen rubble. Rocks had crushed a vehicle. With a feeling of sickness, I recognised one of the settler's trucks.

To the right lay mangled sheeting that had once formed the wall or roof of a temporary shelter.

A man, his clothes caked in dust, was trying to pull it free.

"Help! I can't see my son. Help me."

Deyu started picking up chucks of rock and tossing them aside.

A dust-caked figure came out of the rubble, hopping on one leg, the other bloodied and bent at an odd angle.

"Come here, sit here!" Mereeni guided him away from the rubble.

The man grabbed her hand with both of his. "My brother. Please find my brother. He has a family."

He wouldn't let go of Mereeni's hands, so she lifted him off the ground and carried him to an undamaged vehicle, where someone had spread out a cloth and a few people were already treating injured farmers. I spotted Anyu and Sevayu there as well. Everyone was working together, regardless of ranking or clan designation.

The more I looked, the more debris I noticed.

The rock fall had collapsed right on top of the temporary village.

Why?

Who would do something like this?

I should do something, but I didn't know what. I had little medical knowledge. I wasn't hugely strong like Deyu, who was frantically heaving rocks aside.

I had. . . .

Veyada stood behind me. His face was grim. Sheydu was still in the back of the truck with her rocket launcher. Like me, she wasn't much good with medical stuff, but she was an excellent fighter.

We could make sure that these monsters didn't come back. That was what we could do.

I jerked my head at Veyada.

"Come. Nothing we can do here. Let's fix this."

He pressed his lips together, his face grim.

We met Sheydu at the truck. On the tray of the vehicle stood the rocket launcher. She had cleaned the dust off it and, when she saw me, she slid the barrel into the frame of the weapon's housing with a serious expression that had a finality to it. She jumped in the back. The rocket launcher's stand was still affixed to the edge of the tray.

"You drive," she said to me.

Not a word about what we were going to do. She understood.

She took a reader from her pocket, the screen displaying a scan of the area. She handed it to me. "Take that. Use it for navigation. It's connected to a secret channel. Don't use anything else. We're silent from now on."

I got into the cabin. Sheydu and Veyada went in the back, with the rocket launcher and a box of explosives.

There was so much dust that I couldn't see where the road was, so we set off slowly through the freshly ploughed field.

A couple of Omi farmers followed us on foot.

A group of refugees, dusty and bewildered, were sitting in the field. As we came past, a few people got up and followed our truck, and then more people got up.

They got into their farm equipment vehicles. These were the people who had been working in the field when the cliff face collapsed. Most were adults, but some were children.

I wondered what they were doing, but couldn't ask Sheydu because we "didn't exist" which meant we kept communication silence.

They knew who we were. They followed me unconditionally. We became a convoy, with us at the head.

The dust thinned out. Not much later, we came across a road. I checked the reader Sheydu had given me.

It displayed a scan of the surrounding terrain, with an out-of-focus area at the position of the dust cloud. An entire section of the cliff had given way. The map had not yet recalibrated.

But when I looked to the side, I spotted some people going down the cliff face with ropes: the people from the Ezmi camp at the top of the cliff. They were helping out.

That made me feel much better about the future. People wanted to work together. It was the only way forward.

The three aircraft had turned in a loop and were heading back over the valley, starting downstream from where we were.

I couldn't hear them yet, but Sheydu hit the back of the cabin with her flat hand. I recognised the gesture. In Barresh, Pengali boat people would communicate this way by hitting the side of the boat. Flat hand meant stop. Fist bumps meant speed up.

I stopped the vehicle.

The much slower farm machines and their crew of angry

farmers were still a distance behind us, barely visible through the dust clouds.

I checked the reader. The craft were about to fly over.

There they were, three dark shadows low over the valley floor.

Sheydu thumped the roof.

I accelerated the truck.

More thumping on the roof.

Faster, faster. We were trailing the craft. But on the land, on uneven ground, we were much slower than they were.

We jumped along the uneven track. The distance between the craft and us increased.

Then: the distinctive *fwoomp* of the rocket launcher.

A fireball in the sky ahead. The truck shook.

Sheydu shouted.

A moment later another *fwoomp*.

Another fireball.

The first craft crashed to the ground in a ball of flames.

But the second glided down to our left. The engine was on fire, but the pilot got out, running away from the stricken vehicle—into the fleet of oncoming agricultural vehicles. He realised too late what was going on, and started running the other way.

Someone jumped from one of the farm machines and ran after him. Other people followed the example. Soon the pilot was surrounded by angry farmers.

I approached as closely as I could and jumped from the vehicle.

"Stop, stop!"

The crowd parted, men and women with shovels, brooms, hammers and other tools that could be used as weapons.

It was clear that the pilot was not going to answer any of my questions.

I'd been wrong. It was a woman, her face bashed in beyond recognition.

"Look, we got them!"

A man thrust a bloodied hand into my field of vision. Held between his thumb and forefinger was a blood-caked earring.

An ochre-coloured stone. Talavi.

I struggled with my feelings. My Earth-educated senses were revolted. Everyone deserved a fair hearing and justice should never be meted out as revenge. But the system allowed these types of crimes to be committed, over and over again.

The Coldi justice system absolutely condoned this brutality. The pilot would have known that if she got caught, that would be the end of her.

I was here as a Coldi leader. This was about justice for a group, not about individuals. It was about loyalty networks and looking out for those below you.

I was a Coldi leader. The Omi farmers and the *zeyshi* who had made peace with them demanded that we catch the remaining craft.

I put my hand on the man's shoulder, squeezed it gently, then let go and returned to the truck, all the while fighting the urge to wipe my hands. I was no fighter. I didn't have the stomach for this.

The last craft had disappeared way ahead, although I could still see it on the scan.

We needed a place to hide so that we could ambush it, but we had no time.

It was already turning around.

I scoured the countryside for a hill or pile of rocks to hide behind, for all the good that would do against an aircraft. There were not many options, only a shallow depression with a couple of boulders. It would have to do.

I drove the truck into the loose sand. Sheydu and Veyada in the back unfolded a camouflage sheet over the top of them, the tray and the cabin.

We waited.

But the craft wasn't coming back in our direction. It had

turned in a big loop surrounding the army base and the fork of the valley.

No, they knew that some of our people were still in the house. They cared little about families and children.

No! Thayu.

I watched, horrified as the little black speck approached from the other part of the Twin Valley.

But the craft didn't make for the house either. Instead, it turned in a tighter circle and then, still quite a way upriver, where I couldn't see it, discharged a rocket. It flew like a little black speck across the valley and slammed into the wall of the canyon.

Why would the pilot do that—wait.

The reservoir.

21

———

"**H**OLD ON!**"** I yelled at Sheydu and Veyada.

I debated whether to cross the valley to rescue people or head for high ground, but the water already streamed into the valley. If we tried to cross that, we'd be washed away.

Sheydu had abandoned her silent mode and broadcast an immediate alarm to the team.

They had the craft and it had already proven its ability to act like a boat.

Meanwhile, the opening in the mountainside was still increasing.

Chunks of rock burst outward and then bigger chunks of rock. And then a spray of water that turned into a torrent of white froth that streamed into the valley.

It was going to be close whether we would make it to the bottom of the incline. I had no idea how far up this vehicle would go, and to what level the water would rise. That lake was huge. There might even be water backed up in the Crystal Wastelands.

The truck was going as fast as I dared take it on the uneven terrain. I was *not* a racecar driver. In fact, I rarely drove any vehicle.

My hands were sweaty on the wheel. We had left the farm fields behind and were now on natural terrain. I was constantly on the lookout for trouble, ditches where we might get stuck or where I needed to slow down, boulders I should avoid.

I could hear Leisha's voice through the feeder. "Return to the craft now. This is an emergency. Return to the craft."

Deyu replied, and I could hear Nicha's voice.

Mereeni said, "We're coming."

Then Leisha again, "This is an extreme emergency. I'm starting the downward jets."

The mass of frothing water spread out over the valley floor pushing boulders and debris as if they were little sticks. Yet the torrent of water bursting from the mountain only increased. Chunks of the cliff face fell away under the pressure of the lake.

Then Deyu said, "Everyone's in. How long do we have?"

Leisha replied, "I'm going to hover over the surface using the downward jets. It will be rough. Tie yourself up and pull in as many people as you can reach."

Deyu again, "Give me the ladder."

Even in danger, she always thought of other people.

From where we were, we could see that people downstream were running to the sides of the valley, but it would be too late for many of them. We could hope that their vehicles would float.

We needed to help them. But first we had to get to safety ourselves.

The water was coming up fast around us. I couldn't see where we were going anymore. I had to trust my memory that the land at the bottom of the slope that led to the house was free of obstacles.

We splashed through the water. Every time we hit a ditch, I expected to get stuck.

But we made it to the bottom of the slope. I charged the vehicle a short distance up and stopped and got out. It was quite steep here and I had to make sure I didn't slip on the loose and dry gravel.

"What are you doing?" Sheydu asked. "Keep going."

The fear in her eyes shook me. I had never seen her like this. Sheydu hated water.

"We have to help people."

"What with? We can't save them. They have to save themselves."

"The truck won't go much further up anyway. Can you still see that lone aircraft we didn't shoot down?"

She understood me then. Business first. Do not let fear overtake your judgement.

We peered over the surroundings.

The valley was filled with noise from the rushing water, and the sound of sections of the cliff opposite—those ruins thousands of years old—collapsing into the stream.

The sky was empty.

The valley was still filling with churning, frothing water. I neither saw nor heard any signs of people. The fields had been flooded, the village was gone, the agricultural machines all washed downstream. I didn't even see our own craft, although I was sure they got out. Maybe they'd gone to warn the army base? Surely Asha would send people to help after this disaster?

Then another horrible realisation hit me.

"The city. We must warn people in the city."

"We've been trying already," Veyada said.

The word trying chilled me. Trying, but not succeeding. All those people in their beautiful homes in the shady oases of the aquifers. All the mushroom farmers. How many people would die today because of this despicable act?

"We need to get to the house," Veyada said.

Yes, likely, the craft had already returned.

But Sheydu wouldn't go without her rocket launcher, so she took it from the back of the vehicle. The barrel was still hot so she couldn't put it back in the case because it would melt the packaging.

She fashioned a sling from the case's carry straps so she could carry it on her back. She left the stand attached, too, in case we needed the weapon.

While Veyada and Sheydu solved this problem, I continued to search the churning sea of water for survivors. I saw nothing.

"Come," Veyada said.

We started up the hill in a mad scramble so different from our earlier leisurely walk down here.

I wanted to get out of this exposed, dangerous location.

When we reached the house, the aircraft was already there, as Veyada had said. We went into the security room, where Anyu sat at the hub. She shook her head.

"There is no way I can reach the city. Our reception isn't strong enough to cut through all the panic."

"But people are going to die." I was thinking of all those people who lived in the aquifers and the houses that clung to the cliff faces.

Her eyes had a haunted look. We knew that this would happen, but we could do nothing about it.

"Do you think this justifies contacting Asha?" I said.

I had been told repeatedly that the army did not get involved in civilian conflicts on Asto. Not unless there was an immediate emergency.

"Surely, I think so." As head of the association, calling for this kind of help on this level fell to me.

Asha had already heard of the water, had tried to contact the city and had been met with a similar problem of jammed signals. All he needed was confirmation that help was needed.

I gave it, and the armed forces were underway.

Word from his security team was that the craft that destroyed the cliff had landed on a hilltop not too far from where we had attempted to set up listening equipment.

"The pilot that was captured was Talavi," I told him.

"They're much better armed than expected for a private operation," Asha said.

There were all kinds of ways that could have come about. The Aghyrians, Jasper Carlson and the Tamer group, or even the Ezmi tinkerers.

I wondered why they had chosen to attack the reservoir.

"It's a classic last resort response by desperate people," Asha said. "The Talavi extortionists have annoyed people for too long. Their jealous ways have made them few friends. In despair, they choose to destroy everything."

There was now enough provocation on his doorstep for the army to take action. They must have been ready, because they arrived soon after I signed off.

"Here is the military," Reida said. He was standing by the door.

The drone of engines was clearly audible.

"How many?" Anyu asked.

"Wait." Leisha ran to the veranda. He came back a moment later. "They're not military craft."

I followed him back to the veranda. A formation of five aircraft flew over the valley, followed at a distance by another group.

"Those are military aircraft," Nicha said. He pointed at the platform opposite us where three aircraft were just taking off.

Crap.

"It's time to get out of here," Sheydu said.

Anyu agreed. "Everyone meet at the aircraft."

We'd be returning to Asha's house, I assumed.

I went to our room, and was surprised to find it empty.

"Thay'?" I would have expected her to be in the security room, but she hadn't been there, and I assumed she was resting.

My heart jumped. I walked to the door and pushed aside the curtains that billowed in the breeze.

There was no one.

"Thayu? Where are you?"

What the hell?

The valley outside was filled with water. The roar of the engines of the Talavi craft echoed between the cliff faces. We were like a sitting duck in this house. They could shoot us out of existence in this very exposed locality.

A small sound cut through the noise from outside, like a sob.

Shit. The bathroom.

I ran back inside, pushed open the door that stood ajar.

Thayu kneeled on the floor, her head bent. She had taken off her loose dress. It lay on the tiles, sodden in clear fluid stained pink.

We weren't going to go anywhere.

As I came in, she looked up. "I'm so sorry. I can't stop it anymore."

"I thought you could delay it until after the ceremony."

"Only if nothing bad or stressful happens." She had to stop talking to breathe through a pain.

"Are you all right?"

"Yes. Just I can't go anywhere like this."

Obviously not. "Wait."

She called after me, but I ran into the hallway, where the members of my team were carrying boxes full of Sheydu's equipment out the door.

"Nicha, Veyada, you have to help me get Thayu in the craft. The child is coming. She says she can't stop it."

Sheydu came to the door of the security room. "Go back in there. Help her."

"But we're in the middle of a war zone."

"We will look after that."

"But she'll be much safer—"

"Go back to her. We're not even halfway packed. Asha's people are underway to protect us. Go to her. She needs you now."

A big chasm of insecurity grew in me. I'd read all the accounts of what I was supposed to do. Somehow, I had hoped that someone would come to assist me. What if I did something stupid? What if, contrary to what everyone said, something went wrong and she needed medical assistance?

I wanted to ask for help, but Sheydu stared me out the door.

Back in the room, it was Thayu who told me what to do. Fill the basin with lukewarm water, take off my clothes, leave my electronics in the bedroom.

Hold her. Talk to her.

We sat in the water, while she leaned into me. She was relaxed. Everything I told her about the reservoir breach and our scramble to safety went past her. That I was angry and upset that the Talavi pilot had been so brutally lynched, that I was worried about the Omi farmers, that we'd managed to unite the Omi farmers and the *zeyshi* who lived inside the mountain. That a wall of water was underway to the city and so many people would get killed—

"Shhh," she told me. "These things can be important again later."

But they were important now.

I heard the sound of an aircraft engine close by.

People were coming into the house. Their footsteps clomped on the veranda. Voices sounded in the hall.

It was surreal.

Outside the tiny window in the bathroom, a war was raging. I could see the craft flying back and forth; I could see the top of the ridge on the other side of the valley, where other people were firing down into the valley. Those were the people who had set the explosives that caused the cliff to collapse onto the settlement.

Thayu climbed out of the bath and into the hammock. She couldn't walk properly and needed me to lift her.

The tight skin of Thayu's stomach was slick with sweat, and I could feel the muscles harden and relax underneath.

She was quiet.

As a young boy, I'd always been scared of movies where

women gave birth, because there was such a lot screaming and *violence* involved. Even watching recordings of the real thing. It looked like it violated women's bodies and made them a medical case.

This was nothing like that.

She asked me to take a bottle of disinfecting gel out of her bag, and she asked me to wash her. Already, the skin was stretched. I spread the gel over her buttocks, the muscles underneath worked. I could feel the child's head underneath.

While the battle raged outside the cave, the opening stretched and parted, and our daughter emerged into my hands. It was an intensely calm experience, silent until the little one drew breath and cried.

I could barely believe it. She was perfect, with ten little fingers and ten toes, a fuzz of dark hair plastered to her head. Her eyes were dark, with a surprised expression in them. She worked her lips, as if to rub off the fluids and slime that was fast flaking on her skin.

"Look at her. Just look at her." Thayu laughed and cried at the same time. Tears streamed down her face.

"It's all right, she's healthy."

"I'm so happy. Now I get to do this." Thayu took her out of my hands, cradled her in her arms, with the umbilical cord still attached. In a symbolic gesture, she dipped her hand into a bowl of sand that stood in the corner. I'd wondered what it was for. She sprinkled sand over the little one's head.

"You are born in your home world, surrounded by the people who will watch you grow up."

Then she brushed off the sand with her hands. The little one lifted her tiny hands and grabbed onto Thayu's fingers. Coldi babies did that. They could hold and hang onto things. They also followed you with their eyes.

We wiped her clean, cut the cord and bandaged the stump. We wrapped her in a clean towel.

Strangely, I'd stopped paying much attention to what was

happening in the valley outside our cave.

"You notice that smell?" Thayu said.

I had noticed it: a faint earthy sweet smell.

"That's the smell of our family. It's the smell that she will remember all her life. Once we bury the afterbirth, you will not smell it again."

I'd known that smells had a profound effect on Coldi people and that smells of the opposite sex and reproduction events were strongly linked to instinct.

"I'm going to get changed. Here, hold her."

She gave me the warm bundle.

Already when I looked into her eyes I was filled with wonder and love. She frowned and pursed her lips, and opened her mouth when I passed a finger over her—which she followed with her eyes. Then she sneezed, a tiny little sneeze.

It was so cute.

"Come. Let's introduce her." Thayu had put on a dress.

"Are you all right to walk?"

"Why not? I've had a child, I'm not injured."

A lot of people were at the house. I could hear them talking on the veranda and outside in the yard. As soon as we came into the hallway, with Thayu carrying our daughter, people cheered.

Deyu and Mereeni wanted to have a look at her.

"What did you name her?" Veyada asked.

"This is Emilu. We'll call her Emi," I said.

"After your mother," Nicha said.

"Yes, I couldn't believe my luck that the name was available." I'd fully expected to have to make do with a second choice. My mother, who had never known that after her death, my father and I had gone into space. My mother, who smiled at me from photographs, but who I only remembered as a thin and ill ghost-like wraith that had a fragile, ethereal presence in my early life.

People ushered us onto the veranda, where a large group of people had gathered.

They were covered in mud. Some were injured. All were wet.

They were Omi farmers. Some I recognised as the *zeyshi* who had come to their help from the top of the platform.

As soon as we came out, a cheer went up.

"What happened to the attackers?" I asked Veyada.

"The army patrols drove them away. All these people came up here because their homes and their work were destroyed. The Talavi pilots crossed over the boundary to the military base and they were forced down and killed. Asha has sent their leader a writ."

As I had already done.

"Yita Talavi has some questions to answer," Veyada said.

I didn't think we would face any more attacks with weapons. From now on, the conflict was all going to be personal. "What about the city?" I asked.

I was told that the raging torrent of water had cut a path through the Outer Circle, Eighth Circle and Seventh Circle communities. Thankfully, most of the mushroom farmers had received our frantic warnings. They had gotten out, though their farms were destroyed. People were already talking about a shortage of mushrooms. The Coldi loved their mushrooms.

Some people and houses had been washed away, most of those the cliff-hugging residences of the more well-off. What the effects of their loss would be to society remained to be seen. Recovery efforts were underway, which had recovered more than two hundred bodies. Over a thousand people were listed as missing, and since the list was likely to include only registered people, it was likely that some would forever remain lost. It was a sad fact, for which all the Talavi pilots had paid with their lives.

Coldi justice was harsh and immediate. They didn't like prisoners.

Now that the huge machine of recovery had been set in motion, we could only wait until the parties were ready to talk about the future of agriculture in the valley.

Meanwhile, we had other concerns. The ceremony was tomorrow.

22

THE REFUGEES HAD nowhere to go. Their homes had been destroyed by water.

I told them that they could sleep in the yard, as long as the young children and their mothers slept on the veranda.

While they all settled for the night, and Thayu fell asleep feeding Emi, I got to prepare for the ceremony. I finally knew what I was going to say and how I was going to handle those people who would come schmoozing to get into our sphere of influence: tell me how you're treating your workers. Show me you're treating everyone fairly.

There was also something else I needed to do, and I was the only one person who could do it.

Sitting in the living room while Thayu and Emilu slept in our bed, I wrote to Rashanu and Jeetari. I wrote to Ezhya, letting him know that Jeetari was an important person in the rebuilding of the outer circles. I made a list of all the ways I thought she could be helpful and only at the end did I mention that she had help from her four children, and I asked that those children be allowed to continue to help her. Then I rewrote the writ to the Talavi clan, charging them with the killing of the Omi farmers and others who had drowned. I asked that they repair their reputation by ceasing all activities to collect illegal rents from farmers, and that they attend negotiations. When I was finally done, I found Veyada in the security room, with Ileyu in his arms.

He smiled at me. "She wouldn't shut up in her cot. You'll become familiar with this."

"I guess I will." For the time being, though, my little family were fast asleep.

I gave him the text to read through. He didn't even ask me if I thought it was the right thing to do. I didn't ask him either. It was the right thing to do.

I asked him what to do about the other writ and whether he thought I should retract it.

"No. They did endanger us, and that writ concerns a different matter. If anything, it's an example of what needs to happen. Part of the Talavi clan is out of control. They think they can get away with everything, because very little was ever done to stop them. Things have changed. No more excuses for bad behaviour. Let them do an investigation and provide you with the identity of that woman who calls herself Ilavu and what they plan to do about getting her into line."

I looked at Ileyu for a while. She was fast asleep now, her little hand twitching occasionally.

"Do you think this is what Ezhya wanted me to do?" Build my own large loyalty network and pacify the locals? It seemed rather dangerous to me. I was not a kingmaker, and I wasn't a local.

"I am still not sure that you fully understand the situation. Your work contract may say that you work for Ezhya, but work contracts are not instincts and they don't work in the same way. Ezhya has you on his paid staff because he wants to keep you close. It is the usual way of exerting control over you, but he has none, and he knows that. He knows that because, by rights, you own his position."

"This isn't still about that, is it?" That fateful day that I'd killed Taysha, his bitter rival, who had instigated a coup in Ezhya's absence—I'd done it to help Ezhya, because his rule was important to the peace within *gamra*.

"I am not sure why you think it isn't. The matter was never resolved. He never spoke about it, you have never challenged him because of it, and he would have expected you to, especially since you have developed the instinct since your transformation."

"But I don't want to challenge him." I was horrified.

I'd often relived that moment that Taysha Palayi came into the communications hub that we were holding for Ezhya, who was stuck on Kedras, and how there was nothing I could do except shoot him. I could still remember the look in Ezhya's eyes when he turned up and realised that if I was Coldi and lived on Asto, Ezhya's position would have been mine.

Ever since that surreal event, I had wondered, if it ever came to a challenge between me and Ezhya, whether I would be killed or whether he would send me away. But no, with all the training that Veyada had put me through, and the fact that I had won a couple such challenges, I was wondering if such a challenge was necessary, and if that was what the people on Asto wanted from me. Worse than the fear that I might die, was the fear that I might win. Because that would be too horrible to contemplate.

"I know you don't want anything to do with this. You have this strange notion of friendship that is alien to us. You have spent years trying to avoid this confrontation. But it has to happen. It has to be settled one way or another."

"Is this why Ezhya has kept away on this visit?"

"It is."

And while I was filled with fear, it was good to finally have that confirmation. It didn't make me feel any less miserable. But there was only one way forward.

I didn't sleep very well that night.

Emilu kept making unfamiliar noises. When I stroked her

head, she grabbed onto my finger and held it for a long time until her grip relaxed.

I kept looking at the darkness where the ceiling would be if I could see it. Tomorrow, I'd be facing the dignitaries of the Domiri clan, some of whom had something to say about my joining. There would be other visitors, too. Maybe even Ezhya.

I kept hearing Veyada's voice, "It has to be settled, one way or another."

I made up scenarios where things might not have led to this terrible situation where I would be challenged for a fight with someone I considered a friend for a position I desperately didn't want. But in all of the different scenarios I could imagine, either I or Ezhya, or both, would have ended up dead.

There had been no alternative for shooting Taysha Palayi and I'd known that the moment I'd pressed the discharge.

I lay there in the dark, looking up at the ceiling. As often happened in the dark, all problems got worse and worse. If I wasn't banished from Asto, I'd be lucky to even be alive at the end of the ceremony.

People started moving around the house early the next morning. There were voices in the security room, and people walking through the hallway, but they were polite enough to stay out of our room.

Thayu was awake, feeding the baby. I watched Emi drink, fists clenched against Thayu's breast. I stroked her fuzzy head.

Thayu met my eyes. She didn't need to say anything; we both knew we had precious little time together before we needed to leave, before facing whatever trouble would be thrown at us.

Reluctantly, I pushed myself out of the bed.

Before going to sleep, I'd laid out the ceremonial robe Asha had given me, a loose shirt and wide billowing trousers, both dark blue. A sleeveless vest went over the shirt. It was made from stiff fabric and decorated with intricate embroidered patterns.

Should I wear armour, I'd asked, but no, no armour.

My hair went in a tight ponytail. Since my transformation, it had become a lot thicker and had acquired a golden sheen. My eyes were darker, too. Still blue-grey, but more *intense*. But my skin was pale.

I looked—and felt—tired.

The table in the living room was barely visible under a feast of food. I collected some for Thayu and went back to our room, where she was getting dressed.

"Aren't you supposed to be resting?" I asked.

Emi was still asleep on the bed.

"I'm coming. We're all coming."

It was useless to protest, and I knew it was what an association would do: stand behind the leader, without fail.

So while Thayu got ready and ate her breakfast, I went into the security room to check out what everyone else was doing. Anyu sat at the hub, but she was talking in code to someone, and I didn't want to disturb her.

The people who had camped outside were also packing up. I assumed they would make their way back into the valley to assess the damage and see what they could salvage. If there was one thing I wanted to do before I went back to Barresh, it was to make sure their grievances were heard and their futures secure.

Some time overnight, another party had arrived with their own craft. It must have been during the few moments I had slept, because I hadn't heard them arrive.

The craft was painted yellow with patterns in brown and purple down the side. They were not crude hand-painted patterns either, but properly etched into the surface of the craft.

The door was open and three people stood at the bottom of the entry ramp, one of them a middle-aged woman with her greying hair in a bun, dressed in a stylish mustard-coloured dress.

Jeetari Ezmi.

What was she doing here?

I went down the path to the aircraft.

The other two people turned around. One of them was Olinu, the other a middle-aged woman in a purple garment with wide flowing sleeves and loose trousers. It was reminiscent of a *shayka* but included a tunic worn over the top. This garment glittered with thousands of little glass beads.

The woman's face was sun-worn, with freckles and discoloured patches. Her gold earrings dangled on both sides of her head. Both the same, so she didn't have a contracted partner. The stone was lime green.

She stepped out of the group and met me, her head bowed.

I had to accept her subservient greeting with a touch on her shoulder and that lifting of the chin that I'd always found so belittling. That was just my human upbringing messing up my thoughts. Coldi thought it was a friendly gesture to be allowed to look into a leader's eyes. There was no point for me to wriggle sideways on this issue. It confused people unnecessarily if I did that. Coldi abhorred confusion.

"Well met," I said.

"It's an honour to house the association that will finally help us solve a pressing issue in the lives of my people."

So this was Rashanu Omi. "I'm sorry for your loss," I said.

The valley below was a mess of erosion channels and rocky debris, interrupted with muddy puddles. There was nothing left of the neat fields, or the green haze of growth that had hung over the soil.

"How many died?" I hated asking the question, but I had to know.

"At least forty of the settlers are missing, at last count, but some of the people who got washed downstream may still be found alive."

The way I saw it, that was very unlikely. From here, the canyons only got narrower as they traversed the city. Narrower passageways meant the water would travel at greater speed, and debris would be pulled under at rapids. Coldi people couldn't swim. Most were terrified of water.

"What about the city?" I asked.

Her expression sobered. "It's hard to say. No one knows how many people lived in those aquifers. Many may have been illegal, third and fourth children of farmers who themselves were illegal."

"One thing is certain: the death toll will be higher than any authorities will be prepared to admit."

"We're leaving soon," Nicha said at the door.

Yes, I knew I needed to get ready. But it felt wrong going to a celebration while these people out there were searching for the bodies of their family members.

"I'm very sorry about what's happened," I said to Rashanu and Jeetari. They would both have lost many of their friends. "I wish it could have been otherwise. I had no idea that the Talavi clan was that determined to keep the farmers under control."

"They need to be punished," Rashanu said.

"I'll be sending them a writ as soon as we come back from the ceremony."

"Take it with you. Yita Talavi is likely to be there. The upstart thinks he can misbehave his way into the inner circles."

"Did he get an invitation?"

"All clan leaders are invited to these ceremonies. We rarely attend, but I have a feeling this ceremony will be an exception."

"Are you coming?" She was Asha's lover, after all.

"I don't want to risk it," Jeetari said. "I'll stay and follow it from here."

Rashanu insisted, "We are *all* coming." She waved her beringed hand at the people in the yard.

I asked, "Certainly not all these people?"

There were at least a hundred people on the veranda and in the yard. More camped on the area surrounding the aircraft.

"All of us."

"You won't be allowed in."

"Then whoever is not allowed in will wait outside. We're patient. We've waited for a long time."

I wondered how that was going to go down in a military base.

But I couldn't stop them coming. If Rashanu was invited then she could come in. I just didn't think Asha's people would allow anyone else in.

There was no time to discuss it. My team were coming outside, including Thayu with Emi, and Mereeni with Ileyu. Nicha was coming, and Ayshada was coming, dressed up in his best clothes.

They were making their way through the yard to the aircraft. I had no more time to make arrangements to avoid conflict, to arrange difficult meetings we'd have to attend. We'd have to take things as they came.

We set off when the sunlight just peeped over the horizon. It might be a tense day, but the sunrise was beautiful as always, with rays of colour crossing the sky.

Below us lay the valley, now very clearly green even from this distance, and shrouded in a haze that obscured the damage from the battle of yesterday.

Already some vehicles were going through the field, on the way to once again shifting aside the rocks.

That was the Omi clan. They didn't complain. They did the work.

23

IT **WAS VERY BUSY** at the compound of the military base.

A number of craft had already arrived; I assumed they had come either from the city or from some kind of space settlement.

When we got out of the craft, we were met by someone from Asha's household whom I recognised from our earlier visit there.

To my question where Asha was, he said he was unsure, but we would surely see him later.

"Can you tell him that I need to speak with him urgently?"

"Sure."

I wanted to warn him of the impending arrival of groups of people who had not been invited. Security was already tight and nervous. However, I had no great hopes of actually speaking to Asha before the ceremony. Asha was a law onto himself.

The man told us to go into the building, and if we needed to, freshen up, and maybe it was a good idea to leave the infants in one of the rooms so that one of the nannies could look after them.

Thayu said that she would keep the child with her. Mereeni said the same.

Ayshada was also on his best behaviour. He walked holding onto Nicha's hand, such a big boy already.

"He will behave," Nicha told the man.

We went into a building with a short hallway. The sound of many people chatting drifted from an open door at the end. A lot of people were gathered in a courtyard. Asha had told me previously that this was where the ceremony would be held.

But as we entered the courtyard, another party caught up with us. They were sun-darkened, olive-skinned workers in their best clothes.

At the head were two women: Rashanu Omi and Jeetari Ezmi. A number of young men and women surrounded them. Jeetari's expression was nervous, her gaze darting around the room.

She would know many people in the audience. If they knew her, they might not think much of her. Would the supposed lame-duck Ezmi clan leader be here?

Both of the women took position next to each other and behind me. *Zhaymas*, with me as their leader. They each gathered two layers of associates, which brought their numbers to twelve, excluding the guards.

Those young people were mostly Ezmi, but some wore Omi earrings.

"The remainder of the group is waiting outside," Rashanu said. "They will support us if necessary."

How many others? There had been a lot of people at the house when we left.

From having thirteen people in my association, my network had jumped to having millions, all of them people who had no association with the traditional power structures.

I hesitated at the entrance for what seemed to me like an eternity, pretending to wait until a party with some very elderly guests had taken their seats.

This gamble of mine could end up badly. Very, very badly.

But I had to go through with it.

Even if I knew that everyone would be looking at me, getting to their feet, shouting, shouting at their neighbours, at guards to remove the uninvited Omi and Ezmi rabble accompanying me from the military base, I felt overwhelmed when it actually happened.

It was hot in that courtyard, in that dizzying moment where it seemed that my world collapsed. Surely I'd be hounded to some inhospitable planet where no one would find me for attempting to meddle with instincts I wasn't sure I possessed the way Coldi people did.

I heard Amarru's voice. "*Sheya* is not about your reaction to people who want to be part of your association, but all about their reaction to you."

At this point, it seemed everyone in the courtyard had a reaction to me.

Not all of them a good reaction, I had to admit.

Thayu walked somewhere in the group behind me, with Emi. Nicha walked next to her, with Ayshada. I had to protect them.

An old man yelled, "Everyone, stop!" His voice penetrated the ruckus.

People fell silent.

The old man had been seated on a bench intended for the audience. He rose slowly, with the aid of a walking cane. He wore the ceremonial robe of a clan leader: a loose shirt and trousers with an embroidered thigh-length sleeveless vest.

I knew the woman to his right: the mother of Ezhya's children, the formidable Natanu Vonayi. She was Ezhya's second, and Asha's *zhayma*.

The old man sneered. "You think you can come here and upset our loyalty networks? Insult our people and worm your way into power?"

Now I knew who this was: Chanara Vonayi, the Vonayi clan leader. I gave a polite bow.

"Well met. I ask no power except fair working conditions for these people who come with me. I think your clan should release the hold you have on land outside the city's boundaries, or at the very least, make sure that it's distributed evenly. Parts of the desert are turning fertile. There needs to be a plan to allow people to use that land that doesn't encroach on those who currently have access to it."

"You have cheek, telling me how to do my job."

"Then *do* your job. Give these people land. Stop the exploitation of them."

"I'm too old for challenges, but take on my daughter and I might talk."

Heart thudding, I met Natanu's eyes. I knew she could kill me with her pinky, if she wanted.

A few petrifying seconds later, she shook her head. "Not worth it."

I didn't know whether to be insulted or relieved. I didn't know what it meant, considering the *sheya* instinct. That she didn't want to fight, that she didn't think it was her task, or that it would get her in too much trouble with Ezhya.

The old man snorted. There was no doubt *he* considered his daughter's assessment as an insult to me. "We'll let events take their course, then."

And he didn't think they would be good events, either.

I continued through the courtyard, sweaty and shaken.

Asha had told me there would be seats for me and the others receiving their formal clan induction at the front of the audience.

But while I looked around, someone barged into me from the left with such force that I almost fell over. There was no doubt in my mind: this was an attack.

I couldn't even see who it was. Veyada's training kicked in. In the tussle, I took hold of the man's arm and flung him over my shoulder. Bystanders scrambled out of the way. He landed with his back flat on the ground.

Phew. That was one challenge won.

He slowly sat up, rose to his feet and faced me with his head bowed. It was a fairly young man, in clan leaders' garb, with loose hair over his shoulders.

"What was all that about?" I asked.

"My name is Yita Talavi." The leader of the Talavi clan.

And I had something just for them. In the struggle, my document folder had fallen onto the floor. I picked it up, opened it and took out the card I had prepared last night.

"I'd be honoured to give you this." I handed it to him.

He unfolded it and read, little emotion on his face. "Many mistakes were made."

"Then unmake them."

"It may not be in my power."

"Then find a leader who has that power. The actions of your clan members were driven by revenge, without communication to the parties involved, because you had no right to interfere and you hold no rights in this area. Do you even have formal agreements with the Vonayi clan to collect rent from the Omi farmers in the aquifers? Did you act because you feared losing your ability to extort members of the Omi clan?"

A woman's voice behind me said, "You seem to have increased in status quite remarkably."

I turned around. I recognised that sarcastic voice. What was Ayanu Azimi doing here?

The same as everyone else: having a look at who this upstart new Domiri clan member was. As the leader of the Azimi clan, she would have been invited.

I saw her more often than I liked in Barresh. But this was not Barresh, and the oh-so-polite *gamra* rules didn't apply. She had come to *my* territory and my clan. I couldn't leave her unchallenged. "If you have an issue with me, I would prefer that you raise it now, and not send other people to annoy us on your behalf."

"Whatever are you talking about?"

"You know very well. I have better things to do than bicker over what was or wasn't done in my household to a member of your clan, but if I don't know why you keep bothering me, then I don't know what to respond to."

While I was speaking to her, a number of people joined her, out of whom I recognised Thayu and Nicha's mother Tayanu and Ayshada's mother Xinanu. So that was indeed the relationship between those women.

People in the courtyard were looking at me. No, looking behind me.

My entire association stood there: Thayu, Nicha, Veyada, Mereeni, Reida and Deyu, including the children. Sheydu and her association were there as well. And Rashanu and Jeetari and behind them, a great number of people. They were workers and farmers, Omi people. Olinu and Remiya and the farmers. A couple of *zeyshi* people in *shayka*s.

"Hmmm," Ayanu said.

She glanced from me to the people and back.

The silence lingered. Neither Tayanu nor Xinanu met my eyes.

"Of course, you are more than welcome to have a look at your new granddaughter."

"Yes," Tayanu said.

After another tense silence, in which no one moved, she slipped between me and Nicha to her daughter.

Thayu gave her a blank look, but she lifted the corner of the blanket that covered Emi's head.

Tayanu reached out and stroked the little head with her index finger. Then she met Thayu's eyes.

"Her father is a strong man," she said in a low voice, but not so soft that I couldn't hear. "Your association is very strong. It's good."

Thayu's mouth twitched.

I guessed this meant that a truce had been reached?

Tayanu turned to Nicha, who carried Ayshada on his arm.

Ayshada could be boisterous and noisy, but when a stranger

turned their attention on him, he would hide. This time was no exception. He hid his face in Nicha's shirt.

Tayanu said something that made him turn his head before quickly hiding his face again.

One corner of Nicha's mouth moved up in a kind of half-smile.

Tayanu gave a barely perceptible bow and retreated.

I wasn't sure what all this meant, but I hoped disaster was temporarily averted. The tension certainly went out of the room.

A woman approached who told my team to go and sit in the audience, while I was directed to a line of chairs at the front. As Thayu had said, most of the people who would be inducted into the clan today were children. For Coldi people, this induction happened at the age of thirteen.

Five youngsters sat on the bench, all of them dressed in smaller versions of the same loose tunic and shirt I wore, with very similar embroidery on the vest. They were children from well-off families, well-behaved and compliant.

As I sat down, one of the children turned to me, a skinny boy.

"Are you the one that everyone talks about?" he said.

"I don't know, but I hope the talk is good."

"No. The talk is bad. They say a lot of bad things about you."

Trust the Coldi honesty to play havoc with me. "And do you believe everything they say?"

"My father says them." He lifted his chin in a stubborn way.

"So what does your father say?"

"He says you shouldn't meddle in our ways because you're a foreigner who has no business getting involved with Coldi people."

"Do I sound like a foreigner to you?"

He stared at me, his gaze resting on my hair, curly and much lighter than his.

"Apart from my hair, do I look like a foreigner?"

"You don't live here."

"Many people don't live here. Ayanu Azimi doesn't live in Athyl. Amarru Palayi doesn't live in Athyl. They are still important people for Asto."

He blinked at me with big, dark eyes. Something was eerily familiar about him, about his face, about the way he held his head.

I glanced over my shoulders and noticed a man in the audience looking at the boy. He averted his eyes when he noticed I was looking at him. I knew this man: it was Taysha Palayi's brother.

The boy who sat next to me was Thayu's lost son.

Right.

This put a whole new perspective on clan politics. *This* was why Asha wanted us to attend this particular ceremony. Because, just as the Azimi clan were jockeying to assert influence on Ayshada, *he* was making attempts to stay in contact with his grandson.

These people in Nations of Earth who painted Coldi as aloof people who didn't even care about their own family were wrong, very wrong. They just didn't display affection in a way Earth humans recognised.

Was it a coincidence that I sat next to him? I doubted it.

Did Thayu know he was here?

She sat a few rows behind me, and was talking to Mereeni.

A man in the row behind me said, "Are you proud of yourself now?"

"Excuse me, have we met?" He was middle-aged, with greying hair, and dressed immaculately in dark clothes. Probably military.

"No, and I have no intention of being polite. How do you even dare show your face here after what you've just done?"

After what I had just done? Which of all the things I'd just done?

He was likely to be another supporter of Taysha, although I was unfamiliar with the blue stones in his earrings. Wasn't that

Lingui clan? I didn't have anything to do with those. A lot of them were Traders.

The leader of the Lingui clan? I'd been too busy saving myself and my team to have a look into all their stupid politics.

I had enough of the underhanded jabs. Enough of the thinly veiled threats that were made to see how I reacted to them. Or something.

Enough of the clan politics.

People were dying out there in the outer circles. But this lot just continued their infighting. I rose.

All the people looked at me, but I didn't care, I was that angry. The modus operandi of these people was to blackmail their enemies into submission. In that case, they'd picked the wrong person. I had never fallen for blackmail. Never.

I had fulfilled all my obligations to Taysha's family, Nicha had fulfilled his to the Azimi clan, and besides, if I had to choose sides then I would support Ezhya.

"I am quite fed up with your behaviour," I said. "You all mock *gamra* for its bureaucracy and for dancing around arguments. Look at us, you say. At Asto, we do it so much better. If we have a problem, we go to the heart of it. We don't do delicate political negotiations. If we don't like someone, we don't pretend that we do. We go up to them, we state our issue and give them a writ. We have our *sheya* system of loyalties and therefore, we don't need all this bureaucracy."

Everyone in the courtyard had gone silent and was looking at me.

"But you know what? You're wrong. Your wonderful system of loyalty networks is broken. You jostle for positions, while people in the outer circles do all the work. You play politics, while your money and power no longer reaches those who need it. You have ceased to act in the interest of society as a whole. You look after each other, your friends, your clan, whomever you perceive as deserving benefit of your actions."

The Lingui man said, "You have no idea what you're talking

about. You're just a foreigner and you don't belong here. You have no power here."

"You're wrong and you know it. I've just spent a number of days sorting out *your* problems with your outer circles. You will notice that there are representatives of the Omi and Ezmi clans here. They are here by my invitation, because we spilled blood over the use of the Twin Valley. Many people died yesterday, and many more would have died if not for my team. I think I have plenty of right to tell you to behave. And if you have a problem with that then I'll be happy to challenge you on it."

Several people around me gasped.

But Rashanu Omi and Jeetari Ezmi got up and moved through the crowd to stand behind me. Veyada got up as well, and then Thayu and Nicha, Deyu and Reida, Mereeni, Sheydu and her association. And all the farmers at the back of the courtyard were already standing. They formed a solid wall of determined faces and crossed arms. They would fight, if necessary.

He stared at me, but ultimately couldn't maintain his gaze. He snorted. "Very well."

He rose, turned around and stormed out of the courtyard. At the door, he almost crashed into Asha who was just coming in, dressed in a splendid robe. He looked at his departing guest with wide eyes. And then at me. A shudder went through him.

In the silence, the boy next to me said to the girl who sat next to him, "Look at that. He got Dayna Lingui to leave. I want to learn how to do that."

I sat down on the bench next to him. "You want to know how to do that?"

He turned to me. "Yes!"

"You know when you talk to a friend about why he didn't come to see you yesterday and he's telling you about how he had to help his sister doing some school work? And you know that's nonsense because your friend hates his sister? You should ask your friend the real reason, even if it means that your friend doesn't want to be friends anymore. It's more important to hear the truth than to believe lies. You may lose a friend, and you may need to play with your little sister for a bit, but you will make new friends. Real friends."

"Yeah." He looked down. "I don't have a sister."

"Yes, you do."

He frowned at me.

I asked him, "What do you know about your mother?"

"My mother was a spy. She died in her job."

"Your mother *is* a spy. She's sitting a few rows behind us. You should meet her. What's your name?"

"Nalya."

"Talk to me after the ceremony. I will introduce you to your mother." Because Asha was now coming to the front of the audience, having persuaded his recalcitrant Lingui guest to stay.

He met my eyes. I felt he very much wanted to talk to me, but couldn't. The audience was waiting.

At a sign from him, someone in the corner operated a panel that drew a covering over the courtyard. In the middle hung an installation consisting of metal rods and bits of glass. Little shadows and twinkles of light spread around the floor in front of me and the boys who were about to be inducted into the clan.

He asked us to get up. Each of us had to stand in a particular position, and then the big installation above us started to rotate. The light and shadows fell over our skin, it went faster and faster. Until it stopped.

If I hadn't read up on this I wouldn't have had a clue what was happening. The light and shadows on the floor represented the nearby worlds of the solar system and the world where people from Asto had settled.

One by one we were required to come forward to speak a pledge of allegiance to the clan.

Then we were given our earrings. I had already worn those, but I had handed them in before we left to go to the house. Two different ones. One Thayu's, one mine.

It was a very solemn occasion.

Asha moved down the line starting from the youngest boy until he arrived at me. Again when he looked me in the eye, he froze.

"You've done well," he said.

"I apologise for bringing this large group here. I couldn't stop them coming."

"Nor should you have stopped them. They respect you."

Did I hear *they respect you while they've ceased to respect us* in his words?

"Maybe I should have warned you they were coming."

"It's not of importance. It's important what happens next."

He was unsure what to do. I sensed that he was searching for where to put me now that I had a considerable group below me. He wasn't sure how to treat me.

In the past, I had probably shown subservience to him maybe once or twice, and only if I couldn't get away with not doing it.

He had not wanted to berate me for it and had ignored the issue, because he could, because I wasn't Coldi.

But now everything had changed, and it would need to be sorted out.

24

———————

HOWEVER, ASHA AND I didn't sort out where we stood in relation to each other yet.

The ceremony was finished. It was now time for the newly instated clan members to go through the aggregated members of the clan and other visitors to establish where they belonged, to make new contacts.

"Come with me," I said to the boy next to me.

He glanced over his shoulder, but his father was no longer in his seat. He followed me through the crowd.

Thayu stood with the others of my association. She was talking to Nicha, but when she saw me with the boy, her eyes widened. She knew.

They faced each other awkwardly.

"This is your mother, Thayu Domiri."

"Nalya?" Thayu's voice was barely more than a whisper.

The pain in her tone cut me. The last time she saw him, she'd left him on the floor in the room where she had been kept prisoner.

He looked up at her, his head cocked. He was still a head smaller than most of us, but his face had already acquired an adult look. "My father said you were dead," he said.

"Well, clearly he was wrong." Thayu's voice sounded unsteady. Was she angry, was she happy? I wasn't sure that setting up this meeting was a good idea.

"I told him that he could see his sister," I said.

Thayu pulled back the cloth over Emi's head. She was asleep. Her hand twitched but she didn't wake up.

Nalya came closer. His dark eyes looked over the child and then at Thayu.

"Can I touch her?"

"Sure."

He reached out with his flat hand and ran his fingertips over the soft fuzz of her hair. She turned her head to him, opening her eyes.

He chuckled.

"Would you like to spend more time with her?" I asked.

He snorted again. My question made him uncomfortable. Had his family told him to stay away from us at all cost?

If so, why was he here talking to me? Because his father wouldn't tell him why?

That very man was coming in our direction in big, angry strides.

"Nalya!" He made a sideways movement with his hand.

The boy scurried away.

"He's allowed to talk to his mother," I said.

"But he will not. I don't know why Asha insisted for him to share the ceremony with you."

"Because he would like us to confront the issue?"

"I will. I will send you a writ."

"For what?"

He stared at me, nostrils flaring. I stared back.

Was he going to challenge me?

But he averted his eyes. He didn't bow or acknowledge subservience, but he didn't challenge me either.

It was a strange occurrence, now the second time this had

happened. Someone deferred a decision on superiority. For what reason?

He shepherded his son back to "approved" company. The boy glanced over his shoulder before they disappeared from view.

I went to introduce myself to a lot of people I didn't know. I met members of the military, of the administration, of businesses, all of whom were happy to talk to me. Their immediate display of subservience was not always clear, but for some people it was obvious that they wanted to be in my good books.

Veyada had warned me against those, because they were often people who wanted something and would try to get it by any means possible.

Fortunately, because I lived in Barresh, I didn't need to interact with many of these people, and could put their suggestions aside politely.

I did, however, meet a number of people who I kept in the back of my mind because they might come in useful to give as contacts to Rashanu to administer the agricultural enclave that we had created in the alley.

At all times, when moving through the crowd of well-wishers, I kept an eye on my team. Deyu stood with Nicha and Ayshada and the others. The farmers kept to themselves in the corner of the courtyard. I couldn't see Thayu and I presumed she had gone to a quiet spot to feed Emi. I did see Nalya and his father, now talking to the belligerent Lingui clan leader who was still around, despite having threatened to leave.

Isharu's people had fanned around the courtyard pretending to be ordinary guests.

Ezhya hadn't come. Did he really want to prolong the confusion about our relationship until I had gone back home? That was not like him.

But it might be the sensible thing to do. There was no need for me to interact with him directly in my work. I could continue to communicate with him via messages.

But that wasn't like him at all.

And there was the issue of the agricultural operations in the valley. And those were likely to lead to further operations. And the farmers needed to know where they stood with Ezhya. The Talavi extortionists needed to be punished. The farmers needed contracts for the use of the land. The Ezmi clan had to be granted access to the factories in Eighth Circle. Jeetari had to be forgiven for having too many children.

So there were reasons for me to interact with him.

I had considered him a friend and felt sad that it ended in this strange standoff.

Maybe I should be bold and visit him.

On the other hand, that might be seen as aggression and I would probably be stopped from entering the Inner Circle.

What was I supposed to do?

The past few days had made me very tired, and I was starting to think that maybe we should go back to the house and talk about what to do next when a ripple of tension went through the people who I knew Asha had posted as guards.

Sheydu was looking at the entrance to the courtyard. Isharu exchanged a sharp glance with one of Asha's guards. A couple of other guards came in and cleared the area around the door. Military guards.

Then came two guards in silver temperature retaining suits with sashes in the *shessyu* colour.

Ezhya was in the building.

He came into the door, surrounded by the members of his new guard association. He was in his full ceremonial dress, the silver heat retaining suit, with the sash across his shoulder.

He came a couple of paces into the courtyard, and stopped. His eyes met mine. While this was happening, the people I had been talking to had retreated to the sides.

Neither of us said anything. Was I supposed to do anything? According to all my experiences, the *sheya* instinct would sort itself out. Except when it didn't.

We stood there, facing each other for what seemed in eternity.

My heart thudded like crazy.

As with Natanu, I had no doubt that when Ezhya's instinct fired, he had the strength and skill to kill me in a heartbeat.

I had heard that if it came to a confrontation, which was rare but still happened, that would not be an uncommon result, and more likely the higher up in society the confrontation.

But the longer he didn't move, the more I became convinced that such a confrontation would not happen. Yet I had only ever shown subservience to him once, and I had been very reluctant to do that.

It had been when I first started working at *gamra*, and when I met him for the first time. Thoughts of that meeting came rushing back to me. I respected him and his position, but didn't want to be ordered by him.

The man could be very harsh on people he didn't agree with. Bully, people on Earth would say, but that was a very human-centric view of things.

My heart was full of admiration and fear for this man. He was why I was here, and he was why I had done a lot of things in the past. I believed that he considered the benefits for the people he led.

He took a couple of steps towards me, never losing eye contact. The expression in his eyes chilled me. It was distant, as if he didn't know me at all.

He held out his hand, as if he wanted to shake it, Earth style. He sometimes did this, and then he would address me in Isla, because he was a truly puzzling man, and the customs of Earth amused him. But why do it in this particular very traditional setting?

There was no way I could refuse to shake his hand. Nor did I want to, because over all the years I had interacted with him, I had, perhaps mistakenly, considered him a friend of sorts.

So I stepped forward, and held out my hand.

The moment we touched, he whirled me around with an agility that took me off guard.

He pulled me towards him, grabbed the shoulder of my shirt with his free hand and swung me over his shoulder.

Fortunately I had practised this move with Veyada and managed to land on my feet instead of being slammed back-first into the ground.

I twisted around, managed to yank my shirt out of his grip and grabbed him around the chest.

I pushed and he pushed but, in this position, we were evenly matched and neither of us gave ground.

All around us a lot of people were shouting. People were streaming into the courtyard to watch the spectacle.

He pushed against me and I pushed back.

All the wrestling lessons I had with Veyada were paying off. I understood why Veyada had been so keen to teach me. He had even told me. *Whether you think it's just friendly wrestling, always fight to win. If you trust the other person, fight to win, if you distrust them, fight to win, if you don't think they should fight at all, you fight to win.*

I did *not* want to win.

So I held my position.

Ezhya was trying to trip me up. I managed to avoid his feet, pushing him further back into the audience. Then he tried to get hold of my arm to swing me over his shoulder again.

Veyada had taught me a trick to shift my weight. He couldn't lift me. I turned around, intending to push him away.

But in my stupid overconfidence I managed to trip over my own feet.

Thoughts of *Serves you right* went through my mind as I hit the floor and Ezhya landed on top of me.

Recover from your mistakes, I could hear Veyada say.

I managed to grab his shoulders and pushed him down, but he did the same to me. We rolled over the floor with neither of us able to get the upper hand. People scurried out of the way.

I gained the top position, and then he flipped me over, and I rolled him onto his back. A row of seats got pushed into another row and another one, until the whole lot got so heavy that our weight wouldn't shift it anymore.

Then we stopped to catch our breath.

We both lay on the ground, facing each other.

He met my eyes, his expression now free of the troubled look they had carried earlier.

He let me go and started laughing.

Confused, I pushed myself into a sitting position. What on Earth had just happened? Had anyone lost or won?

Ezhya clapped me on the shoulder. Before my transformation, that would probably have broken my shoulder bone, but now I hit him back.

We laughed.

I had no idea what it meant but the release of emotion was incredible. I wanted to laugh and cry.

People around us looked disturbed.

Ezhya got to his feet. He reached out a hand, pulling me up.

"So what's going on?" someone wanted to know.

People came closer now that it seemed the fight was over. But the atmosphere in the audience remained one of utter confusion.

Ezhya said, "What has just happened is that we've solved a rather large problem that has plagued us going back generations. For many years, all types of agitators have advocated that Athyl was becoming too big, and it was. People suggested that it be split up and a secondary division be founded with its own leadership that was based in the outer circles. Some people even tried that. Remember Hedron?"

Some shudders went through the audience.

"I've been aware of this. My predecessors have been aware of this growing problem. Because as the outer circles grew and grew more out of the influence of the Inner Circle, the problem became more immediate. The Inner Circle networks don't reach that far. I learned, in my youth, that my predecessors, like Mizha and Thania, used to visit Eighth Circle and walk through the streets. When I read that, I knew that the problem had become so much worse in recent years, because I couldn't do the same without a huge contingent of guards. If I wanted to survive, I needed to solve this issue before society fractured. The Ezmi clan was always on the outside, but the circumstances were also pulling out the Omi clan. If our society is a ship, the Omi clan is our engine. We cannot afford to lose them."

He looked directly at Rashanu, who bowed her head.

"We could especially not afford to lose either the Omi clan or the Ezmi clan since other, foreign, agitators have arrived in the outer circles. One thing about agitators is that you can't beat them by fighting them. You can only beat them by joining them, by creating networks that allow you to be part of their plans. Except most of us were not in a situation where we could engage with outside agitators without creating a big disturbance within our own networks. But at the same time, we needed to be represented in those new opportunities created by these developments."

He looked at me. "You knew that I sent you to Tamer for that reason: because I couldn't send anyone from the Inner Circle, because their networks would see that as disloyalty. Through your successful actions, you have become my voice with these new initiatives. In a strange way, we're *zhayma*s. I am here for you. I've never been happy with our level of representation at *gamra*, and now there is the Tamer Collective that our *gamra* delegation has no way to access. We need to be connected to all of those organisations. I'm needed in the Inner Circle. You represent us off-world and manage the connection between them and us."

I said, "*Ichi* and *ata-ichi*." The ones who travelled, and the ones who did not. Local concerns in harmony with larger concerns. *Rimoyu*, balance. All of them deeply important Coldi values.

"Exactly."

In my ignorant past, I had considered the *ata-ichi*, the people who lived local lives and worried about local concerns, to be inferior and narrowminded. It had been when I'd considered my fiancée Eva and her family at Nations of Earth to belong to that group. I had then argued that we were in balance and therefore the relationship would work. But it had been doomed from the start, because I *didn't* think they were equal. Yes, I really wasn't proud of how I'd left Eva, especially when I'd found out, a few years later, how my action had trapped her in her conservative world.

I hadn't really understood the *rimoyu* concept. I was happy with "balance", as long as I could belong to the superior group. Well, that was not how balance worked, was it?

So I asked, "What about the Omi and Ezmi clans?" Because they were a very important part of that balance.

"The outside agitators have a strong pull on those people and I still can't do much about it. For many years to come, most of them will probably feel more aligned with the rogue network than with the Inner Circle. There is a limit to the size of one person's influence. I've reached that limit."

I could argue otherwise, but any additional support for Ezhya was likely to come from off-world as well. He was hugely popular in sections of the Earth community, and many of the progressive Pengali in Barresh had a lot of time for him. But they weren't in his associations in the traditional Coldi sense of the word.

"So, you're setting the Eighth and Outer circles free?"

"They were never really part of our networks, but they're very important in our society. We need fair rules for the use of land and the export of produce. I'm sure you can nominate some people who can sit around the table and negotiate what all the involved parties want. I am happy for you to arrange this, because you represent the part of Coldi society that I have no control over. I trust that you will establish a structure of government which will then feed back into the Domiri clan and my primary association at a high level through Asha."

"That's going to be a really long process."

"We have time. We have a few days before you leave, yes? We'll start negotiations."

25

I **DIDN'T THINK** Ezhya appreciated just how much time would be involved in setting up rules for land ownership and use, employment and payment, and settlement rights in the Outer Circle.

Whenever he ordered something, it was done. He liked his regimented society.

I remained unsure how much of a victory I had really achieved, because the only thing that had changed was that it was now acceptable to talk about Eighth Circle and Outer Circle problems. I guess that was the first step to sorting out all the deeply rooted, unfair, brutal and historical issues.

This was not going to be easy.

After the ceremony, Ezhya went back to the house with us. He had brought both his daughters. Raanu had grown into quite a young woman, who sat with us and listened to every word that was said, while little Nimiyu was running around, teasing Ayshada as she chased him through the house.

It seemed like a heavy weight had fallen off both of our shoulders.

Raanu had been promised a surfing trip with me, and she finally was allowed to go.

Ezhya also explained to me that my new status allowed me a lot more staff, an office paid for, and I would get some local funds.

"I suggest one of the first things you do is to buy yourself a suitable aircraft that will take you to the places where you will need to go," he said.

Implied in that statement was that I would be travelling to Tamer and other places outside the *gamra* network, and that I would be required to have a level of military clearance to use the military sling.

That was possible because of my ties with the Domiri clan.

It seemed like a lot of pieces of the puzzle had come together. He had encouraged me to collect a diverse set of people in my association and it was now clear how that would benefit both of us.

I didn't consider him a *zhayma* of sorts. The man was a political genius. He had planned this from the start.

He also promised to visit me in Barresh.

Over the next few days, Rashanu and Jeetari brought groups of representatives for talks about the future of agricultural communities in Twin Valley and the other areas where agriculture had now become possible, or would be soon.

The agricultural settlements would probably grow, and we had extensive talks with the representatives of the Omi clan to make sure that I understood the limits of what we could negotiate. For the time being, their operations would be limited to the valley, and if they wanted to occupy extra land they would have to apply to the authorities, and the authorities were obliged to respond to them. Veyada drafted the rules governing this process. Midway through this, news came that Chanara had ceded control of the Vonayi clan, citing old age and illness. His daughter Natanu took over. I considered that to be a step forward, of sorts. She was Ezhya's longtime lover after all.

Rashanu was clearly the leader in these negotiations, but many others had input, including Yita Talavi, who had dealt with my writ by donating to our efforts a significant amount of funds that would pay for a permanent base in Athyl for me. Ezhya suggested that it should be somewhere in the Inner Circle.

In the past I would have accepted that recommendation, but now I wondered what would happen if I set up shop in one of the amazing apartments in Eighth Circle, and insisted that he visit there when I was in Athyl. If I had an office there, I could get people to keep an eye on further flouting of property agreements that had brought so much hardship to the Omi clan. I liked the prospect, even if I held off on making a definite decision.

Rashanu was going to move into the house on the cliff. Now that the pressure was off, the mutual affection between her and Asha was obvious. She was a strong, smart and savvy woman who had the rare ability to upset conventions, but do it in a way that made people want to support her.

The thought of the two of them sitting on the veranda watching the machines trundle over the fields gave me comfort. Yes, Asha was a strange man, but ultimately he had needs I understood: a sense of duty to the military, his family and a lover.

As to how to engage with the Tamer Collective, Ezhya said that it was important to involve them in the making of decisions. He gave me permission to do whatever was necessary to gain membership in that group, or be otherwise allowed to attend their meetings.

"This is the essence of Coldi success," he said to me while we were seated on the veranda, overlooking the valley, where the farmers had cleared up the mess and were once again working the fields. "We don't wage wars, we construct networks. This part of the network will be yours."

I asked him how this change was going to relate to the Athens Exchange and the position of Amarru. Earth had officially applied to join *gamra* and the process had been set in place, but there was no getting away from the fact that the Tamer Collective had a strong influence there. The fact that Minke

Kluysters had been defeated in a vote didn't make him go away. The election result had been decisive, but not absolute.

"We will have to organise a meeting with her," he said. "I suspect her position won't be easy, because she has had to speak for the Tamer Collective out of necessity. Because they left their decision about joining so long that other influences have taken hold of the world and they will be impossible to wind back. We just need to make sure that the two organisations can exist with the minimum amount of damage done to both of them."

This was where I came in.

There were also a host of other things he wanted me to deal with and some things he said he had been afraid to ask me to do, because they were dangerous, he would have had to divulge his aims for doing so, and they were all related to the new society order that hadn't been established until now.

He wanted me to sort out the official position of Indrahui, and see whether I could sway that world into joining *gamra*, because it was forever a hotbed of conflict.

He also wanted me to get a handle on the amount of illegal export from and to Asto, much of which was conducted under our noses through Barresh.

It was only a few days after Emi's birth that I walked into the bedroom and found Thayu in her black security outfit. I stopped at the door.

Motherhood had rendered her very shapely indeed, a sight to behold.

"Shut the door. You look like you're seeing a ghost."

"A gorgeous ghost from the past. Are you sure you want to go back to dangerous work already?"

"We have a lot to do," she said. "Now that we'll spend more time travelling to non-*gamra* worlds, I need to brush up on the latest security equipment. Sheydu is starting to teach me today."

"What about Emi?"

"What about her?" Thayu picked up a piece of fabric that I'd not yet noticed and looped it over her shoulder. She then picked up Emi and deposited her in the sling. She sat snugly against her mother's body, remaining fast asleep, with her little hands pressed against her face.

"She'll come with me, or with you. We'll teach her from a very young age."

"Karana can also look after her." She was Nicha's nanny for Ayshada in Barresh.

"Only if there really isn't another option. Emi will come with us. My father did this with me, too."

With all the will in the world, I couldn't imagine Asha walking around a military base with a baby girl strapped to his chest; but, well, the man continued to surprise me.

Thayu had thoroughly welcomed our new position. I strongly suspected she had known for a long time that it was coming. She had worked all her life to be a top-level spy. Here was her chance. Our chance.

So we did the training offered by Sheydu, and we visited the most important of Aghyrian historic sites in Athyl, and we introduced Emi to all the important people, and we looked at some accommodations in Eighth Circle. I took a liking to an apartment on the top floor of one of the modern buildings, one of those connected to other buildings by walkways high above the ground.

We also visited a couple of aircraft dealerships, made a choice and put in an order. That was a very expensive day. Ouch.

When a couple of days later we boarded the aircraft to go back to Barresh, it was with a long list of things to do.

Ezhya said that he had already contacted the authorities on the island, demanding that I be given an office adjacent to that of Ayanu Azimi, his representative in the assembly. The Azimi clan still couldn't stand me, so that was going to be interesting.

But whenever one situation was solved, another one would arise. It seemed like everything was all right now, but things could easily change.

All I knew was that with friends and my new family, I would be strong enough to face all of them.

———

Thanks for Reading

As author of this book, I would very much appreciate if you could return where you purchased it and write a short review. It helps other readers find this book.

Of course the story isn't finished here. Bigger problems loom on the horizon in Ambassador 10: Lost Forest Secrets.

ABOUT THE AUTHOR

Patty Jansen lives in Sydney, Australia, where she spends most of her time writing Science Fiction and Fantasy.

Her career started in earnest when her story *This Peaceful State of War* placed first in the second quarter of the Writers of the Future contest and was published in their 27th anthology. She has also sold fiction to genre magazines such as Analog Science Fiction and Fact, Redstone SF and Aurealis, before making the move to independent publishing.

Patty has written over fifty novels in both Science Fiction and Fantasy, including the *Icefire Trilogy* and the *Ambassador* series.

pattyjansen.com

BOOKS BY PATTY JANSEN

More information:

PATTYJANSEN.COM

For a complete list of books, scan the image below with your phone.